MID-CONTINENT PUBLIC LIBRARY

MW01241889

WITHDRAWN FROM THE RECORDS OF THE MID-CONTINENT PUBLIC LIBRARY

PRAISE FO

The Hackers

Hacking IT
"This high-tech romance is awesome… You don't have to understand computers or security to love this story."
Night Owl Reviews Top Pick

Love Hack
"I am totally enjoying this series and can't wait to see more. Sexy nerds getting hot non-computer people gives everyone a chance at happiness."
Night Owl Reviews Top Pick

Triple X Series

Lexie
"Wrap your ereader in a waterproof bag, because this has all the elements of a perfect beach read… Summer romance books don't get much more fun than this."
Library Journal

Lexie
5 stars
N.Y. Times and USA Today bestselling author Carly Phillips

The Dream Weavers

Dream Man
"This book is sure to please on all levels."
Romantic Times Book Reviews

Dream Walker
It is very interesting idea that leads to a storyline that keeps
your interest and satisfies your need for love and romance"
The Romance Reviews

The Courting Series

Courting Suspicion
"a must-read romance of the summer and one of the best
romance novels I have read so far this year"
The Romance Reviews

Stand-Alone Stories

Ghost Flute
"This eerie ghost story is brimming with steamy sex set in an
interesting plot"
Romantic Times Book Reviews

Everlasting
"This book is temptation incarnate."
The Romance Reviews Top Pick

Private Dancer
2014 EPIC Award Winner, Erotic Division

Fever
"Kimberly Dean does an incredible job creating a scenario
where having a raging fever is unbelievably sexy. "
Romance Junkies

Blade of Moonlight
"fast and sexy crime-fighting story that will pull you in and not
let go"
Guilty Pleasures Book Reviews True Gem

OTHER BOOKS BY KIMBERLY DEAN

Haunted Hearts

Kimberly Dean

Copyright © 2018 Kimberly Dean

All rights reserved.

ISBN: 172310227X
ISBN-13: 978-1723102271

PROLOGUE

Something was in her house; she could feel it. It had a cold vibe, a chilling vibe. The air practically shimmered with malevolence.

The sensation disturbed her, for this was her house. Her space. How dare something invade it?

She pressed her toe more firmly against the hardwood floor, and the rocking chair beneath her picked up its pace. The squeak from the chair's old joints was annoying, but familiar. The familiarity should have comforted her, but she was too distressed to find any comfort in an old routine. The darkness in the air pressed heavily upon her soul.

It was an unwanted, untimely distraction.

She clenched the arms of the rocker more tightly. She couldn't afford to let this new disturbance get in her way. Not when she was this close to accomplishing her goal. Not when she'd waited for so long.

A gust of wind shook the porthole window in front of her, and she looked out over her beloved countryside. Summer had gone on its merry way, and autumn had settled in. The leaves on the trees were brightening. The air was crisper, heavier. Soon, even that would be gone. Winter winds would roll in, and they would bite, snap, and howl.

Yes, the winds of change were coming, and she had to be ready—for this might be her last chance.

The rocker came to an abrupt halt. There was only one thing to do. The dark spirit had to go. It would simply have to move along, because she

wouldn't allow it to stay.
   Not here. Not in her house.
   Not now.

CHAPTER ONE

Callie Thompson stepped on the accelerator of the Mustang and felt the powerful engine surge. A grin broke out on her face as her hair whipped in the wind. It was almost too chilly to be driving with the top down, but she didn't care. The nip in the air was invigorating.

Taking a deep breath, she let her body melt back against the plush leather seat. Now, this was the life—sunshine, a powerful car, and an open road. What more could a girl want? Oh, wait. That was right. She had a list. Add a ruggedly handsome man, a house with hardwood floors, a never-ending supply of peanut butter, and everything would be perfect.

One out of three wasn't bad.

"I'm a homeowner!" she yelled as she lifted both hands into the air. The wind carried her words away down the two-lane road.

With a laugh, she caught the steering wheel again. She couldn't believe how Lady Luck was smiling upon her. She'd inherited a house. Not a flat, an apartment, a brownstone, or a condo, mind you. She didn't care what you called any of those places where people lived smack dab on top of the other. Fate had given her a house.

She still couldn't believe the surprise that an elderly relative had left in her will. She hadn't known Aunt Jeanne well. She was a great-aunt, three times removed, or something along those lines. Callie had no idea why the woman had thought of her when she'd been divvying up her estate. She was just happy she had. The timing certainly couldn't have been better. To say she was sick of city life would be putting it mildly. Boston had been big and exciting for a while, but its charms had worn thin. The relentless noise, the traffic, the constant press of buildings... She didn't know exactly what had pushed her over the edge; she'd just known she'd been getting more and more claustrophobic. Instead of being fed by the city's energy, she'd felt trapped.

No more.

With work going well, she was mobile. She didn't have to live in the city. With email, the Internet, and smartphones, she could live anywhere she pleased. Right now, a house in the middle of Western Massachusetts pleased her very much.

"So long, Boston. Hello, Shadow Valley."

She rested her elbow atop the door and opened her fingers to catch the wind. She liked the rolling Berkshire mountains, the trees, and the birds. Most of all, she loved the fact that she shared the road with early leaf peepers, not harried commuters. People were out just to enjoy themselves. What a concept.

The road took her over the crest of a hill, and her grin turned into a thousand-watt smile.

There it was!

Excitement unfurled in her stomach and, on impulse, she pulled over to the side of the road. She put the Mustang in park and scooted up the leather seat until she was perched on the headrest. She liked the look of the town as much as she liked the name.

"It's perfect," she whispered.

Shadow Valley was tiny and quaint. It sat nestled amongst the hills, filling up the bowl of the valley. It appeared as if houses had tried to make their way up the hillsides, but nature had finally staked her claim and allowed no further advancement. The trees were so thick around the edge of the town that she wondered if a person could walk between them. Either way, they'd be surrounded by beauty. The autumn hues were just starting to appear. Soon the entire landscape would be a riot of color.

But she could see how the town got its name. When the sun went down, darkness would fall quickly. Shadows from the hills would sweep over the town like a protective blanket, and all that color would change to black.

Smiling to herself, Callie plopped back down into the driver's seat and buckled her seatbelt. This was exactly what she'd been looking for. This was a place where she could relax and settle in.

This was a place she could call home.

A news report came over the radio, and she changed channels. A rock station suited her mood. Checking her mirror, she pulled back out and began to cruise. The road snaked down into the valley with twists and turns. The rock-and-roll beat a heavy rhythm, and she stepped harder on the gas.

"Ooh, ooh, baby," she sang along. "Whoa, oh. Shake it, shake it. Huh?"

Her gaze flashed to the radio. That was a terrible guitar solo. Wait… The wailing got louder, and she glanced at the rearview mirror.

"Ah, crud." Flashing red and blue lights.

Not again.

She pulled over to the side of the road. The police car swung in behind her, and she grimaced. This was not the new beginning she'd planned. The police car came to a textbook stop, a few feet back and slightly off-center. She watched as the policeman opened his door. One foot settled on the pavement, and her eyes widened as he emerged from his cruiser.

"Whoa," she said on a swift exhale.

Now that was a big guy. Big, solid, and intimidating. His height continued to grow until he filled up her rearview mirror. With the way he stalked toward her, he looked like a jungle cat approaching his prey. Callie licked her dry lips. Why did she suddenly feel like lunch?

He approached her car carefully, and she rubbed her damp palms against the steering wheel. She couldn't see his eyes behind the mirrored sunglasses he wore, but she could feel him watching her as closely as she watched him. Suddenly self-conscious, she ran her hand through her tangled hair and tried to make herself presentable.

"Ma'am," he said in a low voice as he stepped up to her door. The rumbling tone made a shiver go down her spine.

"Officer." She tilted her head back to look him in the face, but with the way he towered over her, it nearly put a kink in her neck. When their gazes finally connected, she didn't care.

Lordy, he was something—all dark, muscle-bound, and *rugged*.

Awareness sizzled deep down in her belly. So help her, if the man had a jar of peanut butter stuffed in his pocket, she would not be held accountable for her actions.

"Good afternoon," she said breathlessly.

"Could you remove your sunglasses?"

"Oh, sure." She took them off. Giving in to a bit of feminine primping, she ran a hand through her hair again. With the way it had been whipping around in the wind, she must look like a maniac. "Sorry," she said, looking up at him through the fan of her eyelashes.

For a moment, he went still as he looked at her. Then his weight shifted. "Do you know what the speed limit is on this road, ma'am?"

The speed. Right. She had a bad habit of not paying attention to that.

She flashed him one of her best smiles. "My second-grade teacher was a 'ma'am,' but she had blue hair. Could you try miss or even miz?"

He went quiet again—only this time in a completely different way.

Callie's smile faltered. What? What had she said wrong? Wasn't a bit of flirtation expected under these circumstances? Especially when he looked like *that*? She couldn't see his eyes, but the line of his lips had gone flat. His jaw had somehow become firmer, and she shivered as the nip in the air became more pronounced.

Abruptly, she realized he wasn't paying attention to her. He was listening to yet another news report on the radio.

"Authorities are still on the lookout for two escaped convicts from the correctional institute at Concord. People in surrounding areas are warned to be on the lookout. The convicts are thought to be unarmed, but should be considered dangerous. If you have any information regarding the whereabouts of—"

She hit the power button. "I hope I don't look like an escaped convict to you," she teased.

If anything, the lines on his face became even sterner. "Can I see your driver's license, *miz?*"

He said it in such a deadpanned tone, she almost missed it. She looked up at him, hoping to see a smile, but the expression on his face hadn't changed. "Yes, officer," she muttered.

"It's *chief.*"

Of course it was. Callie sighed. This was not going well at all.

"Sorry." She pulled her purse off the floorboard and onto her lap. She felt his attention sharpen, so she kept her movements slow so he could see what she was doing. She pulled out her wallet, but the plastic slot where her license was usually housed was empty.

"I know it's here somewhere." She threw him yet another apologetic look that bounced right off those reflective sunglasses.

She finally decided that discretion was not the best policy, and flirting with him was definitely out of the question. The man might be drool-worthy, but he also appeared to be a by-the-book type of lawman.

And a grumpy one at that.

She grabbed a handful of things out of her purse and began flipping through the business cards, punch cards, and coupons. When that proved unsuccessful, she put the handful of items on top of the box in the passenger seat and reached for another.

The police chief hooked his thumbs in his gun belt and waited impatiently.

Handful number two didn't provide any better results. She was reaching for a third when he finally broke down and asked, "Are you licensed to drive?"

"Of course I am." Callie refused to look at him. Looking at him made butterflies swirl in her stomach, and she was unsettled enough as it was. She searched through her latest collection and found a ten-dollar bill, an expired library card, and two tubes of lipstick.

"Do you remember the last time you saw your license?"

She glanced at the box. "No, but…"

She'd had it out a lot. She'd been filling out so much paperwork with her address change. For a second, her heart tripped. Could she have left it at the lawyer's office or any one of the utilities she'd had to cancel and/or set up? She had such a hard time keeping track of things.

She touched a laminated card, and relief poured through her. "Here it is."

She held it out to him and tilted her head, purposely letting her hair flow over her shoulder. Her *blond* hair. It was time to get this situation back in hand. "I'm sorry if I did something wrong, sir."

He took the license from her, but otherwise ignored her.

Trying harder, she gave him her best doe-eyed look. "The countryside is just so pretty, I got distracted."

She wished she could see his eyes. Sweet-talking worked much better when she could read an officer—or a police chief's—reaction. At least, it had in the past. She needed every advantage she could get with this guy.

"So, Ms. Calina Thompson," he said, reading her name, "you never answered my question. Do you know what the speed limit is on this road?"

Damn. It didn't take a brain surgeon to figure out what that tone of voice meant. She was getting a ticket. She squinted down the road and saw a speed limit sign. "Thirty-five," she said glumly.

"Right. And how fast were you going?"

She threw him a dry look.

"I didn't think you'd have an answer for that." He looked at the contents of her impractically small back seat. "Looks like you're loaded down pretty well."

Ooh, something personal. There was her opening.

"I'm moving," she said, perking back up.

"You should have those things secured with a rope or have the top up. It's a hazard, especially with as fast as you were going."

Which, apparently, he wasn't going to tell her. Callie sank deeper into the seat. Not only was she getting a ticket, it was going to be an expensive one.

He glanced at her license again. "You're from Boston?"

The way he said "Boston" made it sound like something that made his nose hairs curl. Great. That was just what she needed, some cocky small-time chief of police trying to show his muscles.

Well, he didn't need to try so hard. She'd already noticed them.

A sharp reply was on the tip of her tongue, but she managed to hold it back. "I was."

"Where are you headed?"

"Shadow Valley."

His head came up. "You're moving to Shadow Valley?"

Had she not just said that? "That's the plan."

"The Rutger place or the apartment over Ernie's?"

She looked at him blankly. "The address is 1255 Highland."

"The old Calhoun place?"

The abrupt change in the direction of the conversation threw her. Was he actually trying to socialize with her now? *After* he'd decided to give her a ticket? Didn't this guy know how the game was played? "My aunt Jeanne left the house to me in her will."

"You *inherited* the place?"

Something about his reaction disturbed her. "Is that so hard to believe?"

"I didn't know there were any Calhouns left."

Callie drummed her fingers against the steering wheel. She'd heard about small towns being cliquish, but this was ridiculous. Was he checking her pedigree or something? Were outsiders not allowed? "Aunt Jeanne was a Thompson. I don't know anything about any Calhouns."

He stared at her for a long moment.

"That's good." He turned on his heel. "Real good. Hold on, I need to run this."

Callie blinked in confusion. What had that been about?

She watched him in the mirror as he walked away. She could usually charm people without lifting a finger—and, with him, she'd definitely been willing to let her fingers do the walking—but he'd been immune. In fact, he'd been downright surly. Apparently, her list needed a bit of tweaking. Ruggedly handsome or not, she didn't like the man. She hoped the townspeople were friendlier, because their police chief had the personality of a rock.

Which, in fact, matched his backside pretty darn well.

She ripped her gaze away from the mirror once she realized what she was doing. Forcing herself, she stared straight out the front window.

"Tight butt, mean man."

Really, would it be so hard for him to let her go with a warning? It wasn't as if she'd been speeding intentionally. Sometimes her foot tended to get a little heavy. She'd had a long drive, and she was excited about seeing the town. Did that warrant a ticket?

Her mood deteriorated as he let her sit there. And sit and sit and sit. She was stewing by the time he deigned to walk back to her car.

"Sign here," he said.

She snatched the electronic doohickey, scribbled her name, and passed it back to him.

"That's quite a list of infractions you've gathered," he said. He lifted his head, and she felt the force of his gaze. "I'm warning you right now that Shadow Valley isn't Boston. You won't be doing that here."

Callie felt her blood pressure rise. Was that a threat or a warning? "I'm sure I won't have to. The town's not about to have the traffic problems Boston does."

"That's not the only difference you'll find." He looked over her muscle car. "There's very little entertainment here."

She mentally counted to ten. Her friends had told her the same thing. Now, this Podunk police chief was trying to chase her off using the same logic? She'd had just about enough of people telling her how she should live her life.

"I'm looking forward to some peace and quiet."

"Well, we have plenty of that." He handed her the ticket, along with her license. "Welcome to Shadow Valley, Ms. Thompson. Try to keep it under the speed limit."

"Welcome, indeed," she snapped when he was far enough away not to hear.

She glanced down at her ticket, and her eyes rounded when she saw just how fast she'd been going. And he'd fined her for not having her boxes tied down! With a growl, she dropped everything into her purse. "Jerk."

She was from the big city so he had to let her know who was the boss around these parts. She glanced up to her rearview mirror and saw that he was waiting for her to pull out first. Of course. He wanted to make sure she'd gotten the message. She scrunched her nose in annoyance.

And she'd been in such a good mood.

She hit her turn signal and pulled back onto the road. The police chief followed two car lengths behind. Callie fought to ignore the tingle at the back of her neck. If he wanted her to be aware of him, the strategy was working. He followed her to the edge of town, but before she could pull over and ask him to just lead her to her new home, he turned and was gone.

"Some civil servant you are," she muttered.

Being unwelcoming to new residents... Prying into their personal lives... Setting fines when a warning would do... It was a downright shame that all that ruggedness was wasted on such a bullheaded man.

Well, she refused to let him spoil this day for her. Reaching into her pocket, she found the directions that the real estate agent had given her. She held them in front of her, got her bearings, and headed out to find her house on her own.

The old Calhoun place, huh? She'd see about that. "The Thompson place" had a much better ring to it.

Determinedly, she pushed her irritation with the police chief to the back of her mind. As she drove into town, it became easier and easier. Shadow Valley was too pretty for her to stay upset. With each block, her excitement returned.

The town looked as inviting up close as it had from afar. Little houses with pretty lawns dotted the main road into town. Overhead, fall decorations hung from the light posts. A little red-haired girl raced her bike down the sidewalk with the streamers flapping, and Callie had to grin. It was like a postcard.

Eager to explore, she continued down the road straight into the so-called business district. There was a hardware store, a post office, a library, a beauty salon, and a diner. She looked at the sign. *Mamie's*. Perfect.

"Highland Street," she said when she finally saw the street sign.

Really, would this have been so far out of Chief Hardass's way?

Taking a right, she headed back up into the hills. Anxiously, she began looking at the house numbers. It couldn't be much farther… 1023, 1101, 1215… It turned out to be as far as she could go.

"Twelve fifty-five." She pulled into the long driveway at the end of the cul-de-sac, killed the engine, and, for a moment, just sat there.

A mixture of happiness and dismay collected in her chest as she looked at the place. No wonder the police chief had been surprised that she was moving here. The property didn't look like the picture the executor of the will had given her.

At all.

She let out a calming breath. On the one hand, the house

was gorgeous. Absolutely gorgeous. The old Victorian sat far off the road, making it seem aloof, but somehow regal. It was painted white, and picturesque blue shutters surrounded every window. A porch led up to the front door. She could just imagine a swing and potted plants hanging from the rafters.

"*Ah.*" A glare flashed off the porthole window of the attic. Automatically, she lifted her hand to shield her eyes. She squinted at the house again, this time without her rose-colored glasses.

The real view of the house was much less impressive. The realtor had warned her that the house had been vacant for years, but she hadn't expected to find it in such disrepair. Half the shutters were hanging cockeyed. The paint was peeling, the lawn had grown wild, and the garage looked lopsided. In a word, the old Calhoun place was a dump.

But it was her dump now.

Callie sat a little straighter in the bucket seat of the Mustang. Forget Hardass and his condescending attitude. She'd never been afraid of a little work—although this was definitely going to take more than a *little* work. She could make this place into something; she knew it.

She grabbed her purse and the box from the passenger seat. It was time to see what the inside looked like.

She pawed through her purse for the key to the house as she followed the sidewalk up to the front door. The long grass along both sides swayed with the wind, lashing around her calves and grabbing at her feet. Her excitement grew as she found the envelope stuffed near the bottom of her bag. The lock was stubborn from disuse, but it finally turned with a squeal.

Butterflies swirled through her stomach as she pushed open the door. She found herself in an open entryway. The only word that came close to describing it was majestic. In awe, she took a deep breath—and immediately started coughing.

"Air," she said on a hack.

She set her box down in front of the door to keep it open and began searching for windows. Staircases curved up both sides of the entryway walls, and she wandered through the open arch underneath them. A large living room spanned the width of the house. There, she found the boxes of belongings that she'd shipped over the week before. The room had a ton of windows, three on each side, and she opened them all as wide as they would go. Which for some, wasn't far…

Wiping her hands, she turned and surveyed the room. "Oh, boy."

The inside of the house was in just as bad a shape as the outside. Dust and cobwebs coated everything. The fireplace was a disaster area with about half a foot of soot. A thick coating of gunk hid what was surely a gorgeous hardwood floor. And the windows… Yes, she was going to have to do windows.

Somehow, though, just being here made her happy.

She had a house with hardwood floors!

Her creative juices began to flow. The place just needed a good cleaning. The wood itself was in good shape. She didn't notice any decay, although that would take somebody with more expertise than her to decide. The floor plan was wonderful. Her furniture was placed haphazardly around the room and boxes were stacked two, sometimes three deep. Still, her entire apartment full of belongings didn't fill the room.

Her smile returned, even brighter than before. *Space.* Opening her arms wide, she spun in a circle. She had space to move. Space to breathe.

On cue, she started coughing again.

So she'd clean and *then* she'd breathe… She could deal.

She started off to explore the kitchen, but stopped when she stepped on something that crinkled. It was a curled-up piece of packing tape. She peeled it off the heel of her boot, but hadn't taken two more steps before she stepped on another. Her brow furrowed. With as sticky as that stuff was, it shouldn't have come off her boxes like this.

Confused, she looked around the room. She'd been so interested in the house that she hadn't paid much attention to anything else. Now that she actually looked, she could see that boxes had been opened. The tape she'd so carefully applied was curled on the floor like snakes.

"What in the world?"

Had somebody gone through her things?

Slowly, she stepped to the side so she could see into the kitchen. Her box of kitchenware had been ripped open, and dishes were strewn about on the counter. Feeling more than a little unnerved, she walked over to one of the open plastic storage bins. It looked like somebody had gone through her linens, too.

Could the movers have done this? No, something like this would surely get them sued. The neighbors, maybe? How snoopy did small-town people get?

Not this snoopy.

The invasion of privacy made Callie's skin crawl. Something was wrong here. Uncertain what to do, she reached for her phone.

Her purse wasn't at her side. *Darn it.* Where had she left it this time?

She spotted it perched on a window ledge. She hurried to get it, but came to a standstill when she saw the bedroom door standing open down the hallway. She took a step back to look inside. The bed had been made... or someone had tried to make the bed. It looked like a six-year-old had taken on the job—or a man.

A long, drawn-out squeak sounded overhead. Her head snapped up, but the sound didn't stop. It echoed down through the walls and reverberated in the air. Forgetting the purse, she spun for the front door instead.

And promptly ran into a stack of boxes. A piece of paper flew off the top and right into her face. Sputtering, she fought it off, but then she saw it was a note.

Ms. Thompson,

I hope your drive was enjoyable. I've left a bottle of champagne and some food in the refrigerator to welcome you to your new house. Please feel free to call me if you have any questions.

Sincerely,
Tom Henderson

The realtor.
Callie skidded to a stop. The realtor?

She looked around the room again. Boxes had been opened, but she couldn't say if anything was missing. Had Henderson tried to make the big, run-down house homier by putting a few of her things away? She shook off a shudder. He'd volunteered to open the house for the movers when she'd been trying to figure out logistics, but she'd never given him permission to go that far. But he *had* fawned all over her ever since their first phone discussion... Knowing him, he'd think he was being thoughtful.

Thoughtful. Creepy. There was such a fine line between the two.

She chewed her lower lip. What kind of a burglar made up a bed?

"None, you goofball." She tried to think rationally. The place had been locked up solid as Fort Knox. The deadbolt hadn't even wanted to turn to let her in.

Just to be safe, she went outside to double-check. All the windows, even those on the second floor, were shut tight—yet a shutter way up high was moving back and forth in the wind. She stared at it. A squeaky shutter. Of course the house was going to have creaks and groans. It was over a century and a half old. Her knees should sound so good.

She let herself in through the back door and evaluated the kitchen. Boxes had been opened, but it seemed as if her things were still here. She opened a drawer and saw that her cooking utensils had already been stowed, although they were in the drawer furthest away from the stove. Another sure sign of a man.

She was going to have to have a stern talk with her over-friendly realtor. Maybe his boss, too. She tilted her head when she heard the humming of the refrigerator. Although, what was that he'd said about bubbly?

She opened the door and found a nice bottle of champagne as well as a meat and cheese platter. "Henderson, for the moment, you are forgiven."

She let out a self-conscious laugh. She'd almost been ready to call 911. Wouldn't that have just been wonderful? Making a false emergency call on the same day she'd gotten a speeding ticket? Chief Hardass would have loved that. The thought of him showing up on her doorstep was enough to make her scowl.

She grabbed the bottle of champagne and opened a cupboard. A coffee mug suited her needs. She laughed when the cork popped out of the bottle and white foam spilled over onto the dusty floor. The antiseptic wouldn't hurt.

The rhythmic squeak from upstairs started again, and she raised her mug of champagne in salute. She didn't care what the police chief or the rest of the town thought; she liked the old Calhoun place.

"To the two of us," she said to the house. "What a pair we'll make."

CHAPTER TWO

The door to the stationhouse stuck as Carter walked in. It was yet another thing to add to the list of irritations he'd had to endure over the past two days. Putting his shoulder into it, he bulled his way inside. Steel scraped against linoleum, letting out a piercing shriek. Nancy Watkins, his trusty administrative assistant, jumped at the sound, and Bill Raikins came right out of his chair.

"Chief Landry!"

"You're back."

Bill glanced at the door. "I take it the task force meeting didn't go so well."

"No," Carter said. "It didn't."

The door stuck again as it tried to swing shut. He gave it a shove, and the bottom corner left a darkened layer of smudge against the floor. "When are we going to get this thing fixed?"

Nancy already had a phone to her ear. "I'll get Ernie over here right away."

The owner of the hardware store doubled as Shadow Valley's fix-it guy. Carter took off his sunglasses and ran a hand over his face. Too bad his other problems couldn't be solved so easily. "Thanks, Nancy."

She smiled. "You've had a long week, chief."

Yes, he had.

He headed to the coffee pot. With a sigh, he slipped his sunglasses in his shirt pocket. It was tough to judge how long the sludge had been sitting there, but he reached for a cup anyway.

It felt good to be back. He'd spent the entire day yesterday in hell. Actually, it had been Concord, but who was counting?

He took a long drink of the bitter liquid and turned to his office. One glance at the far wall nearly changed his mind. The state map, dotted with colored pins, hadn't changed since he'd left. And it probably wouldn't at the rate things were going. Not even a swig of caffeine was going to help with that.

"So what happened with the task force?" Bill asked as he wove his way through the maze of desks.

The muscles at the back of Carter's neck clenched. "Not much."

"Really? What was the problem?"

"Too many people trying to play king of the hill." He rolled his shoulders and tried to get the kink to pop. Just thinking about it got him riled up. "State officials were tangling with the local police and sheriff's departments. Everybody's trying to either cover their asses or take control. It was like side business that we still have two escaped convicts out there on the loose."

Bill scowled. "Have they narrowed down the search area for Smith and Morton at all? Is Fleiss talking?"

Carter stared into his coffee and watched the swirls go around the cup. "Those are good questions. In fact, they're better than most I heard all day. You'd think we would have talked about something like that."

"You're kidding me. You guys didn't get anywhere?"

"I would have made more progress from here."

"But the governor appointed you to that committee. Couldn't you take over or something?"

Carter let out a harsh laugh. "Don't even think about wishing that on me. Besides, I'm just a small-town police chief. What do I know?"

Bill looked poleaxed. "But we caught Fleiss. Why aren't

they listening to you?"

"Apparently, we just got lucky."

Irritation flared in Carter's gut, and it warred with the caffeine he'd just poured down his throat. Politics. He hated when they got in the way. Just because he and his staff weren't dealing with major crimes on a daily basis didn't mean that they were any less competent than the big-city cops. He'd put his people up against those clowns on the task force any day.

He looked at the map on his office wall. The color-coded pins marked the locations where the prison escapees had been spotted. The blue ones ended in Bernardston, a town close to the state's western border, where they'd assisted in tracking down and arresting Jack Fleiss. Red pins followed Smith's progress, but the green ones worried Carter the most. The green pins were Clive Morton's.

"It's been a week," Bill said. "They could be anywhere by now."

Carter eased his weight onto the edge of his desk. "You and I might be the only ones who realize that."

"What about that retired FBI guy from Boston? The guy the governor appointed head of the task force?"

"Boston." Carter grunted. He'd had it up to here with Boston. He'd spent more time than he could stand at a meeting run by that idiot, and then there'd been that reckless driver just outside the town limits. His tired mind did a stutter step. That smokin'-hot reckless driver... but a Bostonian nonetheless.

"The FBI guy is one of the biggest problems," he said. "He should have stayed retired."

"So what's our plan? Do we need to be more proactive?" Bill asked.

Carter wiped the vision of the blonde from his mind. "No change. Everyone keeps an eye out for anything unusual. Pay particular attention to the back roads, and make sure anything even a little off is investigated. That's as much as we can do. Like you say, they're probably not even in the state anymore."

"But you don't think that."

Carter looked at the pins. Call it gut instinct, but he didn't.

The escapees had no money, no known means of transportation, and no shelter—but Fleiss had made it as far as Bernardston. If the three of them had stuck together, it made a few recent robberies suspicious. A car had been stolen in Bernardston, and an all-night diner had been knocked over in Northfield. He just had a sinking feeling both incidents should be marked with a red pin. "I'd put money on Smith being nearby."

"That leaves Morton still out there."

"He's gone to ground." That was what worried Carter most. Tough guys were easy to handle. Smart guys were another thing entirely. He had no doubt that Morton's IQ was double that of the Boston FBI twit. The guy was cunning and ruthless and, so far, he hadn't made a mistake.

But he would.

"One of these days, he's going to have to come up for air." Carter set his coffee cup down on his desk. Damn, but he wanted to be there when that happened.

He turned away from the map and sat down in his worn, old chair. Frustration gnawed at him, but he had a police station to run. With a little more force than was necessary, he hit the power button on his computer.

Bill lingered near the doorway. "Why don't you just go home for the rest of the day, chief? Nancy and I can handle things here."

"And face even more paperwork tomorrow? Yeah, that sounds like fun." The moment the words were out, Carter realized he was snapping at the wrong guy. Sighing, he ran a hand through his hair. "Sorry. Yesterday didn't go as well as I would've liked, and today hasn't been much better. Hell, I nearly ran our latest resident out of town. Why didn't somebody tell me we have a newbie in the Calhoun place?"

"They're here? I saw a moving truck the other day."

"Not they. She."

Bill paused with one foot out the door. "A woman?"

Having somebody new in town was big news... almost as

big as having three convicts escape from Concord. But a woman? Forget about it. News of this was going to spread like wildfire.

"You heard me."

"Single?"

"Apparently." She'd asked him to call her *miz*. He might have been in a lousy mood, but he hadn't missed what that tidbit meant.

"What do you know?" Bill paused as he considered the possibilities. "Are we talking hot, young babe or retired bingo player?"

"Young." And hotter than a pistol. Carter scowled when his mouse pointer stuck. Was nothing going to work for him today? He jiggled the mouse, and the pointer jumped halfway across the screen.

Bill just wasn't going to make it out the door. "What's she look like?" he asked.

Carter knocked the mouse against the table, but that helped about as much as using a sledgehammer on a straight pin. Finally, he gave up and turned the mouse over. He took out the batteries and opened his drawer to look for fresh ones.

What had Ms. Callie looked like? She looked like heaven, pure and simple.

He was always careful during traffic stops, but he hadn't been prepared for what lay in store for him when he'd walked up to her car. She'd looked up at him with that tangled blond hair and those deep brown eyes, and he'd felt a solid kick in his gut.

Bill let out a whistle. "Wow, she must be something."

Carter ground his teeth together. "She's something, all right. She's reckless. When I first spotted her, she was driving without any hands on the steering wheel. It was like she thought she was on a roller coaster or something."

He blew out a breath. He didn't know why she'd gotten him so worked up. When he'd come across her, he hadn't been able to figure out what he'd been dealing with. She'd been acting so erratically. First there'd been the hand-waving incident. Then she'd stopped on the side of the road and sat for a spell. When she'd then started to drive and the speedometer had just kept climbing, he'd decided it was time to stop watching and do something.

Bill rounded the desk to look at the computer screen, and Carter nearly swore. He shouldn't have pulled up the ticket. Bill's eyes darted back and forth as he read the limited information. Carter couldn't stop him with his mouse on the fritz. Besides, his officer could just go back to his own computer and pull up the ticket.

That didn't mean Carter liked having him look at it.

"A silver Mustang?" Bill put a hand over his heart. "We've got a live one on our hands."

Carter felt the twinge in his shoulder. He couldn't blame the guy. There weren't that many single, available women in Shadow Valley, and this town hadn't seen a woman like Callie Thompson in a long time. He doubted Boston had seen many women like that.

If only she hadn't tried to sweet-talk him...

Irritation surged all over again. Her smile and her routine had been so polished that he'd automatically known she'd used them before. Frankly, to feel that kick and then realize the smile could have been for anyone in a uniform had been a letdown. Worse, it had ticked him off, effectively ruining her chances of getting off with a warning. If that hadn't done it, seeing her list of prior offenses would have. The woman was a regular speed demon—and a speed demon from Boston at that. Giving her a ticket had been a distinct pleasure.

Bill lowered himself into a chair, too intrigued to realize he should be leaving. "Why did she choose the Calhoun place?"

The Rutger house was less than a block away from Bill's apartment. Carter hated to disappoint his officer, but honestly, he was kind of happy that she wasn't moving into the rental. On the other hand, the place she was taking could be worse. "She inherited it."

Bill's head whipped back. "No way."

"That's what she says."

23

"Does she know?"

"I don't think so."

Carter snapped the mouse back together and ran it experimentally over the mouse pad. At last, it decided to behave, and he opened the file that Nancy had marked as priority.

Bill sat back in his chair and balanced it on its hind legs. He wasn't ready to let go of the new girl thing—or the fact that she was moving into the most infamous house in the north county area. "Somebody's bound to tell her."

And that was when the real trouble would start.

They'd had nothing but bad luck with the residents of 1255 Highland. The rumors that swirled around the place made people a little nutty. Carter's staff had been called out to that house at least once a week when the last family had lived there. Once people got something into their heads, it was hard to convince them otherwise. "I'm hoping things will be different this time."

Bill let out a snort. "Good luck with that."

A phone rang out in the bullpen, and the front legs of the officer's chair came down with a bang. Carter turned back to his computer as Bill went to answer the call.

His officer was probably right. Gossip, after all, was a tag-team sport in Shadow Valley. Once people found out that Callie Thompson had moved into the Calhoun house, they'd be climbing over one another to tell her the stories that surrounded the place. Nobody seemed to care that the gossip didn't hold an ounce of truth. People were always trying to outdo each other, and the stories grew every time they were told. If she heard those rumors before she settled into the place, the mind games were bound to begin. Then the distress calls would start again.

Carter pushed the mouse aside. Maybe he should just step in now and head off the inevitable. With the task force, the search for the escapees, and normal town business, he didn't have time to go running out to the Calhoun house every time Ms. Callie heard things go bump in the night.

Then again, bumping in the night with her could have other distinct advantages…

Hell. He wiped a hand over his face. That woman was going to be more trouble than she was worth; he could tell already. It was those big eyes of hers. Not to mention that sassy mouth…

Nancy poked her head into his office. "Ernie said he's busy with a patron right now, but he'll be down later to work on the door."

Carter sat up straighter. "Great. Thanks, Nance."

It was time to get his head back into business. Business that didn't include a blond firebrand. "What did I miss yesterday? Is there anything important I need to know about?"

"Stephanie Evans and C.J. Carlson had a fender bender in the grocery store parking lot, and we had to bring David Hughes in again. Alice Gunthrie caught him snooping around the tool shed in her backyard."

Carter closed his eyes and rubbed the bridge of his nose. The news about the Hughes kid wasn't really news at all. He was one of those types that just couldn't seem to stay out of trouble—or wanted to. "What was he doing there? Did Alice notice anything missing?"

"No, we just got him for trespassing this time."

Carter shook his head. "That kid is headed straight for juvie."

Nancy folded her hands together. She was a sweet woman with a heart of gold, but she also had a backbone of steel. "If this time doesn't do it, the next one will."

It was a foregone conclusion that there would be a next time. With David Hughes, there always was. Carter sighed and leaned back in his chair. "I'll drop by and have another talk with him."

Nancy shook her head ruefully. "You're not going to get through to him. You know he won't listen."

"Yeah, but I have to try. When they go back through his records, at least we can show that we tried to straighten him out." Carter ran his thumb over the lip of his coffee cup. Callie Thompson. David Hughes. The Boston FBI idiot. And everyone thought that the gig of a small-town lawman was easy.

"Hey, chief," Bill called from the other room. "You might want to come see this."

Carter let out a groan and looked at Nancy. "I should have gone home."

"It might have been a good idea."

He pushed himself out of his chair and headed out into the main bay. Bill was standing near the front windows. Something outside on the town square had caught his attention. "What is it?"

"Is that the silver Mustang you ticketed earlier today?"

Carter felt his shoulder twinge. One look out the window, and his rotten mood returned. "Damn."

Parked on the town square was a shiny silver bullet of a car. There were just two problems: 1) The car was parked in front of a fire hydrant and 2) Its owner was heading into the biggest gossip mill in town, Mamie's restaurant.

* * *

Callie's head was spinning as she walked down the sidewalk along Main Street. It hadn't taken her long to figure out that she couldn't unpack before she did some cleaning. The thought of putting food on those grimy counters or walking barefoot across those floors made her cringe. She'd come to town for supplies, but had gotten sidetracked at the hardware store. She'd stopped just for the essentials, but her little visit had taken more time and money than she'd planned. Her Mustang was once again packed to the brim—with the top *up*—and her brain hurt from all the advice that Ernie, the hardware guy, had given her. He was delivering all the things that wouldn't fit in her car tomorrow.

She had a sinking feeling that she was in over her head.

Scraping, sealing, priming, painting… And that was just on the outside. Who knew how old the wiring was? Or the plumbing?

Feeling overwhelmed, she walked into the diner. She was starving, and she knew better than to stop for groceries when just about anything sounded good. Besides, that kitchen needed to be scoured before she cooked anything in it.

The bell over the door rang, signaling her arrival. It was early for supper and late for lunch, but several people sat in the booths that surrounded the main counter. Glances darted her way, along with smiles. She chose an open booth along the far wall.

A pleasant-looking woman dropped a menu on the table. "Can I get you something to drink, dear?"

"A Coke, please." Callie shrugged out of her blue jean jacket. It was a classic small-town diner complete with Formica counters and chrome napkin holders. The silverware gleamed and the red-checkered floor shone. Best of all, the aromas coming out of the kitchen had her salivating.

Ice rattled in a red plastic glass when the woman returned with the drink and set it on the table. She placed a paper-wrapped straw beside it. "Are you a leaf peeper?"

Callie smiled. She loved the colors of the season, but she wasn't a tourist anymore. "I just moved here."

"Really?" The interest in the woman's eyes grew. She had happy eyes, really, and a pleasant face. "Welcome! I'm Mamie."

Her mood was infectious, and Callie laughed. "I wondered if there really was a Mamie. I'm Callie. Callie Thompson."

"Where did you move into, hon? The apartment over Ernie's?"

Callie tilted her head. There had been a vacancy notice in the window of the hardware store, now that she thought about it. "The house at the end of Highland Street." She pointed in the direction of her new digs. "Just a few blocks up."

Mamie's happy eyes rounded. "The old Calhoun place?"

There it was again. Callie's smile faltered when she remembered her encounter with the police chief. "I've heard it called that."

"Oh dear."

"I know. I didn't expect it to be as bad as it is, but I'm going to work on it."

"Oh my. Are you sure you want to stay there?"

"It's all right." Callie found herself in the odd position of comforting the woman, when she'd spent the last hour or so trying to convince herself of the same thing. "It will take some work, but it has good bones. I think I can turn it into a showplace."

"Yes, but… Oh, heavens." Mamie patted her gray hair and looked around the restaurant anxiously. When she turned back around, she was biting her bottom lip. "Do you know what you want to eat?"

"Um…" Callie hadn't had a chance to even look at the menu. "A burger and fries?"

"Coming right up." Mamie snatched up the menu and dashed away without another word.

Callie watched as she scooted back to her command post behind the counter. She clipped the order onto the rotating wheel for the cook and spun it around. Without missing a beat, she grabbed the old-fashioned phone that hung on the wall. When she realized that she was being watched, she smiled charmingly, but then turned her back. Callie watched in fascination as the woman spoke into the phone in hushed words. When she hung up, she smiled that beatific smile again and went back to work as if nothing had happened.

What in the world?

When the bell jingled over the door a few minutes later, Mamie pointed in the direction of Callie's table. Callie blinked and looked swiftly at the door. A short pixie of a woman had arrived. She couldn't have been five feet tall. Her white hair was clipped short, and her blue uniform was crisp. At Mamie's direction, the woman swiftly marched over to the booth. Callie couldn't help but brace herself.

"Hi." The pixie's voice sounded like gravel on sandpaper.

"Good afternoon," Callie said uncertainly.

"Alice Gunthrie." The woman stuck out her hand. "I'm the postmaster in these parts."

"Callie Thompson." For as tiny as the woman was, that voice was going to take some getting used to. "It's nice to meet you."

"Mamie said you've moved into the Calhoun house."

Ah. Callie threw a look in Mamie's direction, and the woman had the grace to blush.

"Yes, I have. I was going to visit the post office next to see if any of my mail had been forwarded yet."

Alice cocked her head. "Girl, why would you want to do a foolish thing like that?"

"Forward my mail?"

"Move in *there*?"

Disbelief dripped from her words, and Callie sat up a bit straighter. It was her house, after all, and she'd already developed some pride in it. "Why not? My aunt left it to me, and I think it has potential."

Alice's jaw dropped. For a long moment, she didn't even breathe. "You *in-her-i-ted* the place?"

"From my great-aunt Jeanne."

"You're family?"

"Well, yes. I didn't know her well, but I sent her Christmas cards every year. Did you know her?"

"Never heard of her." Without being invited, Alice slid onto the padded bench across the table. She settled her chin into her hands and didn't even try to be coy as she gave Callie a once-over. "So you're a Calhoun. I'll be darned!"

Callie shifted uncomfortably when Alice and Mamie shared a look. Worse, people around the diner started murmuring. All she'd wanted was a quick meal before she headed back to the house. That was it. She hadn't expected to be subjected to some kind of town inquest—although after her experience with their chief of police, she should have known better. "I'm a Thompson. I inherited the place from a distant relative, who was also a Thompson. I don't know anything about any Calhouns."

"Gotta be. Gotta be. All the others were renters, but if you inherited it… It just might work this time."

"What might work?"

Alice waved off the question, but she and Mamie shared another look. "Never mind. I've got a good feeling about you."

Callie wasn't sure she could return the compliment. First Chief Hardass and now Postmaster Pokey. Why was everybody getting up in her business?

Alice folded her arms on the table. "Have you been inside the place?"

Callie ripped the wrapper off her straw. Was there a polite way to excuse herself? Could she get her order to go? "I just finished unloading my car."

"How did it feel?"

The odd question had her pausing as she wadded the paper into a tiny ball. "Feel? I don't know. It felt... historic. Lonely. Welcoming?"

"Ha! Well, there you go."

When raised in volume, Alice's voice was a close approximation of a foghorn. More people started to watch them, and Mamie hovered even closer. She was wiping the table next to them with a rag, even though the tabletop was already sparkling.

"Are you here with your husband? Got a family?" Alice craned her neck to look for other people in a car or wandering back from the restroom.

"I'm single."

Mamie's mouth rounded.

"You'll be out there alone?" Alice croaked.

"Why?" Callie asked, pinning her with a look. "What's wrong?"

When Alice went mum, Callie focused on Mamie. She jumped as if she'd been poked.

"Oh, nothing, dear," she said sweetly. "It's just a little... Well, you know... The mess and decay and all. It's so dark up there."

"So she'll buy a light." Alice leaned in. "What do you do, hon? Teach karate, maybe? Or a woman of the cloth?"

"Alice," Mamie hissed.

"What? The skills might help." Alice pursed her lips. "The town's a nice place, but we don't have many job openings."

Callie could see the curiosity in the women's eyes. Suddenly the inquisition made sense. The police chief's she still didn't understand, but these two? They were the generator behind the town's rumor mill. She hid her smile. It would be good for her to remember that.

She dropped the paper ball she'd made onto the table, and it rolled in a lopsided circle. "I kept my old job. With a computer and the Internet, I can work from almost anywhere."

"Doing what?"

"I have a column," she said evasively.

"A column of what?"

"A newspaper column."

"You're a journalist?"

"I'm a humorist."

Alice's brow furrowed. "You write jokes?"

Callie had hoped to put this off for at least a little while, but there really was no getting around it. She might as well give the rumor mill something harmless to work with. "Observations, really. I write about random things that catch my attention, answer people's questions, give advice, that type of thing..."

"Have we ever heard of you?" Alice asked. "Do we get you here in Shadow Valley?"

"I'm not sure. The column is syndicated. Ever heard of *Quick Thinking*?"

The postmaster smacked both hands onto the table, and the tiny paper ball Callie had made from her straw wrapper went tumbling off the table. "Holy mackerel. You're Quick Kate?"

Mamie let out a gasp. "We all read your column, dear," she said, forgetting to pretend she wasn't listening. "You're wonderful. Why, somebody was laughing just this morning about the advice you'd given."

Callie blushed, but took the praise in the spirit it was intended. "Thank you. I think."

Alice was practically bouncing in her seat. "I can't believe you've moved to Shadow Valley—and to *that* house. An observationist. Ha! You'll have something to write about out there. Hey, is that why they've been printing reruns of your column for the past week? Because you were moving here?"

Callie took a sip of her Coke. She should have ordered something stronger. "Uh huh."

"Oh my stars." Mamie fanned herself. "We have a celebrity in our midst." ⸺

People turned in their seats and voices rose. Behind her, Callie heard the bell over the door jingle.

"Carter!" Alice croaked. "Perfect timing. Get over here."

Callie turned in her seat to see who was going to accost her this time, and she stiffened. Chief Hardass. Again. Great.

He reached up to remove his sunglasses, and his attention landed on her. Awareness snapped between them like electricity. Uncomfortable. Enlivening. Powerful. But then he looked at her new friends and scowled.

"Hustle it up," Alice said, waving him over. "You're not going to believe who this is."

Callie let out a long breath as the town police chief walked over and planted himself at the end of her table. God, he was big. He was tall and solid as a brick house. He folded his arms across his chest as he towered over them, and she reached for her drink. Her mouth had suddenly gone dry.

"*Miz* Callie Thompson?" he said.

The emphasis was so subtle that she almost didn't hear it. Yet when she looked up at him, that strange electricity crackled again. "Chief... I don't think I ever did get your name."

"Landry. It's Carter Landry."

"Oh." Alice swiveled her head back and forth between the two of them. "You two have already met?"

"You could say that," Callie muttered.

"So he knows?" Alice said.

"Knows what?" Landry asked.

"That she's a Calhoun."

"I'm not—" Callie started.

"And she's Quick Kate!"

There was a pause. "Who?" he finally asked.

"Kate." Alice rolled her hand as if trying to pull it out of him. "You know, from the paper."

The chief's gaze homed in on Callie again, and she fought not to squirm. He had blue eyes. Really blue.

"Your driver's license said your name was Calina."

Her grip on her drink tightened. He didn't have a clue. Not one. "It's not my real name."

"You gave me a false ID?" he practically growled.

"No, no. It's a pseudonym."

"Calina?"

"Kate," she said impatiently.

"Carter," Alice said with obvious frustration, "she writes the *Quick Thinking* column in the newspaper."

"As Kate," Callie said. Most people had at least heard of the column, even if they didn't read it. Did he live in a cave?

Actually, that made sense.

"So your name *is* Calina," he said.

She jabbed her straw into her glass. "I prefer Callie."

"Carter." Alice knocked on the table to get his attention. "You're missing the point. She writes for the paper, and she's going to be living in the old Calhoun house."

The postmaster waggled her eyebrows suggestively.

Conversely, the chief's eyes narrowed, and the temperature at the table cooled. "Alice," he said in that low, rumbling voice, "so help me, if you've already started telling her stories about that—"

"Hush." Alice cut him off with a swift chopping motion. "It's a good thing. At least, we think it is."

Mamie slipped a large to-go coffee into the police chief's hand. She patted his arm and looked at Callie. "Yes, we have a very good feeling about this."

An impish look came into her eyes. "In fact... Did you know that our handsome police chief is single too, dear?"

"Oh, for God's sake. Mamie." An exasperated look came over Landry's face, and he rolled a shoulder in obvious discomfort. "Just don't listen to a thing they tell you," he warned Callie.

"But Carter..." Alice said with a pout.

"Me?" Mamie said, hurt.

He let one eyebrow lift. "They tend to be… excitable."

Callie hadn't noticed.

With a huff, Alice settled back in her seat. She was so short that she nearly disappeared beneath the level of the table. Muttering, Mamie hurried off to get an order.

"But this time they're going to try to keep the excitement down to a manageable level," Landry called after her. "Ms. Thompson moved here specifically for peace and quiet."

"She did now, did she?" Alice said. "And how do you know that, Mr. Bossy?"

"I told him so," Callie said.

Alice popped up like a jack-in-the-box. "You were called out there already, Carter?"

Landry rolled his eyes. "We had a chat when I caught her doing twenty miles an hour over the speed limit coming into town."

"Twenty! Ooh, honey." The postmaster made a tsking noise. "That's too fast. That road twists and turns like a belly dancer."

Callie folded her arms over her chest. She should have known. She was the outsider, after all, and he was the hunky police chief. Big fish, little pond. "He also fined me for not having my boxes tied down."

"You do the crime," he said softly, "you do the time."

Mamie stopped with a BLT order held high. "Oh, Carter. Stop picking on the dear. She's brand new to town, and isn't she just the prettiest thing?"

Callie felt heat suffuse her face. She'd wanted backup, but not like that.

Even the big fish looked like he wanted to jump to another pond. He cleared his throat and looked down at his coffee. "Uh, so, Alice, I heard there was some trouble out at your place while I was gone."

"Don't you go changing the topic, boy."

He ran a hand through his hair. When he looked at her again, Callie dug her fingers deeper into her elbows.

"Just take whatever they tell you with a grain of salt," he

said.

"Oh, we'll be good," Alice croaked. "We promise to just sit back and see how everything goes."

Mamie zipped her thumb and forefinger across her lips. "We swear."

The police chief didn't look too sure, but he reached into his pocket and pulled out money for the coffee. He gave it to Mamie, but then hesitated, as if he wasn't comfortable leaving them together. Finally, with a nod, he turned and headed to the door. Callie finally let out her breath when the bell jingled.

Mamie spun so fast that her apron flared. "I've got the best feeling about this," she said, clapping her hands together in delight.

"Oh, yeah." Alice's eyes danced. "Things are going to get interesting around here—and in more ways than one."

CHAPTER THREE

He'd ticketed her again!

Callie shoved the front door shut with her hip and stormed into the house.

A quick bite at the diner had turned into much more, and she'd found herself essentially trapped at her table by interested admirers. By the time she'd left, the police chief had been long gone, but he'd left a reminder tucked under the windshield wiper of her car. A parking ticket this time.

"*Aaagggh.*"

Okay, so she'd parked in front of a fire hydrant. It hadn't been intentional. She hadn't even seen the thing. She'd been looking up at shop signs and window displays. Besides, it had been painted green. Weren't they supposed to be yellow or red to draw attention to themselves? No, this thing had blended right in. Although some might argue that green didn't blend with the concrete sidewalk...

She dropped her bag from Ernie's onto the kitchen table with a thud.

Had he ticketed her before or after he'd come into the restaurant? What was his problem, anyway? Did he feel the need to show her who was boss? Was he used to being the big man on campus? Did he not like the attention she was getting at the restaurant for her column?

A column that, apparently, he didn't read.

He hadn't even heard of it. She didn't know why that irked her so much. There were millions of people who had never heard of her. They didn't bother her.

He did.

She shrugged out of her jacket and threw it over a chair. The way he'd spoken to Mamie and Alice had been uncalled for, too. So stern and parental. As if two mature women needed rules on what to say and how to behave. Okay, so they were excitable. What was wrong with that?

Callie grabbed her new broom and started sweeping.

The way they'd stood up for him after he'd left, though! Boy, had they laid it on thick. Her fellow diners had been more than happy to tell her all about the police chief's exploits. Everyone from Alice to Mamie to the busboy had been quick to tell her the story of the "big arrest." Apparently, Landry and his people had been involved in the capture of one of those escaped convicts from Concord.

And, okay, maybe it had been a big deal.

"Maybe he is a stud." She wiped her forehead with the back of her arm. "Okay, granted, the man is a stud."

That didn't mean she was impressed. Throwing around tickets willy-nilly didn't make him Super Cop.

In minutes, she was up to her elbows in sudsy water. Armed with a sponge, she attacked the kitchen counters.

Alice had excused the chief's grumpy mood on lack of sleep, due to the fact that he was on the governor's task force to track down those remaining fugitives, and Mamie had gone on and on about how sweet the man was.

"Sweet as a toothache," Callie muttered. Two tickets and a fine! Didn't he have anything better to do? If he was so hopped up to find those escaped inmates, why was he wasting his time with her?

"Hardass," she muttered.

She looked around at the progress she'd made. The cupboards needed to be cleaned out and the floor begged to be scrubbed, but the kitchen almost looked livable. It smelled better, too. She'd opened the windows to get rid of the staleness. The bite in the breeze coming in put goosebumps on her arms, but the air was lighter now. Lighter and happier.

She glanced up. Funny, the wind hadn't let up, but that shutter on the second floor had stopped squeaking.

"Not complaining." She grabbed her broom and headed to her new bedroom.

She was nowhere near to working off the steam she'd built up over one ruggedly sexy, but irritating man.

It was only after scrubbing her knuckles raw, breaking a nail, and bruising both knees that she decided she could stand to stay for the night. She'd only managed to get the kitchen, her bedroom, and the bathroom into some sort of order. The rest of the house remained untouched.

As it had for years.

She stretched to pop her back. It was time for a break.

She returned to the kitchen and dropped heavily onto one of the chairs she'd shipped from her apartment in Boston. When she looked out the window, she was surprised how dark it was. More time had passed during her cleaning spree than she'd realized. With as far back as the house sat off the street, not even the streetlights reached this far.

The thought was a bit unnerving.

"Alice was right. I need to get some outdoor lighting."

In fact, she needed to start a list for the next time she went to Ernie's. Feeling uneasy, she got up to close the windows. She rubbed her stomach when it growled noisily. Food also needed to go on that list. She hadn't managed to get to the grocery store. In fact, she'd forgotten about it entirely.

"Thank God for overly friendly realtors." She sighed in bliss when she opened the refrigerator and felt the cool air hit her over-warmed skin. "By the time I have that chat with you, Henderson, I may just feel like kissing you."

Although... The man had once again crossed the line by setting her toiletries out in the shower. Just thinking about him fondling her raspberry-scented body wash gave her the heebie-jeebies. "Kicking you, I meant. *Kicking*."

That didn't mean she wouldn't eat his food. She reached for the meat and cheese platter. There was enough to last her for a few days. At least she didn't have to head out again tonight, which was a very good thing. With as hard as she'd worked, she'd be apt to fall asleep before she made it out of the produce section. If the grocery store even stayed open this late…

She grabbed the champagne, too. Not even bothering to get a plate or silverware, she sat down at the table and tucked a foot underneath her. Finally, she felt herself start to unwind. It was her first night in her new home, and she was determined to enjoy it—regardless of the state of the house, the grumpy police chief, or a town full of nice, but snoopy people.

"Just what's wrong with the place anyway?" She took a bite of a rolled-up slice of roast beef and glanced around.

Her heart nearly jumped out her chest when she saw someone looking straight back at her.

She recognized her mirror image in the same instant and pressed a hand to her ribcage. "Stupid window."

The darkness outside was black now. Inky black without a hint of moonlight. With the kitchen light glowing, it made the glass window perfect for reflections… or seeing in from the outside.

Callie shook off the sudden, eerie feeling of being watched. "Curtains."

Her list was growing longer and longer.

Trying not to look at that dark abyss, she evaluated the kitchen. The stove looked like it might be on its last legs. The 1970s-style linoleum was curling off the floor in the corners, but that really was a good thing. It had to go. As did the olive-green walls…

The sensation of being watched hit her again.

She whipped her head to the window, but quickly realized that wasn't where it was coming from.

Thump.

The noise made her turn sharply to her left. The basement.

Thump-thump.

She lurched out of her chair, caught the edge of the table, and braced herself. Her breaths sounded loud in her ears, but she tried to listen past them for anything else. Anything... Something...

Air started blowing from the vent on the floor. The furnace. It was just the old furnace.

Her shoulders slumped in relief. *That* was going to take some getting used to.

A cold breeze swept over her skin. "What the—"

Twisting, she looked under the table at the vent. She could feel heat on her ankles, so why did the room suddenly feel like it had gotten twenty degrees colder? The air wasn't only downright chilly, it seemed heavy. Weighty, somehow.

The hair at the back of her neck rose.

Clunk.

"That's it." She scooped up the tray. It was late, and she was overtired. She put the platter back in the refrigerator, but kept the champagne. She scowled at the basement door.

She hadn't liked it when she'd explored down there earlier today. Hadn't liked it at all. The big, gaping room was unfinished and dingy. Maybe it was that emptiness that had bothered her. Light hadn't even wanted to go down there.

She waited for the furnace a moment longer.

Once again, she was greeted with silence.

"Good," she said. Still, she took another swig of champagne.

She nearly dropped the bottle when a long, drawn-out creak came from overhead. The sound was haunting, coming right down through the outer wall. She lasted only a half-second more before thrusting the champagne into the refrigerator and hurrying out of the room.

It was that annoying shutter, she reminded herself... the one on the second floor.

Not to mention some alcohol that had obviously gone straight to her head.

She found the thermostat in the hallway near her bedroom.

The living room seemed warmer, but she could feel that chill seeping out of the kitchen. Almost as if it was pushing her away from it…

A shiver ran through her.

"Darn it." The furnace needed help. She was going to have to get somebody out here to check on it.

Goosebumps dimpled her bare arms, and darkness pressed on her from all sides. The dim light from the old bulbs in the light fixtures couldn't hold it back. Quickly, she scampered to her room. For one night, she'd have to survive the old-fashioned way of huddling under the covers. Her teeth were chattering by the time she closed the door behind her.

When she did, the chill disappeared, and she was practically bathed in warmth.

She frowned. Kneeling down, she held her hand out in front of the floor vent in this room. Warm air brushed against her fingertips. She sighed. No doubt about it, the heating system was screwed up. *"Ka-ching."*

She was going to have to start writing again soon to earn the money to pay for all these repairs.

Fatigue suddenly hit her hard.

It had been a long day… A big day… The first in her new way of life…

She opened a box to search for something to sleep in. The only things she could find, though, were towels and bedsheets. Giving up, she shrugged out of her clothes. She slapped off the overhead light and dove, naked, for the bed. She pulled the covers up to her chin.

Sucking in a deep breath, she tried to relax.

This was going to have to stop. The house was old and needy. It didn't make any sense why she was letting it get to her. She was used to noise. She'd moved here to get away from the hustle and bustle. On any given night in her old apartment in Boston, she'd had to sleep through music from next door, vacuuming from the obsessive-compulsive upstairs, or fighting from the newlyweds across the hall. A clunky furnace and a creaky shutter should be nothing.

Then again, it could be because she was alone.

Click.

The soft sound was impossible to ignore. Callie's eyes flew open, and she sat straight up in bed. Her heart thudded as she reached over and turned on the bedside lamp. With wide eyes, she looked across the room.

And her heart nearly stopped.

Her bedroom door had just locked itself.

* * *

Her hand hovered over the doorknob, still warm to the touch. This was not how she'd wanted it to be. Not at all.

She glided up and down the hallway outside the first-floor bedroom. Anger burned inside her, filling her being and clouding her soul. A burst of energy left her, and the open lids of the boxes in the living room bent back before flopping forward.

Her home had been infiltrated.

Her secrets were being used against her.

This simply couldn't go on.

Propelled by her frustration, she swept into the living room. Things cluttered the area. Things that weren't hers. She paused in the kitchen, disturbed by the strange scents that floated on the air. They made her draw back. Strange lemon and pine odors stained the atmosphere and—

Fresh air. Fresh, clean autumn air. She let it swim over her.

The winds of change.

Her anger honed into sharp, pointed teeth. The winds of change were here, but the uninvited spirit threatened to ruin it all. She'd waited so long for this place and time. She couldn't linger any longer. She couldn't bear it.

The door to the basement swung open with a beleaguered creak. Darkness awaited her, cold and yawning, and she pitched herself down the stairs.

It couldn't stay. Not here. Not in her house.

Not now.

CHAPTER FOUR

"The tumbler is bad; that's all," Callie told herself.

For the thousandth time.

In the light of day, it made sense. Yet she'd gotten very little sleep last night as she'd listened to the clunky furnace and the squeaky shutter. By comparison, the lock on her bedroom door should have been nothing—but it bothered her. She didn't really know how locks worked. Why hadn't it malfunctioned any other time of the day?

She fought off a shudder. It had just been the sound of that *click*.

Coincidence or not, she wasn't going to spend another night like that. She'd already oiled and tested the thing. Now, it was time to address the squeaking from above.

Wading through the sea of grass, she rounded the house and dropped her things onto a bare patch of earth. The lawn service was supposed to come out in a few days, but she couldn't wait for them to start this project. She looked up at the shutters, particularly the one on the second floor. "You're mine, buddy. As soon as Ernie delivers my ladder, you're coming down."

Until then, she had to make do. Improvising, she set a kitchen chair under one of the first-floor windows. Armed with a screwdriver, she climbed onto the chair and got to work.

Ernie had a cousin who was supposed to drop by to look at the furnace. She could only imagine how ancient that thing had to be, although she hadn't worked up the courage to go downstairs and look at it. It wouldn't matter if she did; she didn't know the first thing about furnaces.

She scowled at the shutter in front of her. Ernie had recommended taking down the shutters to paint them, but some genius before her had decided to take the lazy route and paint right over the screws. With all the blue paint gunking up the heads, it was impossible to get a purchase.

"Why is nothing ever simple for me?" she muttered.

Her screwdriver soon turned into a pickaxe. By the third window, she was hot and sweaty and craving something more thirst-quenching than champagne. Strands of her hair had slipped out from her ponytail and were sticking to her neck. The day was turning out to be too warm for the sweatshirt she was wearing. Working the heavy material over her head, she tossed it to the ground. She wiped a hand across her brow, but paused with her fingers against her temple.

There it was, that feeling again… the feeling of being watched…

She looked to the woods. She saw nothing, but that didn't stop the eerie awareness. She could practically feel the heavy gaze sliding over her, tugging at her ponytail, and stroking the back of her bare neck.

She was off the chair in a flash. She wasn't drunk on champagne now. Palming her screwdriver like a knife, she faced off against her unseen watcher. The warm air turned clammy. Foreboding.

Behind her, she heard music. Instinctively, she began backing toward it. Coming around the front of her house, she found the source. A teenage boy was working on his car across the street. "Hey."

He didn't hear her.

"Hey! You!"

The kid's head was stuck under the hood, and the music

was blaring. She wasn't going to get his attention from way across the street. Sticking her fingers into her mouth, she let out an ear-piercing whistle.

His head jerked up.

She waved. "Hey, neighbor."

It took a moment before he realized that she was gesturing at him. He pointed a finger at his chest, and she nodded. His chin dipped, and he started trudging toward the driver's-side door. He didn't get to the volume control in time before his mother came flying out of their house.

"David, for heaven's sake. Turn that down!"

The kid dove into the car, and the sound disappeared entirely.

The woman caught sight of Callie. "If he's bothering you, just tell him to stop."

"Oh, no. He's fine. I was just—" Callie glanced over her shoulder at the woods. "Never mind. Hi, I'm Callie Thompson. I just moved in across the street."

"Laurie Hughes," the woman said. "This is my son, David."

David nodded and went back to working on his car. For all the loud music, he seemed to be a quiet kid who majored in brooding.

Callie wiped her hands off on her jeans. She crossed the street and stuck out her hand. She'd met quite a few people at the diner, but her neighbors had been more elusive. Laurie Hughes didn't look overjoyed to be making her acquaintance. She shook Callie's hand quickly and folded her arms over her chest.

"I should have introduced myself earlier," Callie said. "I got here yesterday, but the house has taken more of my time than I expected."

The woman looked across the street with distaste. "I suppose it would."

"I know it's not much to look at right now, but you've got to admit, it has charm."

"Is that what you're calling it?"

Callie propped a hand on her hip. She was really trying to

be friendly here. "I do."

"Yes, well, we'll see how long that lasts." Her neighbor started to back away. "I left a client hanging on the phone. If David's bothering you, just tell him to quiet down."

"He's not bothering me," Callie called. It was too late. Laurie Hughes had already hustled back into her house.

Callie tapped her screwdriver against her thigh. Casting a glance over her shoulder toward the tree line, she made a decision. "Hey, kid, does that car run?"

His head snapped back as if she'd jabbed him. "Of course it runs."

"Why don't you move it into my driveway? That way you can turn up the music as loud as you like, and nobody will be bothered." And she'd have some company... "I'm working, and it would be nice to have some tunes."

She'd been looking for her radio, but had yet to find it in her packing mess.

He blinked at her. "You want me to come over *there*?"

"I'll even pay you if you can help me get some of those shutters down."

He turned his head slowly toward the house. The way he was looking at it... well, *leery* was the only way to put it. Leery, but intrigued.

He straightened his shoulders. "Why not?"

Callie let out a breath. "Great."

She knew she was being silly. She'd just had a bad night's sleep. She was unaccustomed to small towns and, especially, this nature thing. Still, she really could use some company.

The teenager dropped the hood of his car and revved the engine before he pulled into her driveway. He shut it down again, but left the radio belting out the Screaming Rockets.

He tensed when he saw the shutters lying on the ground. "Uh... Are you sure you should be doing that?"

"What? Painting? This place is peeling worse than I did when I fell asleep on the beach in Cancun."

"Yeah, but... Do you really think you should disturb things?"

"What do you mean?"

He looked uncomfortable. "Never mind."

Okay… Callie peeked again at the tree line. "So you're a Ford guy, huh? Me too. Ford gal, actually."

"I heard." He wandered closer to take a look at her Mustang.

"Isn't she a beaut?" Callie couldn't resist. Her baby was two years old, but she still loved showing it off. She'd bought it as a gift to herself when her column had gone syndicated. With a wide grin, she climbed back onto the chair. "Leather seats, ragtop, four on the floor…"

"She's all right," he said, leaning in to look at the dashboard.

"All right?" Callie pointed her screwdriver at him. "Do you know how fast she'll go?"

He glanced up, forearms braced on the driver's door. "Twenty miles per hour over the speed limit?"

Callie's jaw dropped.

He smirked. "I told you I'd heard about you and this car—and the chief of police."

"Word does travel fast in small towns."

"Yeah, it's about the only thing."

"Great," Callie muttered. She chewed on her lower lip. "Does your mother know?"

"What do you care?"

"I don't, but I should." Was that why she'd been given the cold shoulder?

She looked at the shutter as the Screaming Rockets… well, screamed. She should have known that the town womenfolk would be on Landry's side. Just look at the man. Still, she couldn't afford to cross the Shadow Valley party line. She was brand new in town. "I might have deserved the speeding ticket, but he could have given me a warning on the boxes."

And don't even bring up that spiteful parking ticket.

Her teeth ground. "I don't know why he has to be such a hard—uh… sourpuss."

David snorted and pushed himself away from her car. "Tell

me about it." He stuffed his hands in his back pockets. "He's not one of my biggest fans, either."

"He's ticketed you?"

"What do you think?"

She glanced at the kid's T-Bird and understood. "Well, forty-five is just ridiculous. A bicycle couldn't go that slow coming into town, much less a muscle car."

"It's thirty-five."

"Crap!"

The corners of the teenager's mouth twitched. He wandered over to her stack of shutters and nudged one with his toe. "The guy needs to get a life. I swear he's a cop from the moment he wakes up until the time he hits the sack."

"Just what is his story, anyway?"

"The chief's?" David picked a shutter off the ground and carried it over to the sawhorses. He found a scraper in her supplies and experimentally ran the new tool over the old wood. "How would I know?"

"Because he's all that anybody wants to talk about around here." Callie returned to her fight with the stubborn screw. "Everyone acts like he's some kind of hero, but all I've seen is a big grump."

"That's because that's what he is. I've never met a guy who needs to get laid worse."

The words seemed to echo across the lawn, and Callie's screwdriver slipped. She nearly did a face plant off the chair before she caught herself. When she looked back up, she saw that she'd left a five-inch gouge in the siding of the house. "Dang it."

"Then again," David said, "who'd take him?"

It was a tough job, but somebody—

Callie felt heat rise in her cheeks. Not her, though. Definitely not her.

"You should skewer him in your column."

Her column? Callie's chair teetered as she spun around. "You read it?"

"Sure. You're not bad."

High praise indeed.

"Thanks." A grin worked itself onto her face. She got a kick out of this kid. They were definitely on the same wavelength, although he was much too serious for her liking.

Paint chips fell to the ground as he worked. "Those other advice columnists are lame."

She chuckled under her breath. She'd heard similar comments before from her younger readers. "They take on some serious stuff. I deal with more common issues. Stupid things, really."

She threw a devilish look at him. "Like what to do when your bra strap breaks during the middle of church."

His lips pulled thin as he fought a smile. "Can't say I've had that problem before."

"Don't go to church, huh?"

His reaction was delayed, but when he laughed, it was as if he'd been caught by surprise. The result was a half-wheeze/half-snort. It was precisely the reaction she'd wanted, and the sound was so funny that Callie pointed at him with glee.

He pressed his lips together, but another snort escaped.

That made her laugh outright. "You sound like a sick whoopee cushion."

That got a belly laugh out of him, which automatically triggered her. Soon they were both bent over and trying to catch their breaths.

Callie was wiping the tears from her eyes when David stopped abruptly. His gaze suddenly homed in on something in the street. Whatever he saw there made his shoulders slump, his hands go tight, and that too-frequent scowl settle back onto his face. Automatically, she lifted her screwdriver.

She relaxed when she heard another vehicle pull into her driveway. Could she be so lucky as to have the furnace guy show up early? Or the lawn service?

Not even close.

One glance at the man behind the wheel made her scowl return. A big black truck had pulled in behind David's car—

and its driver was wearing reflective sunglasses.

* * *

Carter pulled into the long driveway at 1255 Highland and did a double take. That was David Hughes. With Callie Thompson.

Talk about trouble with a capital T.

He shifted his truck into park and stared at the twosome. The delinquent from hell and the blond bomber from Boston… He couldn't have put together a more combustible pair if he'd tried.

"Hell," he muttered, killing the engine and reaching for the door handle. "What is this about?"

Bracing himself, he got out of the truck. Funny thing was, though, he could practically feel the two of them bracing against him. Together. Terrific. He'd come over here to try to smooth things over with their latest resident, but already he could tell that he was being put in the role of bad guy all over again.

Well, he wasn't going to play the part.

Bring it on, honey, he thought. She may want a fight, but he wasn't going to let her get to him. Not this time.

He got out of his truck. "Ms. Thompson," he said, nodding in her direction.

"Chief Landry," she replied. The look on her face wasn't welcoming.

The irritation was automatic, but Carter tamped it down and turned his look on David. "Hughes," he said.

The kid felt the friction in the air, and, apparently, he wasn't up for another go-around.

"I'm outta here," he said. He tossed down the scraper he'd been holding, and it stuck straight up out of the ground like a dagger.

"Hold on there," Carter called.

David stopped short, his hands clenching into fists.

Walking up to the Thunderbird, Carter reached into the car and punched a button. The racket coming from the stereo finally stopped.

"Hey!" Callie said. "I was listening to that."

50

"So was everyone else in town." Making eye contact with the teen, Carter tossed him the keys.

David snatched them out of the air as his lips pressed tightly together.

"What is it with people around here?" Callie said in a huff. "Have you all grown old?"

"I'm just fond of my sense of hearing." David tried to slink away, but Carter had been a cop too long to fall for that. "Hold on. You and I need to talk about what happened at Alice's."

The kid's steps hitched, and his shoulder blades pulled together. "I already talked with the ginger down at the station."

Carter folded his arms over his chest and let the dig pass. Bill could be sensitive when it came to his red hair. "So now you're talking to me. What were you doing in her utility shed?"

"What utility shed?" Callie asked, stepping closer. "What are you talking about?"

Carter ignored her, instead keeping a watchful eye on her newfound friend. With those snug jeans and tank top she was wearing, it was harder to do than he expected.

"Something must have caught your interest in there," he said, trying to keep his mind on task. "What was it? The tools?"

"Yeah," the kid said sarcastically. "Weed whackers are hot on the black market these days."

"Interesting choice of words," Carter said. "*Weed.*"

For once, Hughes' reaction wasn't smart-ass. The smirk left his face entirely. With the way his jaw dropped and his eyebrows rose, it almost looked as if he were offended. "Hey, man. You know I don't smoke that stuff. I've got enough weird things going on in my he—"

He broke off sharply. Shifting his weight, he looked blindly across the house's unkempt yard. "Whatever."

"What's this about?" Callie asked, strolling closer.

One look at her told Carter she was getting ready to champion the boy's side. Probably just because it was the opposite of his.

He felt the pull in his shoulder again. Damn it. He'd

promised himself. Pushing the feeling aside, he leaned back against his truck. Maybe if she knew the trouble that the boy was in, she wouldn't be so sassy.

"David here was caught trespassing on your friend Alice's property," he said.

"Alice the postmaster?"

"The one and only."

She looked back and forth between the two of them in confusion, and Carter felt a flare of satisfaction. He wasn't the big bad wolf here. It was about time she learned that.

"Leave her out of it," David said, stepping forward. "I thought I heard somebody in the shed, so I went to check it out. That's it."

"Right."

"It's the truth."

"Try again."

"Hey, now," Callie snapped. "You asked a question, and he answered. There's no need to be surly."

"Surly?" Carter said incredulously. "*He's* the one being charged with trespassing."

She lifted an eyebrow. "The same could be said of you." She looked pointedly at where he stood on her lawn. "What are you doing here, anyway? Did you come here to badger him?"

Badger?

"I'm delivering your ladder," Carter said, his jaw so tight it would barely move.

Pink dots colored her cheeks. "I bought it from Ernie."

They looked at each other and, suddenly, electricity crackled in the air. Her brown eyes went stormy, and Carter felt the lust for a good fight stir inside him. Screw his promise. If she wanted to squabble, he was up for anything she wanted to dish out.

And then some.

"Uh, can I go now?" David asked. Even he had sensed the change in the air.

"Of course," Callie said. "And for the record, I believe

you."

And so the battle lines had been drawn.

Carter felt the tightness in his shoulder crawl up into his neck. "I'll deal with you later, Hughes."

Right now, he needed to deal with a tall, feisty blonde.

One on one.

The kid made a quick exit toward his house, and Carter turned to face off with Callie. He watched in disbelief, though, as she sauntered right past him. "What the— *Hey!*" He moved quickly to the back of his truck when she started wrestling with the ladder. "I'll get that."

He caught her by the arm, and they both jolted. Carter looked down to where he held her. Her muscles were taut, but her skin was soft. So soft, his palm tingled with the need to slide over it.

She hesitated for a moment, too, but then pulled away. "Fine. Do what you want. You always seem to anyway."

And he was getting more ideas every minute.

Forget it, Landry, he reprimanded himself. *She's too high-maintenance.*

Way too high.

"This is about the parking ticket, isn't it?" he said.

"What do you think?"

Okay, maybe he'd crossed the line there. He could have just asked her to move her car instead. He'd regretted his action all night. It was why he'd come over here, to apologize.

But something about her just got under his skin.

He lifted the ladder out of the bed of his pickup, and her lips flattened when she saw him with it. It pleased him to no end to see signs that he annoyed her, too. "Where do you want it?" he asked.

"Take a wild guess."

"Careful," he growled.

Turning, she headed back to the house. "This way."

He followed, and couldn't help it when his gaze dropped to her backside. The way her butt filled out those well-worn jeans was not a fair battle tactic. And the way she moved?

Not fair at all.

His scowl returned when she stopped beside a kitchen chair under a first-floor window. Had she been using that thing? Seriously? It looked like it was made from twigs. Without a word, he moved it away.

"You need to be careful on this," he warned her as he propped the extension ladder against the house. He maneuvered it until he was sure it was balanced at a safe angle. "Especially when you're working up high."

She shot him an icy look. "I might be blond, but I'm not ditzy."

She moved toward the ladder, but her steps slowed when she saw that he planned to shore it up for her.

"I never said you were."

Pink colored her cheeks again. This time, though, he didn't think anger was the cause.

She climbed up a few steps to where she could reach the shutter she'd been working on. She pulled a screwdriver out of her back pocket, and the screw received a good whack. He ducked to avoid the flying paint chips.

"Long night?" he asked, moving to the other side.

"Is that your not-so-subtle way of telling me that I look like hell?"

Like hell? Was she out of her mind?

"I meant at the diner. I heard you got swarmed by all the locals after I left." He let his gaze roam up her curves to her face. Now that she mentioned it, she did look tired. "Why? Did you have trouble out here I should know about?"

An unreadable look crossed her face, and, for a moment, he thought she was going to say something. The screw turned loose, though, and she moved on to the next one after tucking it into her pocket.

"New place. Excited nerves." She pointed at the shutter above them. "Creaky house. You do the math. It was nothing."

His gut told him it was a lot more than nothing, and he suddenly knew why. She wouldn't look at him. Whenever they went at it, she stared him dead in the eye. Right now, though, she wouldn't even glance his way.

He didn't like it.

"What kind of things did the locals tell you last night?"

She looked down at him impatiently. "Why? What does that have to do with anything?"

"Town gossip? Local folklore?"

"If you must know, all they wanted to talk about was the local boy who done good." With a frustrated sigh, she moved up another step on the ladder. "Don't you have anyplace else you need to be, Police Chief Landry? Like searching for fugitives or something?"

That set his jaw on edge. "Probably."

"Then what are you waiting for?"

Okay, that was the Callie Thompson he knew—and she'd reminded him that they were fighting. "A thank you would be nice, for starters."

"A *thank you*? For what?"

"For delivering your ladder."

"What were you doing with it, anyway?"

"Ernie's truck is in the shop today. He asked me for a favor."

"Oh. In that case... thank you." She turned her attention back to the stubborn screw. "I needed it today, but I think I've got it from here. You have a nice day, chief."

Out of the corner of his eye, Carter saw something falling.

And falling fast.

"Callie, watch out!"

CHAPTER FIVE

Callie barely heard the words before she felt Landry's hands clamp on her waist. Instinctively, she lifted her hand and ducked her head. It was only that—and possibly the way he ripped her off the ladder—that saved her from taking a direct blow. As it was, something hard and rough glanced against her and crashed into the ground.

"Ow!" she yelped.

"Damn." He yanked her another good three feet away. "Are you all right?"

"*Ow!*" she repeated, shaking her stinging hand. "What was that?"

With the way he held her, she was plastered against his body. He felt warm and solid. Her feet had yet to touch the ground, and the contact only magnified her confusion.

"The shutter above you fell." He kicked the offending piece of wood away from where it had bounced close to them. Swiftly, he put her down and turned her around to face him. "Are you all right? Where did it get you?"

She was still trying to make sense of things when he began looking her over.

"Any bumps? Cuts? How's your vision?"

The sensation of his fingers sliding over her hair only

scrambled her head even more. Besides, it didn't hurt—or she didn't think it did. It was hard to tell with the way her finger was burning. The fires of hell had set up residence in her pinky. She tried to nudge him away so she could look, but moving him was like trying to move the Green Monster at Fenway. It just wasn't going to happen.

"My head's fine. It's my hand." She hissed at the pain. It felt like a hot needle was burrowing into her skin. Wiggling out of his grip, she held her hand up in the sunlight to try to see. There it was, right where her pinky met her palm.

He caught her wrist. "Let me see."

The heat of his touch disturbed her almost more than the splinter. Warmth rushed into her chest. Hastily, she pulled her hand away. "It's okay. I've got it."

Her finger stung so badly that Callie wanted to jump up and down like a three-year-old. If he hadn't been there, she probably would have. Breathing through clenched teeth, she fought against the sting and tried to pull out the tiny piece of wood using her fingernails. It didn't help. If anything, the sliver only worked itself in deeper.

"You're never going to get it that way." Ignoring her protests, he took her hand again. He spread her fingers flat and grimaced when he saw where the sliver had lodged itself. "Damn, that's got to hurt."

"You don't say." The thing was right in the crease, almost as if it knew that was where it could cause the most pain.

"Come over here," he said. "I've got a first-aid kit in the truck."

Since he hadn't let go of her hand and didn't seem to intend to, she had no other option.

"Hold on," he said as he opened the door and looked under the seat.

Callie pinched her finger, praying for numbness. It didn't work. All it did was make her finger go white to match the pain.

She looked at Landry miserably. His being there wasn't helping. The problem was that she didn't have a clue where her medical supplies were in all those boxes piled up in her living room. With the way her finger was throbbing, she had to accept help.

Even if it was from him.

"These should do the trick," he said, holding up a pair of tweezers.

He moved in closer, and awareness caught her by surprise. With the truck at her back and his wide shoulders blocking most of the sunlight, she suddenly felt trapped. Her breaths went short, yet her irritation peaked. It was like being hovered over by the Terminator. He had those reflective sunglasses firmly in place on the bridge of his nose. She wondered if he slept in the things.

"Ouch!" Her attention returned to the sliver when he started poking around her tender flesh.

"Sorry."

Tears pricked at her eyes, and she shifted her weight from one foot to the other.

"Hold still," he said.

She pressed her lips together. That was easier said than done. Her hand *hurt*, and funny things were happening inside her chest. He was standing too close. She shifted again, but this time her leg brushed against his.

The tweezers went motionless in his hand. His head was still bent, but his attention had wandered. Callie stood immobile. The tank top she was wearing suddenly seemed skimpy. And tight. He was so close, she could see the rise and fall of his chest as he breathed. The definition of his muscles underneath that uniform hadn't been so apparent from further away.

Although, she had nicknamed him Hardass for more than one reason...

The thought shook her out of her trance. Idiot. This was Landry she was dealing with. So the tweezers in her house would be a little hard to find... She'd just have to amputate. "Never mind, I'll do it."

He caught her hand firmly when she tried to pull it away.

"This time," he promised.

Those sunglasses of his were driving her nuts. "Maybe it would help if you took these off."

The moment she plucked the glasses off his face, Callie knew she'd made a mistake. His blue eyes burned. Like fire. She quickly looked away.

For once, she found herself tongue-tied. She'd thought he'd been hiding behind those glasses. Now, she realized that they'd been her best defense, too.

"*Miz* Thompson," he said in a measured voice, "do you want this sliver out or not?"

She nodded tightly. With one hand, she carefully folded his sunglasses together and tucked them into his shirt pocket. Her hand was surprisingly unsteady. "I can't see what you're thinking when you're wearing these."

"Do you really want to know what I'm thinking?"

She swallowed hard, and her gaze focused somewhere near the ragged bushes that lined the front of the house.

"That's what I thought," he said.

He leaned in, and his energy radiated toward her in waves. It was seductive. She felt herself start to sway toward him, and she locked her spine to stop.

Fortunately, he was focused on her finger. With painstaking care, he caught the tiny piece of wood with the tweezers and pulled it out. She flexed her hand and took a deep breath. When his gaze slid to the scooped neckline of her top, she realized that maybe his concentration wasn't so focused after all.

She maneuvered out from between him and the truck. "Thank you."

He cleared his throat. "Did I get it all?"

She hadn't stopped to check. Steeling herself, she wiggled her finger. She was surprised when it didn't hurt as badly. "I think so." She blew out a breath. "Thanks."

He brushed blue flecks of paint from her hair, but froze when she winced.

"Damn it. I knew it. It did get you."

She reached upward to poke at the sore spot. "I didn't feel it before."

He gave her a disbelieving look. "You screech like a banshee over a splinter, but don't notice a blow to the head?"

"I have a hard head."

"Tell me something I don't know."

He ran his thumb over the area she'd been touching. Callie didn't know what surprised her more—the bump she already felt forming or the way her stomach dropped at his touch. Holding her still, he parted her hair and looked at the injury more closely. "It doesn't look like it managed to break the skin."

Probably because he'd yanked her out of the way too fast for that.

"Ice," he said gruffly.

When he headed for the house, she followed without a peep. Her footsteps slowed, though, when they neared the ladder. Lifting her hand to shield her eyes, she looked upward. "I don't understand. How could that have happened?"

"It was a fluke. You were in the wrong place at the wrong time."

Was she? Her stomach clenched when she saw exactly which shutter had fallen. The middle window had a blue shutter on the left side, but not the right. "Did we hit it with the ladder or something?"

"Not that I saw." He glanced at the second floor, and his jaw hardened. "Come on. Let's get ice on that lump before it gets any worse."

"But that's the one that kept me up all night, blowing in the wind."

"There you go. It must have just been loose."

She dug in her heels. "No. I've been looking at that shutter all day, trying to figure out how to get it down without a ladder to get up there." She leveled an anxious look on him. "It was up there tight."

Carter felt his shoulder squeeze. He didn't like where this was leading. "It was an accident. That's all."

She looked up again, unconsciously rubbing her head.

"An accident." Catching her by the chin, he looked deep into her eyes. "And you're lucky you don't have a concussion." He cocked his head. "Can we go inside now?"

She stared at him for a moment, but then seemed relieved that he was so certain. "Okay. It was just a really long night..."

So help him, he was going to have Alice and Mamie's hides.

Turning so she couldn't see the anger in his face, Carter headed to the back of her house. He opened the door for her so she could step into the kitchen. The room smelled lemony fresh. He directed her to a kitchen chair that matched the one outside. "Here. Sit."

He opened the freezer door and searched for an ice tray. The top one was empty. The bottom one had some dried-out chips left. Using a kitchen towel he found on the countertop, he made an ice pack. "Fifteen minutes on, fifteen minutes off," he said as he held it out to her.

She was looking at him curiously. "You act like you know your way around my kitchen."

He shrugged as he opened the refrigerator. "Most people in Shadow Valley do."

"What does that mean?"

She had nothing to drink except champagne. Shaking his head, he turned to the cabinets. He found a couple of glasses and filled them with tap water. "It means that this place used to be a favorite haunt for neighborhood kids. When the house was deserted, teenagers would sometimes break in and have a look around."

Her eyes were twinkling when he handed her the water along with some aspirin he'd grabbed from the first-aid kit. The expression made his gut tighten. He hadn't seen that look on her face since he'd pulled her over on that traffic stop. "What?" he demanded.

"Why, Chief Landry. Are you saying that you broke into this house as a teenager?"

"No, I'm saying I was the officer who kicked the kids out."

Her smile fell. "Of course. What was I thinking?"

She tilted her head back to down the pills, and he caught himself staring at her throat. Her skin was just as sleek as it looked. Warm and silky.

Damn. He pivoted quickly back to the counter. Why did trouble always have to be so tempting? Turning the faucet on high, he refilled the ice trays. Water sloshed over the edges as he put them back in the freezer.

She was staring at him again when he turned around.

"That," he said, pointing at the ice bag, "is supposed to go on your head."

"Grouch." She scowled, but lifted the cold compress. "Thank you for saving me. That shutter could have knocked me out."

Or worse.

"You're welcome," he said. What were the odds that the thing would fall at just that moment, after years of hanging up there? He sat down in the chair across from her and took a deep drink of water. That pretty pink color dotted her cheeks again, and she glanced away. Silence filled the room.

She looked out the window. "I was hoping to get all the shutters down before lunch," she said in an obvious attempt to fill the quiet. "It would make it a lot easier if they would all just fall off."

"Leave them for the day. I can drop by after work and get a start on the rest for you."

"David can probably help me."

One short word, and their tentative truce was suddenly in jeopardy. They both felt it, and they both stiffened.

"Don't get too close to that kid," Carter said softly. He needed her to hear him on this. "David Hughes is not someone you want to get messed up with."

"Oh, stop it," she said. "He seems like a good kid. You just don't like his muscle car."

Carter tried to keep his patience. "You've just seen the one side of him. Believe me, I usually see the worst."

"Interesting. That's what he said, too." Slowly, she set the ice pack down on the table. "Chief Landry, if you're always looking for the worst in people, that's what you're always going to find."

And there it was, the flare of irritation she always seemed to light inside him. Carter didn't know what ticked him off more, her stubborn refusal to listen to him or her insistence on calling him "chief." "Don't try to use your advice columnist mumbo jumbo on me. The kid's got a rap sheet as long as my arm."

She lifted an eyebrow. "Filled with infractions like jaywalking and illegal parking, no doubt."

She wasn't going to let that parking ticket go, was she?

"Try vandalism, B&E, and stalking, to name but a few."

"Stalking?"

He'd thrown her with that one? Good. "Haley Smothers, the little blond waitress down at Mamie's."

"Ooh," Callie said with a scoff. She waved her hand at him airily. "She's cute as a bug. He's probably got a crush on her."

Carter couldn't believe the casual brush-off. Was she really that blithe or was she trying to tick him off? He took these kinds of things seriously. "You need to be careful around him."

"And I will, but I'm not going to prejudge him. He seemed perfectly nice and respectful before you showed up."

Carter's shoulder felt like it was ready to dislocate. "I'm the problem here?"

She said nothing, and the kitchen clock ticked off the seconds noisily.

"So is this the way it's going to be?" he finally asked.

Her gaze dropped, and she poked at the spot on her hand where the sliver had been. "I don't know," she said tiredly.

Felt pretty decisive to him.

He set his glass back on the table. He'd come over here to sort things out with her, and they just had. He got up to leave, but stopped at the door. "Do you want to know what sealed it for me? The way you tried to work me with the smile and the fluttering lashes at that traffic stop."

Her mouth opened, but then snapped closed.

"I know all the little tricks, honey. It will be easier on you if you just learn to follow the rules."

He was halfway out the door as she came out of her chair, sputtering. They were both caught by surprise, though, when a loud thud sounded from the basement. Whatever retort Callie was going to throw at him froze on her lips. Her gaze flew to the basement door.

He stopped with his hand on the screen door. "Callie?"

She glanced at him, but her concentration was elsewhere. "You're right. Following the rules is much easier. Then we won't have to deal with each other like this."

He watched her closely. "It sounded like the furnace to me. It probably doesn't know what to do with this weather hopping from warm to cold."

"You think so?"

"Yeah."

She drummed her fingers against her leg. "I've got somebody coming this afternoon to look at it."

The furnace clunked again, and she nearly flinched right out of her shoes.

Carter didn't like it. Reflexively, he took a step back inside. "Do you want me to check it out now?"

She hesitated. "No," she finally said. "It's fine. I think we're done here."

His eyes narrowed. Her chin lifted, and that stubborn look came over her face again.

"Yeah," he said. "I think we are." He slipped his sunglasses back on. "Have a good day, Miz Callie. Try to stay out of trouble."

He let the screen door bang shut and cursed under his breath as he strode across the disheveled lawn. He'd come over here with good intentions. Yesterday, he'd been far from his best, and he'd assumed it had been the same for her. Talk about giving her the benefit of the doubt. Why had he thought that she would be any different today?

He climbed into his truck and slammed the door. He'd never met a more frustrating woman in his life.

Still… He hadn't liked the way she'd gone pale at the sound of the furnace knocking.

And she'd looked exhausted.

He shook his head. Hell, they'd gotten to her at the diner last night. They'd told her stories about the house. That explained the lack of sleep and the jumpiness. He glared at the Thunderbird parked in front of him. No doubt the kid had thrown in his two cents, too.

Irritated, Carter twisted the key in the ignition.

This was the last thing he needed to happen. His department was busy enough as it was.

He shifted the truck into reverse and backed out of the driveway. He was halfway into the street when a flash from the porthole window in the attic nearly blinded him. He stomped on the brakes and looked up at the house. The sun went under a cloud, and the glare disappeared.

Still, an uneasy feeling settled in his gut.

He'd never given a second thought to the rumors that the Shadow Valley old-timers liked to tell. They were just stories made up by bored townspeople with nothing better to do. For some reason, though, he found himself pointing at the house.

"Be nice to her," he said quietly. "I mean it."

* * *

The rocker kept rhythm with its ever-present squeak as she rolled back and forth. The visit by the chief of police had pleased her. Such a strong, handsome young man. He reminded her of someone she'd known before. Known. Loved. And lost…

She pushed the heartache aside before it could overtake her once again. Yes, the police chief was the one she needed, the one she'd awaited. He wouldn't put up with the stranger who'd disrespected her so. He'd make them go away.

She rubbed her hands along the smooth wooden armrests as a plan formed in her head.

She must find a way to bring him back.

CHAPTER SIX

The rest of the week was quiet. Callie made sure of it by following "the rules." She walked to town when she could, avoided jaywalking, and kept strictly to the speed limit whenever she had to drive her car. She took advantage of the good weather and finished redoing all the shutters. With David's help, she even got the windows washed. Scraping and painting were next on her list, but she didn't know how far she'd get before it got too cold. She'd take whatever she could get. Especially with the house cooperating like it was...

She let herself in the front door and locked it behind her. Automatically, she hit the light switch and lifted her gaze to take in the two-story entryway. Somehow over the last few days, she and her new/old home had managed to develop a symbiotic relationship. The creaks, groans, and thumps weren't bothering her as much anymore.

She couldn't say as much for her and the chief of police.

She'd managed to avoid him for most of the week, but she'd spotted him tonight at the football game... harassing teenagers smoking under the bleachers.

She rolled her eyes. Okay, it was bad for their health, but did the guy ever take a break?

Ever?

She shrugged out of her blue jean jacket as she walked into the living room. Tiredly, she tossed it and her purse onto one of the boxes that still filled the space. A chill ran through her, and she rubbed her hands up and down her arms. If she'd known that she was going to be sitting on those icy bleachers, she would have dug through all those boxes to find a heavier coat.

As it was, a cup of hot chocolate was definitely in order.

She stretched her arms overhead as she headed to the kitchen. The game had been fun, but she'd lost a couple hours of painting time when Alice and Mamie had shown up late this afternoon, demanding that she go with them. It had been worth it, though. For a big-city girl like her, a small-town high school football game was quite the experience. The game itself had been a nail-biter, but watching her two new friends with their megaphones and pompons had been even more entertaining. Thank God the Phantoms had won. She could only imagine how Alice and Mamie would have sulked if their team had lost.

"Ay yi yi." After sitting next to a megaphone-amplified Alice for three hours, Callie wouldn't have been pleased with a loss, either.

A yawn caught her unexpectedly as she pulled a mug out of the cupboard. Yup, a cup of cocoa and then bed. It had been a long day, and she needed to get an early start tomorrow. Tonight had given her plenty of inspiration for her column, and she wanted to get the ideas written down while they were still fresh in her mind.

She opened the refrigerator door.

And groaned. "Not again."

There was barely enough milk left for breakfast. She sighed in disappointment and bumped the refrigerator door shut with her hip. It was time for yet another trip to the grocery store. With all the physical energy she'd been exerting, her appetite had kicked into high gear. She was practically eating herself out of house and home. Half the time, she didn't even remember eating the food.

She put the mug back into the cupboard. She might as well just go to bed. Maybe another blanket would help fight the chill running through her bones.

"Phantom fever," she said, her lips quirking.

As exciting as the game had been, she could feel her adrenaline waning. She hurried through her nightly routine in the bathroom, alternatively shivering and yawning. She was grateful when she closed her bedroom door and felt actual warmth coming from the heating vents. Ernie's cousin had yet to figure out the cause of the cold spots around the house, but it always felt comfortable in here. Quickly, she changed into her pajamas and slid under the covers.

"Ahh."

That was the thing about painting. It used muscles a person had forgotten she had. Climbing onto the roof of the porch today certainly hadn't helped, but she'd wanted the blue trim around the porthole window of the attic to be as fresh as the shutters.

Just remembering that treacherous climb had her pulling the covers to her chin.

She'd gotten the oddest sensation up there. Almost as if she were being watched again... Only this time, it had felt different.

"No doubt by Laurie Hughes, waiting to see me break my neck," she muttered. She rolled onto her side. She liked David, but his mother was a real piece of work.

Click.

The sound cracked through the darkness like a gunshot.

Callie sat bolt upright in bed and reached blindly for the lamp. In her haste, she nearly knocked it over. When she finally found the switch, the light made stars dance in front of her eyes. Anxiously, she looked through the red blotches until she could focus on the door across the room.

It was locked.

Locked.

This time, there was no doubt. The latch had turned... by itself. She could see it from where she sat.

"No way," she whispered. Her adrenaline kicked back into gear, and her heart thudded.

Determinedly, she pushed back the covers. Her bare feet padded a quick rhythm across the hardwood floor. She hit the wall switch, and the overhead light flooded the room.

The lock was a deadbolt—odd for a bedroom—but it was firmly set. She wrapped her fingers over the thumbturn, but it wouldn't move. "Oh, come on."

She'd oiled that thing *specifically* so this wouldn't happen again.

"I did not just trap myself in my own bedroom." Wouldn't that just be the talk of the town? She could practically hear everyone laughing down at Mamie's about the dimwitted big-city girl.

She wiped her hand on her pajamas and tried again. No luck.

She'd heard of locks freezing up, but not like this. It had been fine two minutes ago, and it wasn't like she'd slammed the door shut or anything. She frowned as she looked more closely at the lock. It wasn't old like the rest of the house. In fact, the finish on it gleamed. One of the more recent tenants had to have installed it. Frustration set in, and she grabbed the knob with both hands. "Don't do this to me. Damn it!"

She slapped her palm against the door. She had tools, but they were upstairs in the room she'd decided to make her office. She turned to look around the room. There had to be something she could use to get herself out of here.

She'd only taken one step away from the door, though, when the handle began rattling.

Callie pivoted like a top. Her heart slammed into her throat, and she jumped backward, coming up hard against the dresser. A scream built in the middle of her chest, but it lodged there when another sound came rolling down the hallway. Thin and high. Otherworldly.

What in God's name was *that*?

The sound grew in strength and seemed to resonate in the walls. She stumbled further away, but stopped in her tracks when she heard footsteps. Loud, heavy footsteps, right outside her bedroom door.

Somebody or something was in her house!

"Oh God, help me."

She dove for her phone on the nightstand and dialed 911. Scooting away until her back was pressed firmly against the far wall, she stared at the door, praying now that the lock would hold.

"Nine-one-one. Please state the nature of your emergency."

"Someone is in my house," she said hoarsely. "They're trying to get into my bedroom!"

"What is your address, ma'am?"

"Twelve fifty-five Highland. In Shadow Valley." She didn't know how the emergency system worked in small towns like this. How far away was help?

"Do you know this person?"

"No! Someone must have broken in."

"Are you alone?"

"*Yes.* Please send someone fast. I don't know what to do."

"If you can, lock the bedroom door. Barricade it in some way."

The laugh that left Callie's throat was a bit hysterical. She had the locking part down.

"Ma'am?"

She gripped the phone like a lifeline, but her thoughts scattered. Could she move the dresser? Not without pulling out all the drawers first. What did she have that she could use to protect herself? Her tennis racket? It was still packed in one of the boxes in her living room. Sweat broke out on her forehead until she noticed the lamp sitting right beside her. It was heavy. She ripped the cord out of the wall and curled her fingers around its base.

"Ma'am? Are you there?"

"Shhhh!" Callie hissed. She was listening for the footsteps. Where were they? She couldn't hear them. Where had they gone?

And that hair-raising noise—*where was it?*

"Stay on the line, ma'am. Just stay calm."

Calm? Was the woman high?

"Is there anyone else there with you?" the dispatcher asked.

"I'm alone."

"We have officers on the way."

Knowing that didn't help. "I won't be able to let them in," Callie said in a rush. "I'm locked in my room."

"I've made the officers aware of that. Just stay where you are."

But she didn't *like* where she was.

Her grip on the lamp became slippery. What was she going to do if somebody came through that door? She was staring at it so hard that her eyes were going dry. What if they burst through, and she dropped the lamp? What if—

A tap sounded on the windowpane behind her.

She screamed. Whirling around, she lifted the lamp up high.

"Callie, open up. It's Chief Landry."

Landry! She dropped the lamp onto the table with a clatter, and the phone bounced on the bed as she dove for the window. She pulled back the curtains, lifted the shade, and found herself face to face with him.

"Oh, thank God!"

"The latch," he said, pointing at it.

He'd used her ladder. Bless him. Quickly, she undid the lock. The window stuck when she tried to pull it up, but her adrenaline surged. She gave a hard yank, and the window screeched although it only lifted a few inches.

"That's good enough," he said. He squeezed his fingers through the opening and forced the window open wide enough for him to climb inside.

Callie had never been so happy to see anyone in her life. Without thinking, she lunged at him.

"I'm locked in," she babbled as she grabbed his shoulders with both hands. "The lock turned, and when I went over to open it, it wouldn't move. I tried everything I could think of, but I couldn't get out. But then it started shaking *on its own*."

"Callie, breathe." Landry dipped his head so he could look

into her eyes. "Are you all right?"

"No! There's someone in my house! They tried to get in my room!"

His look turned hard as he glanced at the door.

She dropped her voice to a stage whisper. "There were footsteps, but then this other noise came down the hall. I didn't know what to do. *I don't know what it was.*"

"You did exactly the right thing. You called me." The muscles in his arms were tense, but his gaze gentled when he looked at her. "Let's get you out of here."

"Yes," she said. That was an excellent idea.

His gaze ran down her form. Her pajamas weren't sexy, just a Red Sox T-shirt and shorts, but she wasn't wearing a bra. And her legs were bare.

"Here," he said, plucking her robe off the foot of the bed. "Put this on."

He slipped the robe over her shoulders and shoved the slippers he found on the floor at her, all while placing himself between her and the locked door.

"Did you hear anything after the noise?" he asked. "Any doors slamming? Which way did the footsteps go?"

Callie fumbled her slipper. He thought the intruder might still be there.

"Toward the kitchen," she whispered. "I think."

She suddenly realized how cold she was. The temperature in the room was freezing, and opening the window certainly hadn't helped. She jammed the slipper onto her foot. All she wanted to do was take one more step toward her rescuer and absorb all the heat she felt surrounding him, but he was in full cop mode.

"We're going out the window," he said.

She nodded. Window. He was full of good ideas tonight.

"You first," he said.

She cinched her robe tight and turned, but froze mid-step. It was jet black outside. Not even the moon was out. Shadow Valley was steeped in darkness.

"I'll be right behind you," he said, nudging the small of her back.

He'd better be. Taking a steadying breath, Callie crawled out the window. She gripped the ladder tightly as Landry held onto her arm and searched blindly for a metal rung with her foot. When she found it, it was so cold that her foot nearly cramped. She forced herself to make her way down the ladder. Wet grass clung to her legs when she touched the ground, and she shuddered.

Landry was close behind her. She stepped away to give him room, but the moment he was beside her, she reached out for him. Screw cop mode; he was big and tough, and she was scared. Her hand tangled in a strap of his bulletproof vest, and she held tight.

"Chief."

Callie spun around and stepped back. She collided against Landry's chest, and his hand automatically settled at her waist.

"It's just Officer Raikins," he said.

The flashlight pointed at them dipped, and a skinny, red-haired policeman approached them. "The front and back doors are secure," the man announced. "Locked."

Callie felt Landry's look turn on her.

"I want you to wait in my truck," he said.

"But…" She really didn't want to be alone.

"Now." He reached into his pocket and handed her the keys. With one hand planted firmly on the small of her back, he escorted her to the big black 4X4 he'd left on the street. "Lock the doors. If you see anything or anyone, lay on the horn. If somebody approaches you other than me or Officer Raikins, drive straight to the police station."

"Chief—" she said weakly.

"I'll be back as soon as I can."

* * *

Carter waited until Callie was safely locked inside the cab of his truck before he turned his attention back to the house. "She heard two distinct noises, footsteps and something else she couldn't identify," he told Bill as they stood on the front walk. "We could have two intruders."

He eyed the layout of the place. "We'll go in through the bedroom. She says the lock is jammed, but I'd rather break down an interior door if we have to cause damage."

Bill nodded, but his face was ashen. They didn't get many break-in calls in Shadow Valley, but Carter knew that wasn't the problem. "Bill, it's just a house. Suck it up."

He gestured impatiently to the ladder. Once he saw Bill take the first step, Carter's mind went back to the woman he'd just stowed in his truck.

"Damn it," he said under his breath. He hadn't liked the look on her face when he'd come through that window. She'd been terrified. Anger bubbled up inside him, but his concentration focused when it was his turn to re-enter the house.

It was time for him to do his job.

Once inside the bedroom, he nodded at Bill, and they readied their weapons. Moving quietly on the balls of their feet, they approached the door from the side. Reaching out, Carter tested the lock. It twisted easily, releasing with a soft click.

He looked at it in surprise.

"Don't touch the handle on the hallway side," he whispered to Bill. "I want it dusted for prints."

Bill nodded and, on Carter's signal, they went through the door. They moved together, their backs bumping, as they made their way down the hallway. It was empty. So were the bathroom and the living room.

Carefully, Carter swept the space. There weren't many places to hide. Callie was still in the process of unpacking. He nudged the larger boxes with his foot just to be sure and checked all the windows. None of them looked as if they'd been disturbed.

The wood floors creaked under his feet, but there wasn't much he could do about that. He carefully moved on to the kitchen. Compared to the living room, there were even fewer places that an intruder could hole up. A quick look at the back door proved it to be locked, just as Bill had said. Carter started for the rear staircase that led up to the second floor.

Clunk.

As one, he and Bill swiveled around toward the basement door. Carter knew that noise. It was the same sound that had made Callie jumpy the other day. He waited a moment before it came again.

He thought she'd had someone come out to look at that.

With a glance at each other, he and his officer crossed the room. The door to the basement squeaked when Carter opened it. Adrenaline started coursing through his veins. The area needed to be searched, but damn, he hated staircases. They were a vulnerability. If anybody was down there, they'd have a clean shot at him.

Still, it needed to be done.

He swatted the light switch atop the stairs, and the lone bulb in the center of the room lit. Nothing showed itself. Determinedly, he started down the steps. Bill was close behind, searching the other side of the open room.

Something suddenly moved in Carter's line of sight.

He held his weapon steady, even as his body went taut.

A mouse.

It scurried underneath a storage shelf, back into the shadows, but his relief was short.

He quickly made his way down the stairs and put the wall at his back. There was a feel to the place, one he didn't like. He scanned the big, dank cellar, trying to put his finger on the source of his uneasiness. It was an open room with nothing more than some shelves of junk, a washing machine, and a dryer.

And a furnace.

It thumped again, and he walked over to look at it. He shook his head and signaled Bill to head back upstairs. They had the second floor and the attic yet to search.

In the end, they found nothing. No intruders and no signs of entry or exit.

Holstering their weapons, they met up again outside of Callie's bedroom door. Carter nodded at the door handle. It was all that they had. "Dust it."

"Uh, are you sure, chief?"

"You got a better idea?"

Bill shuffled his feet. "I… Well, I was just wondering if you were taking everything into account."

"Like what?"

"This *is* the Calhoun place."

Carter's blood pressure tweaked. "Don't give me that. She had an intruder. Somebody rattled that door handle."

"I know. I just didn't see any evidence of a break-in, and I thought—"

"Thought what? That you'd like desk duty for the next two weeks?" Carter rolled his tight shoulder and took a calming breath. "Just see what prints you can get."

"Yes, sir." Bill's head dipped. Without a word, he headed out to his squad car.

Carter ran a hand through his hair. He didn't have time for any superstitious garbage. Callie was already frightened enough as it was. They were going to treat this as a possible break-in.

Nothing else.

He headed out to get her. The moment he stepped out the door, the chill in the air turned his breaths into cloudy puffs in front of his face. Still, he could feel her gaze home in on him like a hot laser beam. He rounded the front of the truck, and she hastily unlocked the door.

"Did you find anything?" she asked. "Did you catch anyone?"

"You have mice in your basement."

Her eyes were wide and dilated. "That's it? Nothing else?"

"The house is clear." He saw her shiver and jumped right back into first-responder mode. "Hell, you could have turned the engine on to keep warm."

He grabbed a ragged old blanket he kept behind the seat and wrapped it around her shoulders before taking the keys out of the ignition. "Come on, let's get you back inside."

She glanced warily at the house.

"I'll go with you," he said.

He stepped back, not letting her dally. She was chilled, and the longer she waited, the harder it would be to gather the nerve to go back inside. Hesitantly, she swung her legs out. Her robe split open and a long, lean thigh was left bare. Carter looked away. He was here on business. *Business.*

He led her up the walk. She moved slowly although the cement had to feel like a block of ice underneath her slippered feet. He glanced at her face. She was white as a sheet. "It's all right. Raikins is the only one in there."

"Are you sure?"

"I'm positive. We searched the place from top to bottom."

She pulled the blanket tighter around her shoulders and nibbled on her lower lip. His gaze was drawn unwaveringly to her mouth.

"Mice, huh?"

He shook his head to break the spell. "Yeah, down by your laundry area."

"I hate mice."

He looked down with surprise when she slipped her hand into his. Their palms met, and she gripped him tightly. When she finally started up the steps, he moved with her. He held the door open for her, and she walked into the entryway. It was as far as she got.

"Why don't you go into the living room and sit down?" he said.

She took a deep, calming breath, but didn't let go of his hand. "Okay."

Bill glanced up when he saw them come into the room. He was in the hallway, kneeling in front of the bedroom door with a print kit.

"Callie, this is Officer Bill Raikins," Carter said. He discreetly pulled his hand out of hers and settled it more impersonally on her shoulder. "Sit down. Can I get you anything?"

She remained standing. Her gaze was on the paraphernalia spread out on her hallway floor. "What's he doing?"

"Taking fingerprints. You said your intruder rattled the door handle."

She nodded. "If it hadn't been locked..."

Carter couldn't help but squeeze her shoulder comfortingly. Together, they watched as Bill pulled the tape off and bagged it.

"Did he—or she—do anything else?" Carter asked. "Touch anything else? Could you tell where they came from? You said you thought the footsteps moved to the kitchen."

"It was a man," she said with certainty, but then her forehead rumpled. "Or an awfully brawny woman. The footsteps were heavy."

She shivered, and he pulled the drooping blanket back over her shoulder.

"I don't know," she admitted. "My X-ray vision was on the fritz. I don't know what was on the other side of that door and, honestly, I get queasy whenever I think about it."

There it was, the biting humor he was used to, although the queasiness factor blunted its effect.

Bill collected his equipment and walked over to join them. "Ma'am," he said, "I'm sorry that this happened."

Callie nodded. "Thank you for responding so fast."

Bill shuffled his feet under her attention. "Is there anything else that you think I should dust? Chief Landry mentioned you heard two noises."

Carter almost winced when Callie went ramrod straight. "What exactly was the other noise?" he asked.

"I... I don't know."

"Could you describe it?"

She shuddered and moved so close that she bumped against him. "It came from everywhere, through the walls and the ceiling."

She glanced around the room nervously, but he pressed the issue. It was important. "Was it mechanical? Or human?"

"It was a *keen*."

Bill's skin paled in contrast with his red hair. He pulled his notebook out of his pocket and wrote down the word. "A keen," he said hoarsely.

Enough. Carter guided Callie to the sofa and made her take

a seat. "This house sits back in the woods. There's more wildlife out there than you would expect."

"You think it was an animal?" she asked, quickly latching on to the idea.

"I know it was. I live close to the woods myself. You hear some strange things every now and then." He threw a glare over her shoulder at Bill for good measure. One word. One word and not only would the officer be pulling desk duty, he'd be pulling night desk duty.

Bill's Adam's apple bobbed, but he nodded in understanding.

Carter gestured at the fingerprint kit. "You get anything?"

"Too much. There were a lot of smudges and overlapping prints." Bill shrugged. "It's a door handle."

"We'll make do with what we have." Carter watched the way Callie took great care in wrapping the old, tattered blanket around her legs. This break-in had rocked her, but he'd seen this kind of a reaction before. Invasion of privacy struck at the core of a person.

He crouched down in front of her. He hated to do this to her, but he had to question her while everything was fresh in her mind. "Do you think you could answer some questions?"

She let out a long, shaky breath. "Okay."

He gestured toward Bill's notebook, and the officer lifted his pen. "Can you think of anyone who might have done this? Have you noticed anyone hanging around the house? Watching it?"

She looked at him with wide eyes that got him right *there*. "You mean like one of your thrill seekers? Shouldn't everyone in town know the house isn't deserted anymore?"

A cold knot formed in Carter's gut. He didn't think that this break-in was some teenage lark. The guy had been trying to get into her bedroom. His hands clenched into fists, but he forced them to relax. "Is anything missing?"

She blinked as if she hadn't even given that a thought and looked around the room. "I don't think so."

"Take your time. If you notice anything later, give us a call at the station and report it."

"Okay."

This was harder than he'd expected. He took a deep breath and let it out slowly. "Has anyone made you feel uncomfortable? Have you had any run-ins with anyone lately?"

A familiar spark lit her eyes. It was dim, but it was there. Relief washed through him. There was that spirit, her strength.

"Nobody's bothered me," she said.

Except him.

He cleared his throat. "We checked all the doors and windows, and they looked secure. Can you think of any other way that this person might have gotten into your house?"

She paled. "No."

"Have you given anyone a key?"

She shook her head.

"Not even David Hughes?"

She flinched, but then her jaw went hard. "He has nothing to do with this."

"I know he's been helping you around the house." Even after his warning... The town gossip mill had kept Carter abreast of everything that had been happening at the Calhoun house.

"David's been helping with the painting, but I haven't given him a key." She folded her arms over her chest. "It doesn't matter. It wasn't him. He would never do something like this to me."

Just like that, that invisible wall sprang back up between them.

Carter put his hands on his thighs and pushed himself to his feet. Irritation bubbled up in his throat, but he kept his voice on an even keel as he looked down at her. "That's enough for tonight. Is there anyone I can call for you? Alice? Mamie?"

"You're leaving?"

God, the look in her eyes. He reached up to rub his shoulder. "Bill needs to get back to the station with that evidence, and I should canvass the neighborhood. It's not that late. Somebody might have seen something."

"But... But... What about the garage?" she blurted. "Did you search the garage?"

"That's where I got the ladder, but I'll check it before I go."

"The chimney? That could have been a—what do you types call it?—a point of entry."

"There's nobody in your chimney, Callie."

Her fingers bit into the musty blanket. She refused to say it, but he could see she didn't want to be alone.

Carter nodded at Bill, releasing him.

"You'll be okay," Carter said as the front door closed. "After all the commotion, this guy is long gone, but I'll have my people keep an eye on your place tonight just to make sure."

Even as he said it, Carter didn't like the idea of others watching out for her. Still, they'd been very clear on where they stood with each other. The two of them weren't friends. They were two people who sparked off one another, yet had very different opinions on things.

He waited, but for once, she had nothing to say.

"Call me if you need anything," he said.

He could see her brain working fast... trying to come up with an excuse. He steeled himself from offering. She needed to be the one who asked.

Her forehead furrowed, and she cocked her head. "You're not on duty."

Carter blinked. Ah, hell. He took a step back from her. "No, I'm not."

She was looking at him as if just seeing him. He'd grabbed his bulletproof vest when he'd gotten the call, but he wasn't in uniform. He'd been at the football game tonight... just like her. It hadn't escaped his attention that she was in the crowd.

She frowned. "How did you know to come?"

He'd hoped she wouldn't notice, but of course she had. He planted his hands on his hips. "I told the dispatchers to alert me if any calls came in from this house. They called me as I was headed home."

"Why?"

He'd wanted to avoid this. "You told me that you were having trouble adjusting to life on your own in an old, creaky, run-down house. It was nothing more than that."

Her chin lifted, and he fought to stand his ground. It wasn't a lie, but she was looking at him as if it was.

"Didn't want me bothering anyone else?" she asked.

No. As a matter of fact, he didn't. If she was going to bother anyone, it was going to be him.

"I'll check on you tomorrow morning," he said. It was time to go.

He turned for the door. Out of the corner of his eye, he saw her spring up from the sofa so fast that a pillow went flying off the end. She followed him until they were both at the front door.

"Lock up behind me," he said, "and try to get some sleep."

She rolled her eyes. "Yeah, I'll be chalking up the Zs."

He hesitated.

"Thank you, chief," she said quietly.

"It's Carter."

"Thank you, Carter."

He stared at her for a long moment before abruptly moving onto the porch. "Lock it."

He waited on the other side of the door until he heard the lock slide into place. Even then, his feet didn't want to move. He'd just made a big mistake there. Huge. Because even though they'd defined how things were going to be between them, it didn't feel like it when she called him by his name.

He stood there, torn, knowing he should go, but wanting to go back inside. And stay...

With a bump of his fist against the doorframe, he forced himself to move down the steps. She was secure, but his job here wasn't done. There was nothing in that house; he'd looked into every nook and cranny. That didn't mean somebody hadn't been there.

He scanned the neighborhood for any houses with their lights on. He wanted to know if anyone had seen or heard anything. His gaze landed on the house across the street, even though it was dark.

He'd start with David Hughes.

CHAPTER SEVEN

Callie sat in her living room with all the lights on and her tennis racket in hand. She wasn't comfortable here, but her bedroom was worse. Although maybe being locked in was better than sitting out in the open...

She couldn't believe Landry had gone... that he'd just left her. Although she hadn't asked him to stay...

The back of her neck prickled, and she quickly looked behind her. Nothing.

He'd said he'd have his people drive by her house. That was great and all, but his people didn't make her feel as safe as he did. She'd seen him in action tonight. He'd taken charge, and it had been impressive. He was big, muscle-bound, and grouchy. She wanted him here, at least until her goosebumps disappeared.

Maybe the bedroom would be better... but it was further away from the front door... because she wasn't going out the back into the woods...

"Get it together," she whispered. She tugged the blanket more tightly around herself. What he'd said about the animals in the forest made sense. Kind of.

But it didn't account for the footsteps.

She listened hard, but the silence around her pulsed. She

swept her palm against the blanket before gripping her tennis racket again. She just had to make it till morning. Everything would be better in the light of day, when she'd be able to think. Too bad daybreak was coming later and later every day.

She tried to even out her breaths, but they went haywire when lights swept across the window before her. There was the sound of an engine and the crunch of gravel. Oh, God. Someone was here.

She bolted off the sofa, moving away from the windows where someone might see her. She pressed her back against the wall in the entryway, but her heart beat hard in her chest. There were footsteps on her porch. She lifted her racket...

But then someone knocked.

It stood her upright. An intruder wouldn't knock.

"Callie?"

The voice was muffled, but she recognized it. All her breath rushed out of her at once, leaving her lightheaded. She rushed across the entryway and peeked out the window. Carter. He'd come back.

Tears of relief pricked at her eyes, but she quickly wiped them away. She tried to be casual when she opened the door, but still, she nearly ripped it from its hinges. "Did you forget something?" she asked.

His gaze settled on her tennis racket. "Would it help if I stayed for a while?"

Her knees wobbled. "Will you stay the night? Please?"

"I might as well." He stepped inside and closed the door behind him. "I already tried to leave once. It didn't work."

Callie wanted to hug him, she really did, but when she nearly gave in, she discovered the tennis racket still in her hand. Trying to be sly, she propped it up against the wall.

"You're cold," she said as she invited him deeper into the house.

"I've been driving around town and talking to people. Not many of your neighbors are up. Those who are claim not to have noticed anything unusual."

"Well, I certainly did," she said, before catching herself. He didn't always get her humor, and she didn't want to squabble with him. "Can I get you something to drink? Hot chocolate? No, I'm out of milk. Coffee? No, probably too late for that."

"I'm fine."

"I could light a fire in the fireplace."

"Probably not a good idea if you haven't had it cleaned."

"Oh. Right."

"Although it would block that point of entry."

She looked up at him swiftly. He wasn't smiling, but there was a glint in his blue eyes. The corners of her mouth quirked. Maybe he did have a sense of humor, deep, deep down.

The tightness around her ribcage relaxed. "I'm glad you came back."

He unzipped his jacket and draped it over the back of the chair. His bulletproof vest was gone, but his gun was still at his hip. "You need to know it will cause a stir if my truck is parked in your driveway overnight."

"I don't care." Although she hadn't even thought of that.

She wasn't in Boston anymore—people there weren't as up in each other's business—but maybe talk was good. It might give whomever had broken into her house second thoughts about doing it again.

"If you can deal with the gossip, then I can too." He settled onto the sofa and stretched his long legs out in front of him.

He was already the town's favorite topic of discussion, although come to think of it, she wasn't far behind. Callie sat down beside him, tucking one leg underneath her. She felt better—much better—but she wasn't sure what to do now. The silence returned, but this time the pulsing beneath it was different.

"Do you want to talk about it?" he finally asked.

"Not really."

"Want to turn on the TV?"

"No." Then she wouldn't be able to hear if the footsteps came back. The other noise, though… She inched closer to him. That, she would notice.

"Feel like hitting something?"

"Someone, but not you."

"That's a first."

Not really. More and more, she was inclined to curl up against him.

He brushed back a lock of her hair. "You look tired."

"So do you." He'd probably been heading home for the night when he'd gotten the call, and he'd spent the last hour or so running around for her. She felt herself softening. Maybe he wasn't such a hardass after all. She toyed with the fringe on the blanket. "Do you want me to make up the guest bedroom for you?"

He propped the pillow next to him up against the armrest of the sofa. "I'll just bunk down here. I don't want to put you out, and, from what I've seen, your extra bedrooms are on the second floor."

Interpretation? That was too far away if he was needed.

It didn't need to be said. Nor did the fact that there was a third sleeping option that would put him even closer.

Callie pushed up from the couch. That option sounded way too tempting. "I'll find a blanket for you."

"Don't worry about me. I'm not a houseguest."

She was already digging into a box. "It's no trouble. It's right here."

It was actually in the third box she opened, along with a full-sized pillow. She plumped up the stuffing that had gotten deflated and added a fresh pillowcase. She passed them both to him. "Do you want a sheet for underneath you?" she asked. "I'm sure there's one in here somewhere."

He stood, and she was reminded again of his size.

"Relax." He caught her hand when she reached for another box. "I'm good. Why don't you go try to get some rest? It will help."

"But—"

"I'll be right here."

She glanced toward the hallway. It was lit up like the Fourth of July, just like her bedroom, but she didn't want to go in there. She didn't want to close the door between them, but she didn't know if she could stand to leave it open, either. Not after those footsteps and the way that door handle had jiggled…

"We'll have another look around in the morning," he said.

"Okay."

He directed her toward the bedroom. "Good night, Callie."

"Good night." She swallowed hard. "Carter."

—*-*-*—

A knocking noise woke Carter hours later. His head jerked up at the sound, and he immediately reached for the kink in his neck.

"Uh," he grunted. The ever-present knot in his shoulder hadn't migrated. It had just expanded its territory and taken over his neck.

Slowly, he looked around to try to get his bearings. It was morning; he could tell that much by the sunshine that was drilling him in the eye. He squinted and found he was on the couch in Callie's living room—a couch that had been much too short. He'd be lucky if he could turn his head by the end of the week.

The knocking was persistent. His eyes narrowed to slits as he glared toward the entryway.

"Make it go away."

The muffled voice made him stop as he swung his feet to the floor. Looking down, he saw a tousled blond head. "Callie? What are you doing down there?"

"Turn off the furnace," she groaned. She turned onto her side and pulled his bomber jacket up over her head.

"It's not the furnace. Somebody's at the door."

He lowered his feet carefully and sat forward to look at her. She'd made an impromptu harem-style bed down there. Pillows and blankets were scattered across the floor. Not only had she commandeered his jacket, his camping blanket still covered her legs.

And it looked good there. He ran a hand through his hair. The proprietary feeling that had been nibbling at him was threatening to take a big bite.

He'd put her to bed hours ago. He must have really crashed not to hear her come out and settle back down beside him. You'd think he would have noticed something like that, especially when he was supposed to be on the lookout for a prowler. And especially since the woman bedding down next to him for the night was Callie Thompson.

The beating on the door picked up to the pace of a jackhammer.

"All right, all right," he grumbled. Callie moaned with frustration, and he ran his hand over the top of her head before pushing himself off the couch. "I'll get rid of whomever it is."

The kinks in his back protested even louder as he walked across the hardwood floor. He was rolling his neck when he answered the door. "Yeah?"

"Oh, Carter, it's you," Alice said slyly. "Good morning."

He pinched the bridge of his nose. Great. This was just how he wanted to start his morning. He glanced at Mamie and prepared himself for more innuendo, but her eyes were round. She held a broom in her hand like a weapon.

"What are you two doing here?" he asked.

"We could ask the same of you." Alice looked like the cat that had swallowed the canary. "Did you spend the night?"

His shoulder twinged. She knew full well that he'd spent the night. His pickup was parked in the driveway, his feet were bare, and his clothes were wrinkled. "Don't get the rumor mill started. I slept on the couch."

"We heard there was trouble."

"So, of course, you hit the ground running to get over here."

"Carter Landry," Mamie huffed. "We came to see Callie. We wanted to make sure that she's all right."

He ran a hand through his hair. Alice's opinions tended to bounce right off him, but Mamie had a moral fiber that jabbed at his conscience every now and then. "She's still asleep."

"Oh, that's good." Mamie patted her hefty bosom. "I wouldn't be able to sleep after something like that."

"You would if you had a hunky stud sleeping next to you."

Carter's shoulder hitched tighter. "Alice, I slept on the couch."

"No wonder you're so grumpy."

She craned her neck to see past him into the house, but he blocked the doorway.

"Was it bad?" she asked. "All the hoopla last night, I mean. Not being kicked out onto the couch."

He ground his teeth together. "It wasn't good."

"Oh my," Mamie said. "Is Callie okay?"

"She was rattled. Why don't you come back later? I'm sure she'd like to see you."

"Who is it?" Callie asked sleepily as she padded into the entryway.

He turned to look at her. It was easy to see that she still wasn't quite awake. Her hair was tangled, and her eyelids were heavy. Seeing her so soft and warm roused his protective instincts. His hand went to the door to close the world outside, but it was too late. She'd been spotted.

"There's our dear girl," Mamie said.

Carter stepped back before he could be swept away in the tide. The door flew open, and the two women carted in several bags full of supplies and one broom.

"We heard."

"Bill told us. It's the talk of the town."

"You must have been so frightened."

"It's a good thing you called Carter."

"Slow down," Callie said as she pushed her hair out of her eyes. "Please."

"Oh, Alice. She looks a-fright."

Callie's eyes snapped open at that, and she self-consciously reached for her hair. Carter had to bite his tongue. She looked pretty damn good, if you asked him.

Alice slapped at Mamie's hand. "She looks just fine."

Callie was trying unsuccessfully to straighten her robe as she searched for a mirror. When she couldn't find one, she looked at him. He shook his head. She didn't need to fix a thing.

"What she meant to say was that you looked as if you'd had a fright," Alice explained.

"Ladies," Carter said. They weren't helping. "What is this? The welcome wagon?"

The visitors both looked down as if they hadn't remembered they were carrying anything. When they did, the expressions on their faces turned determined. They pulled back their shoulders and lifted their chins.

"We're here to help," Mamie declared.

"This house isn't going to get to you, too." Alice lifted the broom like a general leading a charge. "We're here to do a cleansing."

"A what?" Callie asked.

Carter straightened quickly from where he'd been leaning with his forearm against the doorjamb. Oh, hell. He needed to nip this in the bud. "Bill must have told them about the break-in."

"Break-in, my butt. That was—"

He grabbed the broom. "People often feel the need to take back their home after something like this... scrub everything clean."

"That's not what I meant at all," Alice said.

He lifted an eyebrow at her. They'd promised.

It was Mamie who picked up on the hint. She stepped around her friend. "That's right. We're here to help you finish unpacking and straighten up a bit."

"*Ooof*," Alice said on a rough exhale when one of Mamie's elbows dug into her ribcage.

Callie was still trying to clear the fog from her brain. "I had planned to finish up some work on the exterior today with David."

"Probably not a good day for it," Carter said. He took the bag from Mamie and headed for the kitchen. "It's chilly out there."

Mamie and Alice huddled close together as they followed along. They craned their necks to look up the staircases in the entryway and looped their arms together as they shuffled through the living room. It was the quietest Carter had ever seen them.

Callie trailed along behind more slowly. Once in the kitchen, she sat down heavily in a chair. "It's too early to clean."

"You don't have to do anything, dear." Mamie patted her on the shoulder. "You just let us take care of you."

Carter propped the broom up in a corner. He began emptying the bags and frowned as he pulled out sage and incense. Alice lifted an eyebrow at him as she removed salt from her bag.

"Are you cooking, too?" Callie asked.

Mamie and Alice shared a look.

"Mamie has put together a four-course meal with less," Carter said. "Haven't you, Mamie?"

The friendly café owner jumped as if poked. "Oh, absolutely." She began moving around the kitchen with more purpose. "Are you hungry, sweetie? Let me whip you up some breakfast. You too, Carter. You've both had a long night."

Carter threw Alice a glare when he found a wooden stake. What were they cleansing the house of—ghosts or vampires? He slid it into his back pocket before Callie could see. "Thanks, but now that reinforcements are here, I need to be heading out."

Callie whirled around. "What?"

"You want to take that walk around the house with me?"

Her tiredness cleared, and fear flared in her eyes. "Oh... Uh, okay."

"Ladies." With a nod, he said goodbye and headed back to the living room. Callie followed and hovered as he sat down to put on his shoes and gun.

"Are you sure you can't stay for breakfast?" she said.

"I need to get back out there and start talking to people and make sure Bill got those fingerprints entered into the lab's system." He glanced at his watch. "And I have a conference call about the latest search efforts in about an hour."

"Right. The governor's task force thing." She began folding the old camping blanket into careful squares.

"Where's your phone?" he asked.

She pulled it out of her pocket.

He took it. "I'll give you my number so you can call me. You know, if you… need me."

He keyed in his number and sent himself a text. It felt intimate somehow, sharing the private information, even while, out in the kitchen, cupboards opened and closed. He heard Alice's trademark cackle and winced. Oh yeah, talk had already started around town about the two of them.

But there was no way to change that.

"I want you to do some things today," he said.

Callie looked at him, her expression earnest. "All right."

"As soon as you can, call Ernie. His cousin needs to take another look at the furnace, but I also want new locks on your doors. A lot of people have come and gone through this place over the years. We don't know who might still have a key."

She went still for a moment, but then smacked her forehead. "Ahhh. I've been racking my brain over how someone could have gotten in, but that's the first thing that's made sense." She actually looked relieved. "I'll get a new lock on my bedroom door, too."

He glanced at the hallway where Bill had taken fingerprints. Some of the black powder still clung to the handle, while more was scattered across the floor. "That's a good idea, especially if it's been sticking on you."

"It's not sticking. It locks. On its own."

He dipped his head so he could look her in the eyes. "Well, last night, that was a good thing, right?"

Her lips flattened, but she nodded. She shoved her phone back into her pocket. He was glad she'd had the thing on her. That had been a saving point, too. Without her call, he wouldn't have known she needed help.

He rubbed the back of his neck. "Let's start with the first floor."

Together, they made their way through the house, looking

in all the rooms and closets and checking the windows. He knew her feeling of safety had been ripped away. He wasn't quite sure how to get it back for her.

Other than to catch the bastard who'd terrorized her.

The itch to get back out on the hunt became stronger.

"Do you want to cover the attic and the basement?" he asked when they finished with the rooms on the second floor.

"No, I trust you." She rolled her eyes at his pretend-shocked look. "I know. Mark it on the calendar."

A smile pulled at his lips. "I just might."

Color flushed her cheeks. "Thank you for riding to my rescue last night."

"You're welcome."

"And staying with me."

Like he could have gotten himself to leave.

Their gazes locked. And held. Things had changed between them last night. The friction was still there, but trust had somehow taken root.

She took a tiny step toward him. "I know we got off to a rocky start, but—"

"Callie." Mamie's singsong voice floated up the vaulted entryway to where they stood on the second-floor landing. "Breakfast is ready."

Like a teenager caught on the front porch after a first date, Carter pulled back. Damn, that pair's timing was as impeccable as ever. "I guess that's my signal." He didn't want to leave, but he backed toward the stairs. "I'll let you know if we find anything."

"Okay."

"Call me," he said.

She nodded, and, this time, he really did go. He could feel her watching him as he walked down the entryway steps and out to the porch. He was halfway to his truck before he realized he hadn't qualified the request. There'd been no "if you need me" or "if you remember any more information." Just "call me."

He pulled open the door to his truck and looked back at

the house. He hoped she did.

CHAPTER EIGHT

The scrubbing, sweeping, and buffing helped more than Callie expected. Alice and Mamie kept up a constant chatter as they unpacked boxes and helped sort through her things. They hung her pictures on the walls, put her clothes in her dresser, and argued over the best color to paint her office. Their insistence on sprinkling salt outside the entrances confused her, though, and the colliding scents of sage and incense made her nose tickle. Still, their presence pushed away the lingering sense of invasion and helped her stake ownership in the place. They stayed until the first floor of the house was polished and homey. They'd offered to help with the second floor, but she'd given them a reprieve. They'd done more than their fair share of work, but more importantly, she'd noticed "the look."

She took a long drink of the Coke she'd pulled out of the fridge. She'd seen that look on so many people's faces, she was beginning to expect it. Even Officer Raikins had worn it last night, and he'd had a gun on his hip. Carter was the only one who seemed unaffected.

The question was, unaffected by what?

She listened to the bubbles popping inside the can. She knew fear when she saw it. She'd experienced it up close and personal, but what reason could everyone in town have for being so twitchy? Had something like this happened before? Was that why Carter had given the dispatcher special notice?

Trees stood outside her windows, maybe a hundred feet away. To someone of the criminal element, the house would be a prime target. It was dark and secluded, with the woods offering good cover.

She shivered. She felt better with new locks on the doors; Ernie had replaced them himself. She was certain that was how someone had gotten in. Carter had convinced her of at least that.

She brushed her hand along the top of the sofa. Nothing had made her feel safer than he had.

Her insides warmed. She'd tried to be quiet when she'd snuck out of her bedroom last night. She just hadn't been able to stay there, but finding him asleep had made her drop her clutch of pillows and blankets. He'd been too big for the sofa, and his arms and legs had fallen off in every direction. She'd had the most incredible urge to climb onto the couch on top of him, but she'd settled for the floor instead. She'd been out like a light within minutes. Just having him nearby had eased her nerves, made her feel secure and—

She jumped when someone knocked on her door.

"*Ahh*, darn it." She set down her can of cola and licked the splotches off her hand.

She hurried to answer. Even though it was past noon, she took the precaution of looking through the curtains before opening the door.

"David. What are you doing here so early? Is it a short day at school?"

He lifted an eyebrow. "It's Saturday. I'm late."

Oh, wait. That was right. The Friday night game. She ran a hand through her hair. With all that had happened, she'd lost track of her days. "I guess I'm a little spacey. I didn't get much sleep last night."

"I heard."

She winced. She supposed that couldn't be helped. "I hope I didn't wake up the entire neighborhood."

He shrugged and gave the house one of those cautious looks of his. "We're used to it."

There it was again.

"Why is that?" she asked, pouncing. "Why are people so used to the police coming out here? Did something happen in this house that I should know about?"

His guarded eyes connected with hers, and for a split second, she thought he was going to say something. Then, suddenly, his gaze flew over her shoulder to the living room. She nearly reached for him when his face paled to the color of a new moon.

"*And now the latest on the search for those escaped convicts,*" came a voice behind her.

Callie whirled around like a top.

"*As we've been reporting, John Smith was captured in the town of Colrain early this morning. Authorities are still on the lookout for Clive Morton.*"

The television was on. She could hear the midday news report from where she was standing.

She took an instinctive step backward. "How did that turn on? Did you see someone?"

"No," David said.

"Are you sure?"

"I'm sure." He pulled back from her and left her standing in the doorway alone.

"*Authorities are turning to the public for help in finding this last escaped convict. Morton is five foot, ten inches tall and weighs two hundred pounds. He has dark hair, a beard, and a mole on his left cheek. If you see anyone matching this description, authorities request that you contact them immediately.*"

Callie shot David one last pleading look, but he was immovable. It made no sense. The thing shouldn't just turn on all by itself. What had he seen?

"You stay right there," she ordered him. "Right there."

He nodded, and she summoned her nerve. She took two slow steps toward the living room, but then spotted her tennis racket against the wall. She swept it up and held it, poised to do damage as she peeked into the open room. It was empty, but the television was blaring. Morton's mugshot was on the screen, and his blank, soulless eyes made her stomach curdle. No wonder Carter was on an all-out manhunt.

She tiptoed deeper into the room and peered into the kitchen. Bright sunshine lit it up. There weren't any signs that anybody had been there.

She looked at the TV like it was a two-headed snake. It had never acted up like this before. Had someone bumped a switch as they'd rearranged the furniture? Jiggled a cord?

Or had it turned itself on, just like her lock?

She quickly punched the power button. It was time to call an electrician. Two light bulbs had already burned out, and others in the house tended to flicker. Maybe there was something wrong with the wiring. God knew there was something wrong with everything else.

She headed back to David. He hadn't listened to her. Instead he'd moved even further away, onto the front lawn.

"Maybe I shouldn't work here anymore," he blurted when he saw her.

"What?" She nearly tripped over the doorstep. "Why?"

He gave the classic teenager because-I'm-bored shrug, only he didn't pull it off. It came off more as a because-I'm-upset-about-something-but-I'm-not-going-to-tell-you shrug. Callie knew the difference in the nuances. She'd been a teenager once herself.

She rubbed her arms against the cold as she stepped out onto the porch. "You said you wanted to help... that you could use the money to fix up your car..."

"I know."

"So? What's changed?" She wanted to get some of the rotted wood on the porch replaced before the first snow, but that wasn't the real issue right now. Something was off with him. Wrong She clicked her tongue as she considered how to get him to talk to her. "People warned me that you couldn't be trusted. Are you going to prove them right?"

"Who said that? Your cop?"

Her cop? "Whoa, now. He's not mine."

"He acts like he is."

The thought wasn't as unpleasant as it might have once been. "I have my own brain in my head, David, and I use it on occasion. Don't you dare quit on me because you think I'm taking Chief Landry's side on anything. Give me a little more credit than that."

She had his full attention now.

"Are you sure you want me around?"

She frowned. "Why would you even ask me something like that?"

A muscle in his jaw worked. She'd thought he was upset, but now she could see that didn't even come close. He was ready to pop. She took a hesitant step closer to him. Had she done something? If she had, she didn't know what that could possibly be. In this town, she was his biggest supporter.

"I didn't know if you'd want me to work for you after what happened last night," he finally admitted.

The gears in her head turned, but she couldn't figure out what he was talking about. Unless… *Ohhhh*. The truck in the driveway. Carter had spent the night. Suddenly, all David's talk about the police chief made sense. Flustered, she fluffed her hair. "Don't worry. There's nothing going on between me and Chief Landry."

At least, nothing he needed to be concerned about.

There was confusion in the teenager's dark eyes. He stared at her until she started to get self-conscious. "You didn't put him up to it," he finally said.

"Who up to what?"

He let out an unflattering snort. "Landry."

A twitchy feeling caught Callie between her shoulder blades. She knew the relationship between Carter and David wasn't good, but just how bad was it? "What did he do?" she asked.

"Dirty Harry accused me of breaking into your house last night and trying to get into your bedroom."

"He did *what*?"

"He was ready to string me up by my thumbs."

"But why you?"

"How the hell would I know? Convenience? I'm always at the top of his suspect list."

Outrage clogged Callie's chest. "But you... You'd never do anything like that!"

David dragged his hand through his too-long hair. "Thanks," he said roughly. "I wasn't sure what you were thinking. He was pretty hot, and I thought maybe he'd gotten to you."

Carter had gotten to her, but on a different level, and she was a fool for letting that happen. She couldn't believe she'd been walking around all day, daydreaming about "sweet" Chief Landry. "What exactly did he say and what did he do?"

"I was at the park when he came at me on a rampage. Man, I've ticked him off before, but I've never seen him like that." David stuffed his hands into his pockets. "I didn't even know what had happened. When I heard, all I could think about was you. I told him the truth—that I had been with my friends all night—but he didn't believe me. He wasn't happy when he left."

Callie's hands opened and clenched into fists. "I told him it wasn't you."

David shrugged again, but he didn't seem as unhappy as he had when he'd first knocked on her door. "So does this mean that I'm not fired?"

"It means that you're getting a raise." She ground her teeth together. Fuming, she spun around on her heel. "Start working on the porch. I've got something else I need to do."

* * *

Carter was typing up a report when he heard the door to the station open and stick. The sound made him scowl, and he hit the enter key with a sharp tap. That damn thing. He was pushing himself out of his chair to go take a look at it when Bill went flying by his office window. He'd never seen the guy move so fast.

"I'm sorry," came a feminine voice. "Did I do that?"

Carter swore and pulled his hand away from his holster. With the way his officer had responded, he'd thought they were being ambushed. He shook his head. It wasn't an ambush; it was Callie.

"It's all right, dear," Nancy said. "We've been having problems with the door."

"Ah gee, let me get that for you," Bill said. Carter heard a swift kick, a groan when his officer stubbed his toe, and the sharp creak of the door closing.

"Thank you, Bill."

"You're welcome, Ms. Thompson," Bill replied, his voice strained.

"Call me Callie. Is the police chief in?"

"He's in his office," Nancy said. "Let me tell him you're here."

"I'll just surprise him, if you don't mind."

She was surprising him, all right. He hadn't expected her to show up at the station. Uneasiness unfurled in Carter's stomach. Had something happened at the house after he left? Alice and Mamie hadn't gone back to that cleansing nonsense again, had they?

He realized he was tapping his fingers against the desktop and made himself stop. So she was setting foot in his territory. They might be a small operation compared to Boston, but he was proud of the place. He made sure that his people were well trained and had the best tools their budget could buy.

At last, she appeared in his doorway. "Hello, Carter."

He stood there, poleaxed. No wonder Bill had lunged to get the door for her. She always looked good, but this was something else entirely. She was dressed to kill, and his gaze was drawn to her legs like a moth to the flame. The short leather skirt and matching boots were enough to make him want to cry.

He shook his head to clear the cobwebs. His staff was already looking at him funny as it was. "Everything okay at the house?"

"It's spick-and-span." She leaned against the doorframe.

"May I come in?"

Looking like that, she could do just about anything she wanted. He pulled out the chair in front of his desk. "What are you doing here?"

Her heels clicked against the floor with an even staccato. He knew he was staring, but he couldn't look away. Her walk had a predatory strut to it that made him hard. He lifted his head slowly. He didn't know the reason, but she was on the hunt.

And Lord help him, he was her prey.

"I thought we could chat." She glanced over her shoulder and waved at the redheaded cop planted behind her. "Thanks, Bill. I've got it from here."

"*Ooof.*" The officer promptly bumped into the corner of a desk.

Carter walked over and closed the door. When he turned, he found Callie shrugging out of her jacket. Her pink sweater was soft and clingy. It didn't show skin, but it showed shape. He felt a light sweat break out on his brow. Damn, what was she up to? "What do you want to talk about?" he asked.

"David Hughes."

The tension in his shoulder pulled tight. He'd been wrong; this *was* an ambush. No wonder she'd come dressed for battle.

She lowered herself into the chair he'd offered her and crossed her legs. "You accused him of breaking into my house."

Carter looked her straight in the eye and saw the fire she barely kept banked. "I questioned him. He had opportunity and motive."

"What motive?"

Did he really need to spell it out for her?

At last, Carter found that he could move. He rounded his desk and opened the lower drawer. He grabbed the biggest file in there and unceremoniously dropped it on his desk. "There it is, the David Hughes file. You're new in town, so you might not have known, but he's our most notorious juvenile delinquent. If I'd known you were thinking about hiring him to work on your house, I would have warned you earlier."

Her hands closed around the arms of the chair, but she kept that temper of hers on tap. "I don't care about your little file. I only care about what I know, and that's that David would never do anything to hurt or scare me."

"Don't be so gullible, Callie. It doesn't suit you."

Color dotted her cheekbones, and for the first time, Carter realized he'd made a tactical error. She ranted when she was irritated. This went deeper.

"You told me that it appeared as if the intruder had a key. I told you I didn't give him one."

"That doesn't mean he doesn't have one." Carter began feeling a little hot under the collar himself. He jabbed his finger at the file. "The kid is a known shoplifter, and he broke into Alice's shed right before you moved to town. It's not that big of a leap."

"But why would he do it? I'd let him in if he asked." She tapped her fingernail on the file in question. "This is not a motive."

"The kid has a crush on you," Carter growled. "There isn't any bigger reason for a man to go lurking around a woman's bedroom than that."

"What?" She blinked, and he knew he'd caught her off guard. "He does not."

"Huge crush." She'd wanted to hear it. He'd give it to her straight.

She shook her head. "He's just a kid."

Carter ran his hand through his hair. She sat there dressed like a manhunter, but he couldn't believe the naivety that was coming out of her mouth. "I could see it in his eyes last night. He's sixteen, and you're the sexy blonde next door who pays attention to him. It's not rocket science, honey."

Her mouth dropped open before snapping shut.

Carter picked up a pencil and nearly broke it in half. The hell of it was that he knew how the kid felt. "You need to be careful of him."

"I need to be careful *with* him. He's incredibly sensitive, and

I don't think many people listen to him. His mother certainly doesn't."

"His mother might not, but I've listened to him plenty. I've listened to his excuses why he spray-painted the school, why he cherry-bombed the toilets, why he played mailbox baseball with the city council's—"

She held up her hands. "Enough. I'm not saying that he doesn't have a wild streak. I'll give you that. I just… Well, I've seen another side to him. I think there's more to him than most of us know."

Carter felt the knot in his back tighten so hard, it was amazing his shoulder didn't separate. "I know all I want, and I don't like him sniffing around you."

"For God's sake, Carter, he's not 'sniffing around me.' I've been blond all my life. Do you think I really would have made it this far without knowing how to pick up the signs? I know when a guy is interested."

Their gazes met—and held.

"Fine." She leaned back in the chair, but the swinging of her leg gave away her inner turmoil. "Keep him on your stupid suspect list. Just do one thing for me."

A muscle in Carter's jaw ticked. "What's that?"

"Dust my house." She uncrossed her legs, and her heel came down on the floor with a crack. "Dust every last inch of it. You won't find any of David's fingerprints. I guarantee you that."

"If he's been in that house, we will."

Her eyes flared. "Exactly. David has never been in my house. He won't even set foot inside the door."

Carter paused. Ah, hell. He hadn't thought of that.

"And you know why!" She leaned forward and pointed at him. "You know why everyone is so damned afraid of my house."

"Nobody is afraid of your house."

"Liar. You tell me, Carter Landry, or I swear I'll… I'll… I'll park in every restricted zone in town."

He dropped the pencil on his desk and rubbed the bridge

of his nose. "I'll have your car towed."

"I'm not leaving this office until you tell me."

"Damn it, Callie." He reached for his shoulder.

"Would you do something about that already?"

She jumped out of her chair and was around the desk before he realized what she was up to. He swiveled around to face her, but she caught the arm of his chair and twirled him back the other way. He started to stand, but nearly collapsed when her hands settled onto his shoulder and began kneading it.

"How am I supposed to fight with you when I'm feeling sorry for you?" she grumbled.

Her thumbs found the center of the knot and pressed deep. Carter nearly whimpered with relief, but he didn't like how she'd turned the tables on him. Instinct made him look up. He found two very shocked staffers looking at him through the windows of his office. He started to push her hands away, but she bopped him lightly on the head.

"Sit still."

He couldn't help but watch the back of her long legs as she went around the room closing the blinds. He swore. He was going to have a lot of explaining to do, but at the moment, he didn't have the will to stop her. Every time she lifted her arm to twirl the controls, her skirt hitched up a little higher.

When she finally blocked the room from prying eyes, she turned around to face him. "You're going to tell me about my house."

He paused. With that look and tone of voice, she could teach his staff a thing or two about interrogation. "There's nothing wrong with that house."

"Was somebody murdered there? Was it a meth house?"

"No."

She lifted an eyebrow. When she circled behind him, he prayed he was in for more delirious torture. His head dropped forward when she again began massaging his shoulder.

"If there's nothing wrong with the house, why do I practically have to kick people in the butt to make them go inside?" she asked.

"You didn't have to kick my butt."

"I will."

"It's been abandoned for a long time."

"What does that have to do with anything?"

"You know how big, abandoned buildings are. There are stories," he finally admitted. He couldn't help his weakness. He was feeling jolts of electricity all the way down to his fingers. He hadn't realized how much circulation the tightness had cut off.

"What stories?"

She began working on his neck, and he was putty in her hands. Her thumb applied pressure to a particularly sensitive spot, and his eyes drifted shut. For the first time in what felt like weeks, he relaxed. "God, you're good."

* * *

Callie felt the change in Carter's body under her hands, and her fingers tingled at the power submitting to her commands. Nerves suddenly hit her. He kept in shape. Like, *mouth-watering* shape. With those arms and that chest, he could probably bend her into a pretzel if he wanted. She needed to remember that when she was antagonizing him.

"What kind of stories?" she asked, trying to keep control of the situation.

"Town legend, gossip, that kind of thing."

He rolled his shoulder, and a knot as big as a quarter popped under her fingertips. "You idiot," she said softly. "You shouldn't have let this get so bad."

She couldn't imagine how long he'd let the tension build for his muscles to become so rigid. She was still upset with him, but her touch automatically gentled. He needed about an hour on a massage table. She exhaled slowly. Now, wasn't that just the picture?

"It couldn't be helped. We're swamped around here." He settled his elbows onto the desk and began rubbing his temples. "There's the search for Morton, the break-in at your place, and the Halloween pranks have started already. They're about a week early this year for some reason."

"All I've ever seen you do is work. Why do you have to handle everything?"

"Because there's nobody else who can."

She rolled her eyes. "My, aren't we a little full of ourselves?"

He shook his head, and she had a crazy urge to slide her fingers into his thick, dark hair.

"I'm not full of anything. I'm shorthanded. I've got one officer on maternity leave and another out with a broken arm. It's a small department. What would you have me do, Quick Kate?"

Her hands stilled on his back. He was asking her for advice? Her anger with him came down at least three notches. "See this contraption?" She nudged the trash can on the floor with her foot. "You put things in it, and they disappear."

"Callie."

"It was a joke," she said with a sigh. He still had a long way to go in the humor department. "I'm usually wittier than this, but you delegate. This cop with the broken arm, can he still use a computer?"

"I can't order him to come back. He's on medical leave."

"You don't have to order; you can ask. Maybe he's banging his head against the wall with boredom. See if he can come back for a couple of hours a day. He might be more willing than you think."

Carter grunted, and she knew that she'd made a point.

"That doesn't help with the legwork," he said.

Still stubborn. "There's this newfangled tool we have called a phone. If he can't run a computer, he can certainly run that. Teenagers can run them with only their thumbs."

His shoulders were wide and muscled, but even they couldn't support the whole world. She put her elbow against the huge knot in the center of his shoulder blade and applied pressure. No wonder his body was buckling under the load. "You can't tell me that everyone in your department is as busy as you are."

"They're carrying their weight."

"And you're carrying about three elephants."

He glanced over his shoulder at her, and she was secretly pleased to see that his neck had limbered up even with the small amount of work she'd done.

"You're bossy when it comes to this advice stuff."

"I'm a professional." A fuzzy feeling settled in her chest when he faced forward and sat there compliant, ready for more. She couldn't avoid the temptation any longer. She slid her fingers into his soft hair and began rubbing the base of his skull. He groaned, and she nearly joined him.

The fuzzy feeling drifted lower and became an ache. What had started as an act of compassion was quickly turning into something more dangerous. "Let's try something else," she said unevenly. "What case is your top priority?"

"Have you been living underneath a rock? What do you think?" He pointed toward a map on the wall. "That's the priority of every lawman in the state."

She squinted across the room. "What is it?"

He mumbled something and rubbed his eyes. "You really do have tunnel vision. It's a map pinpointing the sightings of Concord's escapees."

Callie did a double take. She'd forgotten about his conference call this morning. She'd meant to find a distraction, but that particular case was bigger than that. She looked closer at the map and the pins. "What do the colors mean?"

"Red is Smith—or I should say 'was.' Colrain PD got him this morning." He settled his elbows on the desk and looked at the map with her. She'd bet he saw it in his sleep. "Fleiss was blue, and Morton is green."

"I saw Morton's picture on TV earlier today. He scared me."

"He should."

The flat, unemotional tone flustered her. She remembered Alice's story about how Carter had tackled Fleiss in order to arrest him, and didn't like the feeling she got in the pit of her stomach. By his own words, Morton was the most dangerous of the three. What risks would he take to capture the man atop the most-wanted list? "How long do you think it will be before you find him?"

His shoulder muscles bunched up, and she realized she'd asked the wrong question.

"We're doing our best, but he's a slippery son of a bitch. He needs money, food, shelter, and transportation. We think he was behind the theft of a Dodge pickup not far from Concord, but we found it broken down in the Berkshire foothills. We haven't figured out how he's fulfilling any of his other basic needs. We're dead in the water until he makes a mistake."

"All right, big boy. Ease up." She looked at the map again and quickly saw the problem. Whereas blue and red pins were dotted across the state, there were hardly any green pins at all. Morton had been lying low. "You'll get him."

Carter went very still. "I'm going to need a bigger calendar. That's twice in one day."

"Funny." She smoothed her hands over his shoulders. "Okay, so I'll give you that one. The Morton case is yours. What's that you've got on your computer screen?"

"Nancy had a load of laundry stolen off her clothesline earlier this week."

"That doesn't sound too major. Give it to Bill."

"Nancy is my assistant. I can't give the case to someone else."

"Why? Bill looked perfectly competent to me last night."

Carter pinched the bridge of his nose, and she smiled. She liked poking at that unbending conscience of his.

"Raikins is my best worker."

"Then let him take lead on the case. Nancy won't be offended. Bill will ask you if he needs help."

Callie waited for the next excuse, but Carter said nothing. She took her chances and pointed at David's file. "Why don't you give that to someone else, too?" She stepped back quickly when he put his hands on the desk and pushed himself to his feet.

"No."

"It's obviously stressing you out."

"I said no."

He turned and, all of a sudden, she felt like she'd let a tiger out of its chains. He rolled his shoulder and tilted his neck to the side. Lord help her if he'd been operating at anything less than a hundred percent.

"I haven't ruled out David Hughes as a suspect in your break-in, and that's one case I'm not delegating to anyone. It's mine."

Oh, was it? Callie lifted her chin. "Maybe it shouldn't be."

He took a step toward her.

"Just when did I become the bad guy?" he asked, his voice dropping low. "Last night, you seemed pretty happy to have me around."

And she had been. She'd been glad he was there, but she'd also been in a state of shock. "Last night, I didn't know that you'd accused my friend after I'd specifically told you that he didn't have anything to do with it."

Carter's eyebrows rose. "So you came here looking for a fight?"

"I came looking for justice."

He moved closer and braced his hand against the wall beside her head. "Dressed like that?"

His gaze swept down her body, and heat trailed behind it. Callie willed herself not to tug at her skirt, which suddenly seemed too short. She'd dressed for power when she'd decided to come down here to confront him. He had his sunglasses; she had her leather skirt. Only one problem: its power was backfiring on her. She felt strong, but she also felt sexy. And hot and bothered...

"I can dress any way I want."

"But why all the touching? What was that about? It didn't feel like you wanted justice when you were running your fingers through my hair."

She swallowed hard. His jaw was rigid, his lips were tight, and his eyes... Oh God, his blue eyes burned. When their gazes finally connected, the air practically ignited.

"Maybe I didn't."

She didn't know why she said it. Maybe it was a challenge. Maybe it was a tease. Either way, he picked up the gauntlet.

He came right at her, and her breath caught when his arm snaked around her waist. His head dipped down and, before she could form a complete thought, his mouth was on hers. Hot and hard. Her heart began thudding in her eardrums, and the ache that had started in her belly when she'd first touched him clenched tighter. *Oh, God.* He slowly crowded her back against the wall, and something close to a moan erupted from her throat.

"Carter." Her fingers dug into his shoulders, and her knee brushed intimately against the outside of his.

His dark gaze smoldered as he judged her reaction. Then his mouth settled over hers again, and he took his time. The kiss wasn't a tentative, first-time brush of the lips; it was the type of kiss that had been stored up for weeks and allowed to age. Callie shuddered and slid her hands up from his shoulders into his hair.

He let out a sound that was half desperate/half demanding and tilted his head to the other side. His tongue slipped into her mouth as his hands found their way under her sweater. The skin-to-skin contact made heat rush through her, bold and sweet. Instinctively, she lifted her leg higher, wrapping it around his thigh. Her other leg nearly buckled when he situated himself more intimately against the niche at the top of her legs and pressed firmly.

"Do you have any idea how crazy you make me?" he whispered into her ear.

She clutched at him. "As wild as you make me?"

It was the wrong word to use, and way too accurate.

His eyes sparked. "That's good to know."

His hands began sliding upward, and her skin prickled in anticipation.

An unexpected knock at the door jolted her back to reality. "Chief?"

He swore hard. *His secretary.* Callie pulled back, but bumped her head against the wall.

His fingers tightened around her ribcage as he tried to catch his breath. "Yes, Nancy?" he finally called.

Callie quickly sidestepped away from him. He reached for her, but she batted his hands away. Her movements were clumsy as she tried to smooth her clothes back into place.

"I hate to interrupt your...uh, meeting," Nancy said through the door, "but the dispatcher just received a 911 call. I thought you'd like to know."

Callie could feel Carter staring at her hard, and she put more distance between them. She rubbed the back of her head, not so much for the pain, but to get her brain working. What had just happened? That was *not* what she'd had planned.

He wiped her lipstick off his mouth with the back of his hand. "Come on in."

She spun around and feigned interest in the map on the wall. Out of the corner of her eye, she saw him sit behind his desk.

"What happened?" he asked when Nancy hesitantly opened the door and poked her head inside.

"The Lutheran church is reporting a robbery." The older woman folded her hands primly in front of her. "Sally MacDonnell, the church secretary, had some money locked in her desk and now it's gone. It looks like someone pried open the drawer."

"She kept church money in her desk drawer?"

Callie could feel the curious glances being thrown in her direction. She ignored them and stared at the map as if it were the most fascinating thing in the world. Fortunately, Nancy was discreet enough not to say anything.

"They had that pancake breakfast this morning. Sally didn't finish cleaning up until after the bank was closed. She thought the money would be safe in her desk until Monday, but it was gone when she went back to get her coat."

"Did she see anyone?"

"I thought you'd like to talk to her yourself, chief. That's what you usually do."

Callie felt another look hit her in the middle of the back. Enough. She wasn't going to stick around to generate any more gossip. She'd already given the town plenty. She steeled her spine and turned around. She hoped she didn't look as thoroughly kissed as she felt. Her belly was still doing flip-flops, and her lungs felt like bellows. "I'll be going. You're busy, and we were through here anyhow."

Nancy stepped aside, but Carter's blue eyes flared. "The hell we were. Hold on. I'll get Bill to handle this."

This was not the time for him to take her advice.

"No, no. You're needed at the church." She grabbed her things and moved quickly to the door.

He started to stand, but stopped. Callie knew why. She'd felt the evidence he didn't want Nancy to see pressing between her thighs. She used the opportunity to make her escape.

She needed time to process this. She needed to figure out why he threw her thoughts into havoc.

And she needed legs that weren't the consistency of Jell-O.

She was halfway out the door when she stopped. She'd come here for a reason. She took a deep breath and schooled her face. Slowly, she turned. "And remember what I told you about David. Back off... Please."

CHAPTER NINE

Halloween arrived on a bright and crisp day. Callie looked around the neighborhood, and her grin widened. Shadow Valley did the holiday up right. Jack-o'-lanterns smiled toothily from doorsteps, ghosts hung from trees, and orange and black lights twinkled in the downtown area. She even heard the song "Monster Mash" blaring from a stereo somewhere.

She looked at the freshly painted columns of her front porch, now strung with spider webs for effect. A stuffed woman sat on the swing she and David had hung on the porch. It had taken more time than she'd expected to stuff leaves into old clothes, but she'd achieved the effect she'd wanted. She just hoped the scarecrow wouldn't frighten her trick-or-treaters too much.

A random thought occurred to her, and her eyebrows lifted. Maybe that was what had happened to Nancy's load of laundry. Oh well, it was up to Bill to figure that one out. That was, if Carter had taken her advice.

Carter.

A sizzle went down Callie's spine, and she shook it off. She still didn't know how things had spiraled so far out of control down at the station. She'd been mulling it over in her mind, but all that mulling had turned her brain to mush. She was just as confused now as she'd been then.

David came out of his house across the street, and her thoughts cleared. Of him, she was still certain. "Happy Halloween!" she called.

"Hey," he said. "What are you doing?"

"Waiting for the trick-or-treaters." She'd thought she'd have had more by now. Actually, she'd hoped to have at least one. The official time for trick-or-treating had started half an hour ago, but nobody had dropped by. The children she'd seen coming up the street had turned around before they'd gotten to her house.

David's footsteps slowed. "You might not get any."

Callie felt a pang of disappointment. "Why?"

He shrugged. "Because."

She rolled her eyes. "Could you be a little more specific?"

"Because they don't normally come out here." He reached into his pocket for his keys. "You might have better luck if you brought your candy out to the sidewalk."

"Really? That's not a half-bad idea." Her house had been big and scary for a long time. She grabbed the big plastic pumpkin she'd filled with treats and carefully navigated the porch steps. The long black skirt she was wearing made walking interesting. The long slit seemed to catch even the slightest puff of wind. Between it and her high heels, it made the walk to the front sidewalk take twice as long.

She looked down the street. She had the good stuff—strictly chocolate. There weren't any cheap knockoffs in the bunch. She wasn't about to be labeled as the lady with bad treats, not on her first Halloween in town.

"Nice costume," David said as he opened his car door.

Callie adjusted the cape that was tied around her neck. The thing was going to strangle her before the night was over, but Alice had already told her that she wouldn't be let into the party if she wasn't wearing a costume. Looking down, she decided she'd just have to suffer. There was no way she was taking the cape off.

"I was hoping they'd have a bunny rabbit or something

more mundane," she admitted.

"It wouldn't matter. You could make a bunny look hot."

Callie felt her cheeks flush. Ever since Carter had insinuated that David had a crush on her, she'd been self-conscious around him. Poor kid. He hadn't done anything wrong.

"Where are you going?" she asked.

"Out."

Of course, "out." Where else did teenagers go?

"Do you want a Hershey bar or something? I have a feeling I'm going to be eating this stuff for weeks."

"Sure, I'll take one."

She pulled a candy bar out of her pumpkin and tossed it to him. "Have fun."

"Thanks. See ya." The Thunderbird rumbled when he turned the key in the ignition. He nodded at her one last time and revved the engine before pulling away.

Once he was gone, the street felt lonely... and kind of eerie. It was starting to get dark, but Callie couldn't see any pirates or dinosaurs as she peered down the street. She rubbed the goosebumps on her arm to fight the chill in the air. She hoped that David was wrong. She'd gain ten pounds if she had to eat all this candy alone.

"Come on, kiddies."

"Trick—"

She spun around.

Carter stopped dead in his tracks. "—or treat," he said slowly.

Callie's gaze darted down, and she gasped. Her cape had flown open. She hurriedly pulled it back into place. "Don't sneak up on me like that!"

His gaze didn't move, and she looked down to make sure the cape was in place. It was, but he was looking at her like he had X-ray vision.

"Elvira?" he asked, his voice raspy.

Her face flared with heat. "It was all they had left at the costume shop in Pittsfield. It was either this or a Teletubby."

"Good choice."

His gaze finally slid up to her face, and the heat in her cheeks spread. She folded her arms around her waist. The dress was way more revealing than she'd thought when she'd rented it. "What are you doing here, Carter? Where did you come from?"

"I'm parked a block over. I've been doing some foot patrol to make sure we don't have any pranksters going too far."

She glanced at the walking path along the tree line where many of her neighbors liked to hike.

"You've been avoiding me, Miz Callie."

Her chin came up. Well, why didn't he just dive right in? "I haven't been avoiding you. I've been busy."

"I noticed. I haven't seen your car speeding through town for days."

Her fingers curled around the handle of the pumpkin. She shouldn't have to explain herself to him, but she felt compelled to say something. She didn't want him thinking that one little kiss had sent her hiding.

Okay. One major, toe-curling kiss.

"I've started working on my column again."

"Your column? That's the excuse you're going with?" A corner of his mouth twitched. "Okay, here's one for you, Quick Kate. How can a dress defy the laws of physics?"

The dress was formfitting, with a neckline cut way too low. Apparently, he'd gotten an eyeful. "None of your business," she mumbled.

"I don't seem to remember Elvira wearing a cape."

Why had she chosen the Mistress of the Dark? What was wrong with a purple Teletubby? It was a perfectly acceptable children's show. Family friendly. "It's the cape or no dress at all."

"Now *that* would be illegal."

She flushed. "I meant—"

"I know what you meant." His eyes sparked, but he turned to look at the house. He was standing so close that his shoulder brushed against hers. It made her even more aware of him. She could smell the pine trees he'd passed on the trail and feel the heat his body generated.

Callie hated how flustered she was, but she didn't know how to act around him anymore. Things had been so much simpler when they'd been rivals. Or uncertain friends. This attraction that had forced its way to the forefront ignored all the rules they'd agreed to follow.

"The place looks good," he said.

She softened. He might as well have complimented her newborn baby. She looked at the house in satisfaction. The change in the place was really something, she had to admit. The new paint job was like a facelift, and the blue trim around the windows added some pizzazz. The porch had taken a while to repair, but it was her favorite part of the house. Her swing was there, and once spring rolled around, she'd hang planters full of flowers. The house was almost as she'd pictured it when she'd pulled into the driveway her first day here.

"David helped." She pretended not to notice the way Carter's jaw flexed. "We just reattached the last of the shutters yesterday."

And one had squeaked throughout the night. At least, that was what she'd told herself the sound was.

"Any trouble?" he asked.

Callie stiffened. There it was, the real reason why he was here. It was Halloween, and he was checking up on David. "Why must you always assume there's going to be trouble?"

"Because with the two of you, there usually is." He planted his hands on his hips. "I see that his car is gone. Do you know where he went?"

"Out."

Carter shrugged. "I'm sure he'll be called in by someone before the night is done. Knowing him, he'll be blowing up jack-o'-lanterns somewhere."

"Oh, stop it. He will not."

"Want to bet that cape on it?"

Callie bit her lip. She wasn't *that* sure. Her fingers curled in to the heavy cloak. "I'm going to Alice's party," she said, by way of explanation.

His eyebrows lifted. "Make sure I don't have to come get you, too."

Callie could feel his gaze like a touch, but she couldn't tell if he was making fun of her or not. He was adjusting to the change in their dynamics better than she was. "Are you going?" she asked.

"I'm on duty until late tonight."

"That's too bad."

"Tell me about it."

She looked down into her pumpkin and began organizing the candy. She needed something to do. "How's the search for Morton going?"

"Don't ask." She caught her breath when he reached into the pumpkin and pulled out a bite-sized 3 Musketeers bar. The wrapper crinkled as he opened it. "It's not a good subject."

"You don't have anything new?"

"The task force has had a few leads, but none of them have panned out."

He looked even more tired than he had the last time she'd seen him. There were shadows underneath his eyes, his hair was rumpled, and he was rolling his shoulder in that uncomfortable way that told her it was tight again. Her hold on her candy tightened. The need to take care of him was strong. "You should take a vacation. You need to get away from that case."

"I'll take a vacation once he's behind bars again."

They needed to find the man first. It unnerved her to think Morton could be anywhere, with his soulless eyes and ruthless mouth.

The sound of laughter and excited chatter suddenly filled the air. Callie perked up and spun around. A group of candy seekers was running down the street toward her.

"Trick or treat!"

She couldn't help it; the expressions on the kids' faces made her laugh. They stampeded toward her with their eyes big on the house. They stuck together in a tight group, and she realized that they were in on some kind of a dare.

"That's more like it," Carter said only a few inches from her ear.

She could feel his body heat warming her back. "Like what?" she said as she handed candy to a hairy blue monster.

"You're smiling."

His breath stirred her hair, and her stomach flipped. It was hard to smile around him. Whenever he got close to her, she felt uptight. Wound up. It had been that way from the very beginning.

The trick-or-treaters moved on, and she turned uncertainly to face him. Without warning, a gust of wind caught her cape and threw it over her shoulder. She grabbed for it, but he caught it first. Her heart jumped against her ribcage when he slowly pulled it back into place. His fingers trailed over her skin as he smoothed it over her chest.

"I've got to get going," he said quietly. A muscle ticked in his temple as he looked at her, but he took a step back. He reached into his coat pocket and pulled out a pad of paper and pencil. He scribbled a note, ripped off a page, and handed it to her. "Sooner or later, you're going to have to face up to that kiss."

Her heart rate zoomed into the red zone.

"What's this?" Her fingers brushed his as she took the note.

Only it wasn't a note.

"Another ticket? Are you kidding me?"

A slow, heated grin spread across his face. "If that isn't indecent exposure, I don't know what is."

Callie looked down at herself. Not only was her cape wide open, her skirt was flapping around like bat wings, displaying a good amount of thigh. Her face flamed, and she whipped her cape closed.

Carter smiled as he backed away from her. It was the first true smile he'd given her, and her belly dropped.

"Is this real?" she asked, waving the ticket in the air.

"It is if those are."

Callie lowered her arm and threw him a glare. "You... You..."

"Feed your trick-or-treaters," he said, laughing as he turned. "And don't take that cape off for anyone but me."

* * *

It was late when Callie pulled her car into the driveway. The wind had picked up over the hours, and she fought with her cape as she got out of her car. It was flapping around like it wanted to take flight. The air felt so good, she finally gave up and let it go.

"Ah," she said with relief. Sensing her presence, the motion detector light she'd had installed on the garage came on.

She'd had fun at Alice's house but hadn't found the guts to take off the cape. Having Carter see her was one thing. Strutting around wearing half a dress in front of the whole town was another.

She tugged at the long black wig she'd added to complete the ensemble. It had been a mistake. She shook her hair free and closed her eyes as the wind cooled her scalp. It was a wonder she hadn't passed out from heat exhaustion.

Other than nearly sweating to death, she'd had a blast at the party. Everyone was celebrating, from the toddlers to the octogenarians. She'd even met the elusive Sherman. It was hard to tell if she'd ever be able to identify Alice's husband again, though, because he'd been dressed as a Hell's Angel, complete with dark sunglasses, a bandana, and leather chaps.

The wind started to bring cold drops of rain with it as she hurried up the steps. She'd just let herself inside when the sky opened up and it began to rain in earnest. She hit the light switch, but jumped when the wind caught the front door and slammed it shut.

Her heart gave a start, but she turned the lock. She pulled back the curtain and watched the rain smack against the window. She was glad she'd decided to come home when she did. She hated to think what the Elvira dress might look like soaking wet.

"Like a wet seal," she muttered.

With a relieved sigh, she untied the noose from around her neck and let the cape drop onto a chair. She ruffled her hair as she walked into the living room. Her reflection in the mirror caught her eye, and she paused to look at herself.

Her breasts warmed when she remembered how Carter had stared—and his question about how the dress stayed in place.

Suddenly, she couldn't stand the thing one minute longer.

Reaching under the material, she pulled at the double-sided tape. It had been tickling ever since he'd drawn her attention to it. Kicking off her heels, she walked to her bedroom. She worked the dress down over her hips and let it drop to her feet. It looked harmless when she laid it on the bed, but looks could be deceiving. That dress had a mind of its own, and a one-track mind at that.

All it said was sex, sex, sex, sex, sex...

She headed down the hall to the shower and sighed when the spray hit her. She let the water sluice down her body until goosebumps popped up on her skin. It was only then that she turned up the heat and reached for the soap. Ten minutes later, she stepped out of the shower feeling warm and sleepy... and still a bit turned-on. She heard the wind whipping outside. It was a good night to curl up under the covers.

Nobody needed to know what she did there.

She was reaching for her towel when the room went black.

She experienced a full-body flinch before she heard the wind again. "Damn," she whispered.

Was the power out everywhere or had she blown a fuse? Her fingers brushed against terrycloth. She yanked the towel from its rack and wrapped it around herself. The pitch darkness in the tiny bathroom made it impossible to see anything. Groping around, she finally found the door handle. More darkness greeted her as she opened the door to the hallway. "Great," she said as she began to shiver. "Just great."

Uneasiness prickled the back of her neck. Where had she put that flashlight? She remembered unpacking it. The nightstand. It was in the nightstand by the bed.

Her eyes were having trouble adjusting. With the rain falling outside, clouds covered the moon. There wasn't much natural light to guide her. Her heart beat fast as she shuffled along, inch by inch.

She made it into her bedroom okay but grunted when her shin bumped into the footboard of her bed. She felt her way along its side until she encountered the nightstand. She prayed for decent batteries as she pulled the flashlight from the drawer. A stream of light hit the wall when she pushed the button, and she sighed with relief.

She'd been trying to fight it, but the darkness had unnerved her. Water dripped from her wet hair onto her shoulders, and goosebumps ran down her back. She wasn't certain, but she'd bet money that the fuse box was in the basement.

"Of course it is."

Once a week, she forced herself to do laundry, but outside of that, she avoided going down those steps. There was just something about the cellar that made her nervous.

And it wasn't the mice she'd hopefully exterminated.

Quickly, she toweled off and blotted the wetness from her hair. She used her flashlight to find her robe. She belted it tightly around her waist before squaring her shoulders and heading for the hall.

Was the whole neighborhood out? She moved in the direction of the living room, hoping she could see through the front window to the Hughes house, but she moved too quickly.

"Ow!" Her toe mashed against the baseboard hard. The flashlight dropped from her hand as she doubled over in pain. She grabbed her toe, but it throbbed so badly that it brought tears to her eyes. After an interminable time, she set her foot on the floor and gingerly let it take her weight.

When she was sure she could walk, she looked for the flashlight. It had rolled several feet away. She bent to pick it up, but another light at the end of the hallway caught her eye.

She looked up at it and froze.

Something was moving.

Toward her.

She stumbled backward, but heavy footsteps in the kitchen suddenly split her attention. Her head snapped to the side, but she couldn't see through the wall. Her gaze darted back to the blob of light. It was halfway down the hallway when it began to take form.

A woman. It was an old woman.

Callie opened her mouth to scream, but nothing came out.

The hazy apparition lifted a withered hand and pointed at her.

"Run, Calina. Run!"

This time, the scream ripped from Callie's lips. She scrambled backward and collided with a table. The sharp corner dug into her back, but she pushed it out of the way. It tumbled over with a bang. She spun toward the entryway, but her feet slipped on the hardwood floor.

A floorboard in the kitchen creaked. She risked a glance over her shoulder. The old woman hovered a foot above the ground.

"Run!" she yelled.

Callie's mouth dropped open when the woman, or apparition, or *whatever it was* just melted through the wall.

"God. Oh, God!" She fell against the door, and her fingers were clumsy as she fought with the lock. It gave way, and she lurched down the front steps.

Rain pelted her, but she didn't even notice it. All she knew was she had to get away. Air rasped harshly in her lungs as she ran. She didn't know where she was going, but she spotted David getting out of his car across the street.

"David!"

The teenager spun around.

"Help me," she said, sobbing as her feet pounded against the cement. She launched herself at him, and he caught her.

"Callie! What's wrong?"

"The house! I saw something in my house!"

His gaze landed like a laser on her front door. She could feel the muscles in his body clench.

"It was… a woman." She clenched handfuls of his T-shirt in both fists. "But… You've got to believe me. *I could see right through her.*"

He finally understood. She knew the precise moment, because his face went pale. He swallowed hard. "What should I do?"

He wanted her to tell him?

"Carter," she said without even thinking. She bit her lower lip and risked a glance at the house. It chilled her to the bone. "Call Carter."

* * *

Adrenaline pumped through Carter's veins as he drove across town with the siren blaring and lights flashing. His foot dropped a little harder on the pedal, and he had to force himself to slow down as he came to the town square. The streets were wet, but, as it was, he took the turn on nearly two wheels.

Something had happened at the Calhoun house. *Callie's* house. He didn't know quite what, but it must have been bad. David Hughes had called him.

Tires skidded as he braked to a stop in front of the Hughes place. He jammed the transmission into park and hopped out of the cruiser. David answered before he could knock on the door, and Carter spotted Callie in the front room. She was sitting in an easy chair, dressed in her robe. Her hair was wet, and her feet were bare.

At least she didn't look as if she were hurt.

Some of the tension left his shoulders, but it all came back with a punch when she turned those chocolate eyes of hers on him. He walked to her. The paleness of her skin made him uneasy. She looked like she'd had the life scared out of her. Again.

"What happened?" He crouched on his haunches in front of her.

She looked at him with wide eyes and pressed her lips together. He looked at David.

"She saw something in the house."

Carter took a second to evaluate the kid. He looked as if he were ready to jump out of his skin. "What do you mean, 'something'? Did the intruder come back?"

David shook his head. "She'll have to tell you. You won't believe me."

There was a knock on the door. When David pulled it open, Bill was standing there, his expression stern.

"I'm just trying to find out what we're up against," Carter said. He looked back at Callie. She looked as if she were trying to pull herself together, and he reached out to catch her hand. "What happened? You've got to tell me so I can do something about it."

She took a ragged breath, and he got a bad feeling in his gut.

"Come on, honey."

She clutched at his hand. "I was taking a shower. The lights went out, so I grabbed a flashlight. I was going to find the fuse box."

Bill looked over his shoulder. "It's the only place on the block without power."

"I never made it there," she said, her voice hitching.

"Take it slow," Carter said. He wove his fingers through hers and their palms sealed together.

Her teeth worried her lower lip. "When I came out into the hallway, it was so dark. I stubbed my toe and dropped the flashlight. When I reached to pick it up, I noticed…"

Carter felt his hackles go up. "Go on."

"I noticed another light." Her grip tightened. "When I looked down the hallway, I saw someone. It was a woman."

"Could you describe her?"

A nervous laugh came out of her lips, and she clapped a hand over her mouth. "I don't think I'll ever forget her."

Bill shifted his weight in the doorway. "Female burglars are rare."

"It wasn't a burglar," David said quietly.

Carter's jaw clenched. If the kid said what he thought he was going to say, he was going to drag him out of here by his ears.

"It was Adelaide," the teen said, plunging in headfirst. "She saw Adelaide Calhoun."

CHAPTER TEN

"David," Carter said, but it was too late.

"Adelaide Calhoun?" Bill's face blanched, and he spun away. "Oh, jeez."

"Adelaide? What?" Callie looked around the room. "Who?"

Carter swore. "Everyone, *quiet*."

He pinched the bridge of his nose. This was not going to happen again. "Callie, this woman... What did she do? Did she say anything?"

"Who is Adelaide Calhoun?"

"Nobody important right now." He squeezed her hand. This was getting them nowhere. If somebody had been in that house, they were giving him—or her—too much of a head start. "You wait right here. Bill and I will go take a look. Then I'll be back to take your statement. I'll want every detail you can remember."

His temples throbbed as he pushed himself to his feet. She'd had another break-in; that was serious enough. He didn't want things to get all twisted around with gossip and lies. He caught both his officer and the kid with a look that pinned them to the wall. "This better not be a prank, Hughes."

"I just got here! Besides, it happened inside her house. How could someone get in there? She had all the locks changed.

You told her it was safe."

Carter clenched his hands into fists. "Not one word about Adelaide Calhoun until I get back. You hear me?"

A belligerent look settled onto David's face.

Carter stepped right up to him. "I'm through playing games with you. She's already scared enough as it is. You're not going to put any thoughts into her head to make things worse."

"All right, all right. Take it easy, man."

"Stay here and watch over her." Carter glanced over his shoulder and saw the way Callie was rubbing her bare feet together. With that wet hair and thin robe, she must be freezing. "Get her a blanket and something hot to drink."

"Sure. I can do that." Turning away, David left the room.

Carter didn't care if he was being fair or not. He'd played the levelheaded police chief for long enough. This was the second time something had frightened Callie Thompson, inside her own home. He wouldn't put it past David to scare her so he could play hero. Still, it would have been hard for the kid to be in two places at one time. Somebody had, in fact, seen him lighting off firecrackers in stolen jack-o'-lanterns down at the park. Carter had been looking for him when the call had come in. Still, he took nothing for granted.

He looked out the window at Callie's house. It stood dark and quiet. "Come on, Bill, let's check it out."

Bill didn't move. He just stared at the house with a muscle twitching in his jaw. "You know how much I hate that place. I've hated it since I was a kid, and it's *Halloween*."

"Get it together," Carter snapped. He didn't have time for this. He believed that Callie had seen something, just not Adelaide Calhoun. If something had been in that hallway, odds were that it had been of the human variety.

Because there were no such things as ghosts.

Bill pressed his lips together and fell into step. Wordlessly, they crossed the street. The rain had tapered off, but the raindrops that hit were still cold. As they neared the house, they turned on their flashlights and fell into a familiar rhythm. They wouldn't have to crawl through a window this time; the front door stood wide open.

"We'll take the main floor first," Carter said.

Bill's Adam's apple bobbed. "Check."

Carter took the lead, and their twin beams of light swept the entryway.

"Why did it have to be overcast tonight?" Bill muttered.

Carter had to agree. Even a little bit of moonlight would have helped. The house had dark corners and muted nooks and crannies.

Together, they moved into the living room. Alice and Mamie's handiwork was on clear display. The house looked clean, tidy, and homey. All the boxes had been unpacked, and the room was easier to maneuver through and search. His beam of light swept over something. Swinging it back, he saw the outrageously high-heeled shoes Callie had been wearing earlier in the evening. She'd been smiling and enjoying herself when the night had begun.

She didn't deserve this.

He directed Bill to the kitchen. He didn't want to split off, but he did as ordered. Carter took the hallway. He approached it cautiously. There was an overturned table, and Callie's flashlight was lying where she'd dropped it. Its beam cut through the shadows.

Her terror still hung in the air. The hallway was charged with it. He could see her crouching in pain... Looking up in horror... Stumbling away... Damn it. He didn't know who was behind all this, but he was going to find out.

Somebody was going to pay.

"Clear," Bill called from the kitchen.

Carter turned into Callie's bedroom. A wet towel lay discarded on the floor beside a trail of wet footsteps, and the million-dollar dress was draped across the bed. She'd been caught naked and vulnerable... in darkness so pitch black she couldn't see a foot in front of her face...

A muscle throbbed in his temple.

"Clear," he called to Bill.

He met the officer coming out of the bathroom. With a

hitch of his head, Carter indicated the back staircase. They were moving in tandem when a thumping sound came from below.

The basement.

They both pivoted, and the beam from Bill's flashlight swung back into the kitchen. It landed on the door to the steps that led down, and the circle of light quivered.

Carter's heart started to pound. Again. The basement.

He hadn't liked going down these steps the first time he'd searched her house. This time, it would be worse. With the power out, they couldn't turn on the light at the foot of the stairs. Their flashlights would make them glowing targets.

Taking a deep breath, he opened the door. He and Bill each took a side as they used the doorframe as a barrier. They swept the basement with their lights as well as they could.

"Furnace?" Bill whispered.

"She's had somebody out to work on it twice."

Carter wrapped his hand around his gun and nodded at his backup. Going slowly, he took two steps down the staircase.

The silence from below was gaping. Like a true black hole, it sucked up all sound. All light. As powerful as his police-issue flashlight was, it couldn't seem to pierce the darkness. He made himself continue down the steps, listening for any sign of movement. His vision was practically useless, so he concentrated on his other senses to determine where the noise had originated. As still and dark as the room was, it felt alive. Charged, somehow.

And creepy.

By the time he made it to the basement floor, Carter's heart was pounding and beads of sweat coated his temples. Bill, to his credit, was right on his shoulder. Together, they swept the place.

The basement was empty.

Pitch black, cavernous, and empty.

"There's the fuse box," Bill said. He directed his beam of light at it, and air hissed through his lips when he got a load of it. All the breakers had been blown.

"Don't touch that," Carter said, grabbing his wrist. "We need to fingerprint it first."

Bill turned with a stunned expression on his face. "You still think this was a break-in? There's no sign of entry."

"It's Halloween. Don't you think it's a mighty big coincidence that 'Adelaide Calhoun' chose this night of all nights to magically appear? We search the rest of the house first."

"In the dark? Hell, Carter. You must have balls of steel."

Bill knew procedure as well as Carter did.

They checked out the rest of the house, but found nothing. Carter wasn't surprised; whoever had been here was long gone—and it sure as hell wasn't a ghost. Maybe this time, though, they'd left a little piece of themselves behind. He went to his cruiser for the fingerprint kit. He wasn't taking any chances; he was collecting the evidence himself. Results from the last samples they'd taken had turned out inconclusive. There had been too many overlapping prints, and most of them had been smudged.

Dusting the fuse box took time, but he worked meticulously. Once he got the evidence he needed, he threw the switches. Bill flinched when the basement remained dark. Carter reached up and pulled on the old-fashioned chain hanging overhead.

Light mercifully appeared, and Bill's shoulders slumped in relief. "That's better."

"I disagree," Carter said. "None of this is good."

With the power back on, they took another look around, going all the way up to the attic. It was the polar opposite of the basement, filled with items previous residents had left behind. A rocking chair, an old trunk, and other various antiques gave the space a sad, lonely feel. As desperate as the room felt for human companionship, the coating of dust made it clear that nobody had been up there for years.

"Let's go talk to Callie," Carter said.

Bill glanced at him cautiously. He started to say something, but then stopped. Then started again. "You two seem to have worked out your issues."

Carter's steps slowed on the narrow attic stairs. That wasn't even close to being the case, but he knew what the man was asking. "She's off-limits."

Taken. Off the market. However you put it, Callie Thompson was his.

Or she would be soon.

"Okay. Good to know." Bill ruffled his red hair. "She doesn't happen to have a sister, does she?"

Carter threw a glare over his shoulder. Teasing was not going to shake him out of this mood. He knew that he and Callie had gotten off to a rocky start, but things had changed. His protective instincts had been roused.

Hell, they were surging.

Bill must have picked up the vibe. Instead of going to the Hughes house, he swung off toward his cruiser. "I'll take the prints in, and then I'm going to head back out on patrol."

"Good idea," Carter said. He reached up to rub the back of his neck. He knew he'd snapped at the guy earlier. He was just a little sensitive when it came to this particular blonde. "Thanks for the backup."

"You do the same for me." Bill nodded and everything was back at an even keel.

Carter headed across the street as Bill drove away.

"How is she?" he asked David as he stepped inside the house.

"Better."

Callie was sitting in the same chair, only there was a blanket around her legs and a cup of hot chocolate in her hand. Her eyes turned big when she saw him.

"Did you find anything? Did you see her?"

"There was nobody there. Bill and I checked the entire house."

"She went into the kitchen. I forgot to tell you that. I heard noises in there, and she just sort of melted through the wall."

She was starting to shake again. Carter crouched in front of her and rubbed his hands up and down her arms. She felt like a block of ice. "Easy. I checked everything out myself. There's nobody there."

"But I saw—"

"Whatever it was is gone."

She pressed her lips together and looked him in the eye. "It was Adelaide Calhoun."

He wasn't going to fight with her. Not now. Later, when things had settled down, and preferably after the sun had come up, he'd sit down with her and they'd talk through things.

"Calhoun," she said more insistently. She set her hot chocolate down so fast that the mug banged against the table. "As in *the Calhoun place.*"

He nodded reluctantly. He'd give her that much. "Adelaide Calhoun was the original owner. The name just kind of stuck."

"It stuck because she's still there! *That house is haunted.*"

"Enough. You're upsetting yourself."

"Upsetting myself? No, no, no. I'm upset because I had a ghost chase me down, yell my name, and tell me to get out of my own home. There's no need for me to upset myself. Old Adelaide did a bang-up job."

"That's it. Let's go." He took her hand. "We can talk about this later."

She snatched her hand back. "Why didn't you tell me? That was the story, wasn't it? The town legend, as you called it. Don't you think I had a right to know?"

"I didn't tell you the stories because there's no validity to them. I didn't want to scare you for no reason."

"No reason?" She pounced to her feet, and the blanket tumbled to the floor. "I just saw a ghost in my house."

"You saw something." He slowly pushed himself to his feet until he stood eye to eye with her. She'd had a scare. He'd let her do her thing, but he wasn't going to add fuel to the fire. He was more interested in the sounds she'd heard in the kitchen... at the top of the basement stairs...

"What did she look like?" David asked. Carter turned on him. The teenager held up his hands and took a step back. "I'm just asking, man. Callie had never heard of Adelaide before tonight. She has no reason to be making this up."

Carter hated it, but the kid was right. "I do need a description."

He reached into his pocket for his notebook and pointedly ignored the glare that Callie was giving him. She should have used that look on her house. The paint would have peeled right off the siding. "Okay, tell me what you remember."

"I remember an old lady," she said, her lips barely moving. "She had gray hair pulled back into a bun. She wore a blue dress with a white collar. She was about six feet tall, give or take, because *she was floating nearly a foot off the ground.*"

Carter's shoulder twinged. "Anything else? Any distinguishing characteristics?"

"Well, I could see right through her. Is that distinguishing?"

"That was her," David said quietly. "It was Adelaide."

Carter wheeled around. Enough with the side comments. "How would you know? Have you got something to do with this?"

"I told you to back off him," Callie snapped.

Carter held up a hand. His concentration was on the teenager. "How do you know what Adelaide Calhoun looks like?"

The kid stuffed his hands in his pockets. "Everyone in this town knows what she looks like. I've seen pictures."

"There are pictures of this thing? This ghost?" Callie asked.

"Adelaide Calhoun lived in Shadow Valley in the mid-1800s," Carter said. "There are pictures of her in the history books, although I'm surprised that David has seen them. He's got an aversion to school."

"That's not all I've got an aversion to."

"Stop it, both of you!" Callie cried.

Carter felt like kicking himself. He knew better than to let David Hughes get under his skin. It was just that everything about tonight had been off, and his feelings toward Callie Thompson were just a little too raw. She didn't need this now. What she needed was peace and calm. A little rest. "Why don't I take you home?" he said.

The color drained right out of her face.

"Not to stay," he added quickly. "To grab some things. Then I'll take you to Alice's."

She shook her head. "I don't need anything."

"I'll go in with you."

"I don't want to go back in there."

"Okay. Scratch that plan. I'm sure Alice has an extra toothbrush." Her look of relief caught Carter right in the gut. Gently, he took her by the elbow. "Let's go."

He nodded to David, silently acknowledging his help. Despite their differences, he had to admit the kid had come through tonight. Outside, the rain had stopped, but the wind was still howling in the trees. Callie's eyes were big on the house across the street as the wind tugged at her robe and her hair.

To hell with it. Carter swept her off her feet and into his arms.

"What are you doing?" she said, even as her arm came around his shoulder.

"It's cold, it's wet, and your feet are bare. And if I'm not mistaken, you're not wearing much under that robe."

Her lips clamped together, and she clutched the robe together at her neck. "Gentlemen aren't supposed to notice such things."

"If you haven't noticed yet, I'm an officer, not a gentleman."

He carried her to the street where his cruiser was still parked and tucked her into the front seat. Leaning over her, he turned up the heat. "Anything in particular you need?"

"You're not going back in there?"

"I'll just grab a few things for you and be right back." She caught his arm, but he pulled away. "Don't worry. I've got a gun."

Her eyes narrowed. "Maybe you haven't heard, but bullets go right through ghosts."

"They do the same with people, only they cause a lot of damage. Keep the doors locked until I get back."

* * *

Callie started shivering all over again as she watched Carter cross her porch and disappear into her house. He didn't believe her, but she knew what she'd seen and what she'd heard. Now that she'd figured out the secret that everyone had tried to hide from her, things were beginning to make more sense.

Her house was haunted.

That was why the repairmen hesitated to go inside—and why David flat-out refused. It was why her bedroom door kept locking, the lights flickered, and the television misbehaved. It also explained why the temperature could drop twenty degrees in under a second.

She wrapped her arms around her middle. She'd been living in that house with the undead for almost a month. The sounds... the squeaks and thumps. Why hadn't she figured it out sooner?

Other people had. She'd been told about all the renters who had come and gone over the years. No wonder Adelaide had appeared and ordered her out of the house. She'd been the dense one. Nothing else had worked with her.

A nervous laugh escaped her. The ghost wanted her out of the house. She'd gotten the message loud and clear this time.

Her teeth began to clatter, and she turned the heat on high. What was taking Carter so long? She wanted him out of there *now*. He didn't know what was in there. He refused to believe. She'd give him two more minutes and then she'd...

She'd what? Go inside herself?

Two minutes passed by, and her hand went to the door handle. She was just about to get out when she saw the light in the windows turn off. Carter stepped outside, and the breath she hadn't realized she'd been holding rushed out. He closed the door behind him and crossed her lawn with a box tucked under one arm.

Cold air breezed into the cruiser when he opened the door and slid in behind the wheel. He grabbed some things out of the box before putting it in the back seat. When he handed her slippers and his old blanket, tears pricked at her eyes. She quickly put the slippers on her feet and huddled underneath the warm throw. "Thank you," she said, her throat thick.

"I hope I grabbed the right stuff. I'm not too good with these kinds of things."

She bit her lip. She supposed it should embarrass her that he'd gone through her personal items, but she was just happy she hadn't had to do it herself.

She was quiet as he swung the car around and headed down Highland, away from her house. She felt better with every inch of distance he put between her and that place. "You should have told me," she said quietly.

He made a turn toward Alice's house before glancing at her. "That was the mistake that was made when other renters moved in. They'd hear about Adelaide before their boxes were even unpacked. Every little squeak and groan would set them off. You didn't need that."

"Ignorance wasn't bliss. I heard the same squeaks and groans."

"But you took them in the right light. It's an old house. It's supposed to squeak and groan."

"But the sounds weren't from the house. I have a ghost."

He let out a sigh. "Callie."

He was a skeptic; she got it—but was he calling her a liar? "I saw her. She chased me out of there."

"I know that's what you believe, but your mind can play tricks on you, especially in the dark."

She stared at him, dumbfounded. His jaw was set, and he refused to look at her. It ticked her off. "I don't know why I asked David to call you."

He hit the brakes, and, reflexively, she reached for the dashboard. Gravel crunched under the cruiser's tires as he pulled over to the side of the road and threw the engine into park.

"Carter!"

She was stunned when he reached over, undid her seatbelt, and hauled her across the console.

"You damned well better call me when you need me." His blue eyes glowed in the light of a nearby streetlamp, and her heart skipped a beat.

His hand fisted in her hair. She gave a gasp, but he sealed their mouths together in a kiss that silenced her. His mouth was hot and possessive, protective, and her reaction was like a solid kick in the gut.

"I don't care if it's Adelaide or a mouse or something as little as a hangnail," he said as he came up for air. "You call."

The hard knot of fear in the pit of her stomach finally loosened. A soft sound left her throat, and she turned into him. She was wound tight as a top, but she'd been afraid to turn loose. For all his gruffness, he was letting her. With relief, she rested her head against his shoulder. He ran a hand up and down her back, and her eyelids drifted closed.

"I hate seeing you scared," he said. "Absolutely hate it."

"All I could think was that I wanted you there."

"I turned on a dime when the call came over the radio."

He kissed her again, and Callie was lost. It was a slow, heated connection meant for comfort, but the passion was still there. She let her tongue move against his. The rasp was hot, wet, and intimate. She felt heat building in her belly and seeping through her system. After being chilled for so long, the sensation was heady. Enticing. She caught his shoulders and let one hand slip behind his neck. She began massaging the tight muscles she found there.

He groaned in pleasure.

She tilted her head to the side as he ran kisses down her neck and arched into him as one of his hands went down to the small of her back.

"*Ah.*"

He stopped and pulled back. "What's wrong?"

She reached around and tested the soreness in her lower back. "That must be where I ran into the table."

"The one that was knocked over in the living room?"

"That was me."

"Let me see."

"Wait," she said. She caught his hands, but he still managed to part the robe nearly as suggestively as her Elvira costume. The opening plunged all the way past her navel and her breasts nearly spilled out.

He froze, the look in his eyes blazing. "You're not wearing *anything* underneath that robe."

She clutched the material back together, even as her nipples tightened and her belly clenched. "I told you, I was caught in the shower."

His hands caught her hips when she tried to move off him. "Let me see how badly you're hurt."

"It's just a bruise."

"That was a heavy table."

"With a very sharp corner," she agreed.

His eyes narrowed and his hands kneaded her hips gently. The temptation to lean back into him was strong, but Callie reached out to brace her hand against his shoulder. Her heart was still racing, and her toes had yet to uncurl. If he kissed her again, she had no doubt she'd lose her robe entirely, but they were sitting on the side of the street just off the town square.

"You get hurt nearly every time I see you."

"Clumsy, I guess."

"Danger-prone." The car grew quiet as they watched each other. Finally, he sat back in his seat, breathing a little too hard. "I need to get you over to Alice's."

"Do I have to go there?" The question was out before Callie could stop it.

The blue in Carter's eyes flared.

She traced the line of his shoulder with her fingertip. "There might still be people there from the party, and you know she'll just pester me with questions. And don't say Mamie. She's at the party too. By breakfast, everyone at the café will know what I told them."

A muscle clenched in his jaw, and she knew she'd scored a point. He'd been trying to shield her from the gossip about her house, but that time had ended.

"There aren't many other places you can stay," he said.

The town didn't have a hotel or even a motel.

Callie looked away. She didn't have the energy to argue with him. Knowing that he didn't believe her hurt, though. She knew what she'd seen, and she knew what she'd heard. "Take me to your place."

"You can't go to my place."

"Why not?"

"You know why."

"I'll sleep on the couch."

His silence answered that.

She pushed herself off his lap and settled back into the passenger seat. Away from him, the warm air blowing from the heater just didn't cut it. She grabbed the blanket from where it had fallen and tugged it over herself. All of a sudden, she had a tension headache to go along with the dull ache in her back. "Just give me one night before all the hoopla starts—because you know it will."

He took a deep breath and shifted the car back into gear. "All right. You're coming home with me, but let's get one thing straight. You're not sleeping on any damn couch."

CHAPTER ELEVEN

Callie sat quietly as Carter drove up into the hills. Apparently, he lived in one of the houses that was still fighting the uphill battle against the tree line. It was dark this far out, away from the streetlights… She plucked uneasily at the camping blanket that covered her legs. With the wind howling and the rain splattering against the windshield, the darkness seemed alive. *Angry*.

"Is it much farther?" she asked as he followed the winding path away from the town center.

He glanced at her. "Are you all right?"

"I didn't realize you lived this far out of town."

"It's probably only a few city blocks in Boston."

"But Boston isn't this dark." As exhausted as she felt, adrenaline threatened to start pumping back into her system.

"Relax."

"I'm not—"

He covered her restless hands with one of his. "We're almost there."

She took a calming breath. It might be childish, but she'd suddenly developed a healthy fear of the dark. With everything inside her, she wanted to crawl across the console and back into his lap. He'd taken the most direct route possible to snap

142

her out of her panic with that kiss. He'd made her feel safe. He'd made her feel wanted.

Adelaide hadn't wanted her around; she'd made that abundantly clear.

Callie didn't think she'd ever forget the image of that gathering shadow… the old woman staring at her with penetrating eyes… or the sound of that strange voice echoing down the hallway…

Carter braked and turned down a road that seemed even more remote. Even more desolate. Neighbors seemed few and far between, but then he turned into a driveway.

"This is it," he said.

Curiosity took the edge off Callie's worries. A small clearing had opened up. A house was tucked away in the far corner, surrounded by trees like big bodyguards. The rain made it hard to see, and the trees bent and curled under the wind, but there was no battle going on here. The trees had accepted this place a long time ago. The house stood waiting for them like a haven.

"Home sweet home," he said. He hit the garage door opener and pulled in to park. "Let's get you inside and warmed up."

Callie let herself out of the car as he got her things out of the back seat. The concrete floor felt like ice against her feet, and she moved quickly to the doormat next to the door to the house.

"Go inside," he said. "Your lips are turning blue."

He held the door for her, and she entered. They'd stepped into a laundry room, which led to the kitchen. Beyond that, she could see a living room with a huge stone fireplace taking up one entire wall.

"My grandfather built this place," Carter said.

"Really?" She moved aside as he set her box on the kitchen table. "He did a wonderful job."

Her attention was captured by that fireplace. Every stone fit against its neighbor like parts of a jigsaw puzzle. Some were no bigger than her fist, while others looked heavier than she weighed. "He didn't do the stonework by himself?"

"He had to. It was a requirement of my grandmother's if she was going to live so far away from town. There wasn't anyone else to do it, so he knew he had to get his act in gear."

Callie headed over for a closer look, but saw something out of the corner of her eye as she walked into the dimly lit room. Her head snapped to the right, and she nearly jumped out of her skin.

Carter was at her side in an instant. "What is it? What's wrong?"

"Nothing. Sorry." She dropped her head in embarrassment. She'd been scared by a light-colored coat hanging on a hook by the front door.

He frowned when he put two and two together. Reaching out, he caught her chin. His gaze was soft but steady on her face. "Nothing is going to hurt you here. Anyone or anything that wants to try will have to go through me first."

She nodded.

"Do you understand?"

She blinked fast. She didn't doubt that, but she hated being such a scaredy-cat. She was an independent, self-sufficient woman... who had just happened to see her first ghost. She pushed back her hair. "I guess I'm still a little jumpy."

He trailed his fingers across her cheek. "It's late. You're tired. Let's get you situated." He grabbed her box of things. "The guest room is this way."

Callie followed him, feeling uncertain and out of sorts. This was not like her. She tried to approach everything with a sense of humor, but she couldn't laugh this off. He turned into the second room on the left, and she saw a spartanly decorated but comfy bedroom with a full-sized bed waiting for her.

He set her box on the dresser and stepped away. "Is there anything I can get you?"

A spine? A Ouija board? "Some holy water?"

The light bulb went on inside her head, and she clapped her hand over her forehead. "That's what the 'cleansing' was about."

"Enough. You need to stop thinking about this." He strode to the bed and turned back the covers. "Hop in. I can't take the shivering much longer."

The way he looked at her made Callie curl her toes inside her slippers. The wall of friction was down. Not trusting herself, she wandered over to look through the box of things he'd collected for her. She found clothes, her toothbrush, her blow dryer... bras and panties... Her cheeks heated. Had he intentionally picked out the sexiest and laciest lingerie she owned, or was that a coincidence? She dug deeper. She needed to change out of her damp robe before she crawled under those covers. She frowned when she got all the way to the bottom without finding any pajamas. "Uh, did you bring anything for me to sleep in?"

He went still. "Ah, hell." A helpless look crossed his face, and he rubbed the back of his neck. "Sorry. You can wear something of mine."

She stepped aside, self-conscious, when he walked over and opened a drawer of the dresser. He pulled out a black T-shirt. "Will this work?"

She unfolded it and saw "SHADOW VALLEY POLICE DEPARTMENT" written on the front. Size large and soft from wear. *His.* "Yes."

It was perfect.

"Okay. I need to call the station, but I'll come back to check on you."

She nodded and watched as he left. She wasn't quite sure how to deal with him. He wasn't the stoic, by-the-books police chief anymore—and that was the problem. She didn't know quite what he was.

She glanced at the bed. It would be so much warmer with two...

She untied the robe and found a hanger for it in the closet. She pulled the T-shirt over her head, and it came around her like a big, warm hug. Her nipples beaded as the material brushed against her. Her thighs clenched, and she scampered to the bed. The sheets were cool, but the comforter was heavy.

It wasn't long before she heard a tap on the door.

"Come in."

He'd changed, too. The uniform was gone, replaced by sweats and a worn T-shirt. She licked her lips. He looked good. Younger and athletic. Not so uptight, almost approachable...

Her belly tightened.

Very approachable.

"Everything okay?" she asked.

"Bill caught another Halloween prankster in the act—but no news about your house."

That hadn't been a prank, but she didn't want to argue about it.

He looked at her sitting propped up against the headboard, and his tense stance relaxed. As big and tough as he might be, he carried a lot of stress on those broad shoulders. She drew her knees up under the covers and wrapped her arms around her legs. It felt intimate, being tucked in bed in his house, away from the craziness of town.

"Well, you look like you're settled in," he said.

"It's a comfy bed."

His lips twisted into a feeble smile, and he shook his head. With a heavy sigh, he reached for the light switch. "I'll be just down the hallway."

"Wait." Her gasp and forward lunge stopped him from dousing the room into darkness.

"Callie."

She winced, but she didn't want to be alone. "Talk to me? Just for a little while?"

Like clockwork, he reached up to rub his shoulder. Strong and silent, her big toe. He kept things stored up like a pressure cooker. She shivered. One of these days, he was going to blow.

After what seemed like an hour of contemplation, he crossed the room and sat down on the foot of the bed. "What do you want to talk about?"

Anything. The Patriots. Daylight saving time. Pumpkin spice lattes.

"Do you believe in an afterlife?"

He stopped, hand cupping his collarbone. "You mean like heaven and hell?"

"And other places in between."

His hand slowly dropped across his chest and down to the bed. "Are you asking if I believe in ghosts?"

She shook her head. "I know you don't. But do you believe in energies? Lost souls? Dying has to be like everything else humans do; we've got to mess it up every now and then."

His lips twitched. "You *have* been spending more time writing."

Her eyes narrowed. "Why do you say that?"

"It was a very Quick Kate thing to say."

She popped up off the pillow. "You've been reading my column."

He tilted his head. "I had to find out what all the fuss was about. Alice and Mamie have been on me nonstop about you."

She went still. "And vice versa."

"They're trying to play matchmaker."

Her pulse pounded in her ears. "I know."

And why had she been fighting that so hard, again? She eased back against the headboard. "You didn't answer the question. Don't you think a soul could get stuck?"

He shrugged. "Maybe."

"Then why not this time?"

He shook his head. "Adelaide Calhoun is not in your house."

"How do you know?"

"I just do."

"How can you be so sure?"

"Because I can't fight a ghost."

Callie felt something flip inside her chest.

"Tell me more about your column," he said.

She bit her lip. "I'm worried about it."

"Why?"

She plucked at the comforter that was already warming her up. "It's been hard to get back into the swing of things, and my world has changed so much."

That was an understatement. Not only had she moved to a small town, she was now dealing with the supernatural. And it had affected her writing. She didn't know if her readers would stay with her now that she wasn't writing about her adventures in big-city life. Her new columns hadn't hit publication yet, and she was worried and excited to see how people would react.

"Alice said you've been getting some mail. Do people still do that?"

"Some, if they're older or they don't want someone else to see their email." Talking was helping. Or, at least, the distraction of him was. "I got a couple of good ones today."

"Yeah? What were they about? Or can't you tell me that?"

She smirked. It wasn't as if she was bound by any client confidentiality agreements, but she'd avoided Alice and Mamie with the same questions. "I had an email from a guy whose teeth-whitening procedure went too well. An even better one was from a woman who discovered that the swimsuit her boyfriend bought her for their tropical cruise was too small."

"What did you tell her?"

"I told her that a too-small bikini might be the best way to change a boyfriend into a husband."

He chuckled. "Now that's damned good advice."

She felt herself go soft. "You think so?"

His gaze ran over her, and he cleared his throat. "How did you get started with that, anyway? The column, I mean."

Callie was suddenly acutely aware of what she was—and wasn't—wearing. "I fell into it, actually. I used to be a reporter. A poor one."

"Oh, come on. You're one of the most popular columnists out there today."

"I said that I was a poor reporter. There's a difference. I like the creative side of writing, rather than just regurgitating facts. My boss was about ready to fire me when one of our regular columnists got sick. He had white space he needed to fill, and he put me on it. The rest, as they say, is history."

"It sounds like everything turned out for the best."

"It did. The column became popular enough to go into

syndication. That meant more money, and then the house dropped into my lap…"

She hesitated. He was good at this interrogation stuff. He'd made her forget what had brought her here. She plucked at the comforter again. Sometimes he really could be sweet. "What about you? What did you do before you became Shadow Valley's chief of police?" He wasn't the only one who was curious.

"I spent time on the beat in Pittsburgh. Then I moved up to detective in Springfield."

She tilted her head. "I thought you hated big cities."

"I never said that."

"You most certainly did. You haven't had anything good to say about Boston since I got here."

He scowled. "It had nothing to do with the town itself. I've been dealing with a brain-dead bureaucrat from Boston on the task force. You just happened to catch me at a bad time."

"Guilt by association?"

"Guilt by breaking the speed limit by twenty miles per hour."

Agh. Was she ever going to live that down? "You could have let me go."

His gaze caught hers, slow and heated. "Not on your life."

Callie didn't look away. "Is the FBI guy the reason why you're having problems finding Morton?"

Carter sat up straighter. "Let's not talk about that."

"Don't do that," she said softly. "You always pull back when I ask you about your case. Why don't you just tell me what's wrong?"

"You shouldn't have to worry about it."

"I'm not worrying about it. You are." She dared him to argue. The hunt for the escaped convict had crawled under his skin and set up housekeeping. She could see the dark circles under his eyes and the lines of fatigue around his mouth. She wasn't the cause behind all of that.

"Morton's a bad character," he said. "He's out there somewhere, and it's not going to be good when he pops out of his hidey-hole."

"But he's got to be out of the state by now. Maybe out of the country."

"Maybe." He rubbed his eyes. "It's hard to tell."

"Carter," she said softly, "did you at least take my advice and start delegating some of the other work?"

He sighed. "Yeah, my cop on medical leave has been helping out with some of the investigative work. It's good training for him."

"And Nancy's stolen laundry?"

"Bill took it over—along with some of the other Halloween pranks."

Some. Callie felt the friction come back into the air. She knew he wasn't talking about what had happened at her house. He'd made it clear he was taking lead on that. So what... Oh. David.

The mattress shifted as he stood. "We both need to catch some shut-eye. Tomorrow's going to be busy."

Because of Halloween. Because Adelaide Calhoun had made an appearance. And because Callie Thompson had spent the night at Carter Landry's house. The townspeople would be all atwitter.

"Thank you for letting me stay here," she said.

"Glad to help." He opened and closed his hands by his sides. Stiffly, he reached out and turned on the lamp on the nightstand. "I'll be in the last room on your left."

Callie watched him go, her muscles straining as she held herself back. He switched off the overhead light as he walked out, and her chest ached. He'd left her with a night light on, but it didn't spread all the way across the room.

She tried not to think about it, but her gaze flashed to the corners where shadows lurked. Darkness was no longer just the absence of light. It was a different world—a world that held things some refused to see. Frightening things. Dangerous things. She tried taking deep, slow breaths, but her ears listened intently for any creaks or groans. The woods outside provided plenty.

For what seemed like an eternity, she concentrated on breathing in and out. At last, she couldn't stand it anymore.

She crept from the bed and grabbed the pillow and the old blanket she'd never returned to him. She was as quiet as she could be as she padded down the hallway. She hadn't made a conscious decision, but she knew exactly where she was going.

Dim light spilled out of the room she left, and she could see Carter's door standing halfway open. She slipped inside and glanced at the bed. There was enough moonlight now to see that he was sleeping with his back to her. Just knowing he was there eased her racing pulse. She dropped the pillow onto the floor and shook out the old blanket.

"Don't even think about it."

She yelped when he rolled onto his back and stared at him like a deer caught in the headlights. "I... I didn't mean to wake you."

"I heard you the moment your feet hit the floor."

What was she supposed to do? Go back? She didn't think she could—

Reaching over, he caught the covers and flipped them back. "Get in."

* * *

Air raked in and out of Carter's lungs as he watched Callie in the moonlight. She stood motionless before she let her blanket—*his* blanket—drop to the floor. She slid in beside him, and his pulse took off.

He been doing his damnedest to be a good guy, but he wasn't a saint. It had been a long night, and he'd been fighting his inclinations for most of it. This time, he went with them. Reaching across the bed, he caught her around the waist. He heard her inhale sharply as he pulled her across the mattress.

The tension in her body left almost instantaneously when he locked his mouth over hers. He pulled her up against him, and she pressed even closer. Threading his fingers through her hair, he swept his tongue through the sweetness of her mouth. A shudder went through him when the tip of her tongue flirted with his.

"The dark?" he asked.

She nodded against the pillow.

"Good things can happen in the dark, too."

"Show me," she whispered.

He rolled her underneath him. Sweeping his hands up her sides, he started to remove her T-shirt—*his* T-shirt—but his hands stopped on her hips. She wasn't wearing panties, and he *knew* he'd grabbed some of those for her. The hard-on he'd been fighting went to steel.

God, she owned him.

He stroked his hands over the smooth skin of her waist and the sides of her breasts. She lifted herself off the pillow to help extricate herself, and then she was naked beneath him. He shoved his hands into her honey-colored hair and kissed her again.

Everything about her was sweet as honey, except for her spirit, and that had an irresistible tang.

He pushed the T-shirt aside. He wanted clear access to her. There was nothing about her he didn't want to touch.

"Hey, I liked that T-shirt," she said.

"Me too. It's yours." His thighs clenched when she settled her hands against his lower back. "It looks better on you than it ever looked on me."

Her touch tickled his ribcage, and she spread her fingers wide over his chest. "I doubt that."

His heart beat fast. She'd given him such a hard time since she'd come to town. Challenged him and sparred with him. Foreplay.

He wanted her more than anything.

He wrapped his hand around her hip as he kissed his way down her throat, along her breastbone, and, finally, to her breast. She was long and sleek, but she had enough curves to make him break out in a cold sweat. He licked his tongue over her already taut nipple, and she let out a cry.

She liked that? He settled in for a longer stay. He suckled at her, swirling his tongue and gently nipping with his teeth, until she arched beneath him.

Her fingernails scored his skin. "Ah, Carter!"

She tugged his T-shirt up his back. When he levered himself up to take it off, she started working on his sweats. Between the two of them, they got them off fast.

She wrapped her leg around his hip, and his erection settled in snugly between her legs. Carter's head dipped. He had a thing for her legs. A really bad thing. He was tall, and she was long and sleek, just right to fit him.

He thrust slowly between her legs, forward and back, rubbing himself against her. She was like silk. Warm, wet silk. Her hips fell into a rhythm with his, and a groan rumbled up from his chest.

Why had he played good cop for so long?

He pushed himself up over her. Bracing a hand beside her head, he watched her as he worked his other hand between their bodies. Her stomach sucked in as he caressed her, but he kept going. Lower and lower. Finally, he swept his finger along her slit and around the secret little nub at the top. Her body bowed, her neck stretching too temptingly to resist.

He pressed his mouth against her pounding pulse as he dragged air into his lungs. He couldn't wait a moment longer. He had to get inside her.

Reaching out blindly to the nightstand, he yanked open the drawer and found protection. He tore open the package, but nearly lost it when her hands were there, "helping him."

"Gah, Callie."

He gritted his teeth as she unrolled the condom over him, but she'd barely gotten it on before he lined himself up and pushed into her, driving from his toes.

Her cry of pleasure lit the room.

"Oh, God." She clenched her thighs around his. "You're big everywhere."

Her breath was right against his ear, and his balls cinched up tight. The feeling of being inside her messed up his brain processes, but he forced himself to go still. "Too much?"

She rubbed her toes against the back of his knee. "How long can you hold it there? *Oh, yes*. Right there?"

Not long.

He failed the challenge, because his hips began pumping uncontrollably. He kissed her again, their mouths melding. From that point on, there was no talk. Only touching. And stroking. And sensation.

It was faster than he wanted, but this thing between them had been building for a while. Too long.

And, tonight, someone had threatened her well-being.

Carter lost it a little—and then he lost it a lot. He began thrusting into her, fast and deep. She cried out as she came beneath him, and the feel of her body clenching him inside and out pushed him to the brink. His hips jammed forward, and his spine locked. He came hard, and he came long.

She was limp when he sagged down atop of her, but still, she wrapped her arms around him. Her breaths slowed, and her body turned languorous. She found the stubborn knot along his shoulder blade and began massaging it.

Carter's cock twitched, still inside her. "*Mmm*. Keep that up, and you'll never sleep alone again."

"That's not a bad deal." Her gaze was soft as she looked up at him. "You watch out for me, and I'll do the same for you."

He caught those sassy, plump lips one more time. "Done," he murmured.

He'd watch over her for nothing.

CHAPTER TWELVE

Callie awoke in the middle of the night, immediately alert. The house was quiet. Dim light from the guest bedroom spilled down the hallway, barely reaching the door of the master bedroom. It was eerie being on the other side for once, watching the light from the shadows, but she didn't see anything. Still, she listened carefully.

Outside, the wind blew, but that wasn't it. Wait. *There.*

A soft click tapped in faster rhythm... until air started to blow out of the vent next to the far window. She relaxed. This house had sounds that she wasn't used to. At least it wasn't a *thump*.

"It's the furnace." The low grumble was close to her ear.

Her stomach did a dipsy-do. "I know."

Carter radiated heat behind her. She was pressed against his solid chest, and his arm was wrapped around her waist.

"Sorry if I woke you."

He brushed his lips against her shoulder. "Go back to sleep."

She quieted, but she was awake now. For reasons more than just sounds... She rested her hand over his on her stomach. She hadn't meant to push him when she'd snuck in here earlier. Or maybe she had. The intimacy was something she needed right now, as well as the distraction.

The strength in the legs tangling with hers was impossible to ignore. So was the hand sliding up to cover her breast. Her nipple perked up at the caress, and it poked into his palm when he gently squeezed.

"You're not relaxing," he said.

"Kinda hard to when you do that."

He pressed his hips more snugly against her bottom. "*Kinda* hard?"

Her breath slid out between her lips. "My mistake."

Their bodies brushed against one another's as she rolled over to face him. As she looked at him in the moonlight, her heart melted. She trailed her fingers over his chest. He'd ridden to her rescue twice now, and, stubborn as he was, listening to his opposing opinions kept her from going off the deep end. Surprising as it was, they fit well together.

Like, really well. It felt good to be with him like this.

His forehead rumpled as he watched her.

"I'm okay," Callie whispered.

She crawled atop him, and his eyelids went heavy. Straddling him, she traced the cords of muscles wrapping around his ribcage. "Since you're up…" she said.

His cock stirred between her legs. "Might as well do something."

His mouth was ready for hers when she leaned down to kiss him. She explored lazily. Her breasts rubbed against his heat, and she felt his hand slide between her legs. The idea of being on top of this strong, determined alpha male made her cream.

He was a protector; it was at his core, but the way he acted… She shuddered in pleasure as his thick finger penetrated her. This thing between them just might go further than that. She reached down to close her hand over his. All the ghosts, creepy noises, and faltering home appliances would have to wait.

Something unbelievable was happening right here.

* * *

"Are you ready to talk about what happened at your house?" Carter asked. Morning had arrived, although clouds blotted the low-lying sun. He and Callie were still in bed, but he could tell from her breathing that she was awake. Neither of them had made a move to get up. It was that quiet, calm part of the morning where nothing felt urgent and everything seemed possible. She had to feel safe now; she had to be calm.

"No," she said, burrowing deeper into the pillow.

"I think we should."

"Can't we just say we did and be done with it?"

"What would Quick Kate have to say about that?"

"Something smart, no doubt."

She let out a huff and rolled over. Her blond hair was tangled, and her cheeks were pink. She looked so sexy and relaxed, Carter felt himself stir beneath the covers.

"She'd probably chew me out for not taking advantage of a haunted house on Halloween and charging admission."

"Don't you think that *is* a big coincidence? That this happened on Halloween night?"

"Not really." She traced the pattern on the pillowcase. "That's when the spirit world is closest to the land of the living."

Carter lifted an eyebrow. Her words had been so quiet that he almost hadn't heard her, but she was serious. "You believe in ghosts?"

She raked a hand through her hair. "Well, *yeah*! How could I not after one kicked me to the curb?"

"Before, though. You believed in them before last night."

She rolled onto her back and stared at the ceiling. Finally, she nodded. "Yes, I did, but you've made it clear that you don't."

"I can't," he said.

She folded her arms atop the comforter. The relaxation was gone, but at least she was talking. "If it wasn't a ghost, then what do you think it was?"

He'd given that some thought. "All of the breakers in your fuse box were thrown. You either had a power surge or somebody did it on purpose."

"Her name is Adelaide Calhoun."

"Just hear me out." He propped himself up onto an elbow. "It was dark last night, and your nerves were on edge."

"And the sky is blue. Get to the point."

"I checked the scene outside your bedroom last night when I searched the place. Your flashlight was still on the ground, pointing away from you. It was reflecting off a picture at the end of the hallway."

"You think I saw the picture?" She shook her head. "It's of a flower basket."

"You saw yourself, Callie. I saw my reflection as I stood where you must have been."

She let out a scoff. "If that's the case, I must have been hearing things, too. I specifically heard someone say, 'Run, Calina. Run.'"

"Isn't that what you were thinking?"

"No, I was thinking how bad her shoes looked with that dress!" Holding the covers to her chest, Callie sat up in a flurry of motion. "I didn't make this up in my head, Carter. I know what I saw."

He knew what she *thought* she saw, but eyewitness accounts were among the most unreliable. And she'd been on edge for weeks. He gnawed on the side of his cheek. She was so worried about spirits haunting her home that she'd glossed over the possibility of another intruder—or the same one that had gotten in the last time. That was what had been keeping *him* up at night.

"You don't believe in Adelaide," she said flatly.

"Oh, I believe in her," he said. "Only I believe in the woman who died in 1854."

Suddenly, he knew what he had to show her. He pushed back the covers and walked to the bookshelf filled with sports stories, biographies, and more than a few mysteries. It took him a while to find what he was looking for, but he pulled a book out and turned back to the bed. He didn't miss the way she stared at him, even though she was peeved with him. His body responded—hard—but that could wait.

This couldn't.

He slid back under the covers and began flipping through the pages. "Here. This is what I believe in."

"What is that?"

"A history book." At the surprised look on her face, he gave a little shrug. "I used to be somewhat of a buff back when I had that life you keep telling me I need to find."

Her arms were still crossed defensively over her chest, but she scooted closer to look at what he was trying to show her. "Is this what you were giving David a hard time about?"

Irritation fluttered through him, but he let it pass.

"Adelaide Calhoun isn't just famous for being the so-called resident ghost of Shadow Valley. She worked with Harriet Tubman."

Callie's eyebrows lifted. "The Underground Railroad?"

He lifted an eyebrow. "You're not so bad on history yourself."

He had her. Now if he could only convince her.

He propped himself up against the headboard and turned the book so she could see. "Harriet Tubman was the most famous conductor to lead slaves out of the South to freedom, but there were others, too. She couldn't have done what she did without help."

"Like Adelaide's?"

"Adelaide joined the abolitionist cause in the early 1850s. She didn't travel in and out of the South like Tubman, but she contributed in her own way. As the story goes, she'd meet conductors right here in these woods and then lead their groups to a safe spot for the night. If she couldn't do that, she'd provide blankets, food, or whatever was needed."

"It sounds dangerous."

"It was, but she was crafty. Not many people knew about what she'd done until after her death."

By now, he could see Callie was intrigued. He wrapped his arm around her and rubbed his thumb against her arm. She didn't have anything to fear, at least of the supernatural variety.

"Adelaide was a schoolteacher by trade and very much a women's libber—especially for back in those days. She never married. She had that house built, and she paid for it with her own money."

"No wonder she still thinks it's hers."

She was so stubborn. Why couldn't she see? Adelaide had been a great woman, but she'd made her mark. She'd passed, and time had moved on. Period. End of story.

"What happened to her?" Callie asked. "Was she ever caught?"

He sighed. He might as well tell her the whole story so she heard the truth at least once. "She came close, but always managed to get away. None of her charges were ever caught, either. It was pneumonia that finally brought her down. She was caught in a rainstorm one night while delivering food to a group of slaves on the run. She gave her jacket to a young girl and caught a fever. She passed away within a few weeks."

Callie turned the page and flinched so hard that the entire bed shook. She pointed at a photograph. "That's her! That's who I saw in my house."

Carter frowned and looked at the picture. It was a grainy black-and-white photo, taken in a schoolhouse. Although formidable on the inside, the woman in the picture looked petite and unassuming.

He closed the book and put it on the nightstand. Callie was shaking like a leaf. He gathered her close. "Don't do this," he said.

"How could I have imagined her so perfectly if she wasn't there in my house? That picture proves everything. It even looks like the same dress."

All it proved was that other people in town had history books too, but he didn't have the heart to tell her that. He pressed a kiss to the top of her head. This wasn't helping. "Let's get out of here," he said.

Her eyes were still on the book.

He caught her by the chin. "How about a hike?"

She sat there mute, which was a first. Her eyes were glossy, and her skin was pale. He didn't like it. This wasn't her.

"Come on. We both need to clear our heads."

The day could wait a little longer.

He tossed back the covers and tugged on her hand. When he pulled her into the shower with him, it was with every intent to take her mind away from Adelaide and her house and bring it back to him. Steam filled the bathroom and clouded the mirror by the time they were through, but it did the trick. Even the knot in his shoulder had to turn loose after that.

"Want something to eat?" he asked when she came into the kitchen, wearing the sweatshirt and jeans he'd packed for her. He itched to know what she was wearing underneath the ensemble, but he could wait.

Sometimes immediate gratification wasn't as sweet.

"What do you have?" she asked.

"Cereal. Eggs." He opened the cupboard for a look. "Or how do you feel about peanut butter toast?"

She looked at him sharply.

"Sorry. Grocery shopping hasn't exactly been at the top of my to-do list."

"No, it's just..." She pulled the peanut butter off the shelf. It was a large jar; he never ran short on peanut butter. For some reason, she blushed. "Toast with peanut butter is fine."

They ate at the kitchen table, and she looked out the window, down at the town. It was as close to an eagle-eye view of Shadow Valley as a person could get. "You can see the whole town from here," she said.

"Grandpa picked this spot for a reason."

She glanced at the fireplace. She'd been enthralled with it ever since she'd first entered the house. This time when she walked over to take a closer look, nothing popped out to scare her. She ran her hand over the face of the smooth stones. Pictures decorated the mantel, and she picked one up. "Your dad?"

Carter knew he looked a lot like his father, and the picture had him in uniform. "He was the police chief around here before he and my mom retired to Florida."

"Did you always want to follow in his line of work?"

He shrugged. "The Landry line of lawmen goes way back. I never even thought about doing anything else."

"You're good at it. Look at what you did with Fleiss." She carefully set the picture back on the mantel. "Look at what you've done for me."

With her, it was becoming less and less about enforcing the law.

He cleaned up after their meal and met her in the living room. The sun was trying hard to break its way through the cloud cover. At least the wind had gone down. He grabbed a jacket from the coat rack and stopped. His grab 'n' dash at her house had really been subpar. He'd forgotten to bring a coat for her, too. Her eyebrows shot up when he passed her the light-colored jacket that had scared her so badly last night.

"There are some nice trails here," he said, refusing to acknowledge her reaction. It was a jacket. It would keep her warm. "We'll do an easy one."

She scrunched her nose at him, but pulled the jacket around her shoulders. It hung down to her thighs, and she had to roll up the sleeves, but the thing looked damn cute on her.

For a moment, he reconsidered what he was about to do.

But then he steeled his spine. Her fears were starting to consume her. He needed to shake the hold they had on her, but there was only one thing left he could think of to try.

He just hoped she wouldn't hate him afterward.

* * *

Callie stepped out of the house and took a deep, cleansing breath. Sharp needles of cold hit her lungs, and she coughed. If she wasn't awake before, that did the trick.

"We'll warm up once we start moving," Carter said.

He took her hand and began walking across the open meadow toward an opening in the trees. It was a well-worn path she hadn't noticed last night in the dark. She followed quietly at his side. She knew what he was doing, and she was grateful for it. She no longer felt the need to run, but seeing that picture of Adelaide had shaken her.

The woman in that old-time photograph had come back to life at her house last night. She'd talked, and she'd moved.

Callie nibbled on her lower lip. Could she have possibly seen a story about Adelaide when she'd been doing her research about her new house and the town of Shadow Valley? It was possible, but she didn't think so. The woman's story was memorable.

So was her ghost.

They started along the trail, and the trees closed in around them. Callie moved closer to Carter. "Where does this go?"

"It connects with another trail at the creek bed up to the north. That one loops around the top half of the valley. There are a lot of smaller trails people use for shortcuts."

The most hiking she'd done in Boston had been along the Freedom Trail when visitors had come to town, and that left her with blisters on her feet. Probably because of her cute boots. This, though... This was better. With Carter and the quiet and the peace... "Are we going anywhere in particular?"

"I want to show you something."

The farther they walked, the better Callie felt. The fresh air cleared her mind, and the exercise made her feel strong. She was wrong about the quiet, though. Once she listened, she heard birds twittering, squirrels scampering, and leaves crunching underneath their feet. It was late in the year, but a few trees still stubbornly clung to their remaining leaves colored in reds, oranges, and yellows.

"This is beautiful," she said. She snuggled deeper into Carter's jacket when a breeze ruffled her hair. "I still find it hard to believe that I can step outside my door and be in the middle of nature."

He glanced her way. "Do you miss Boston?"

"A little, but I like small-town life better."

For the past year or so, she'd felt an itch to leave the big city. A desire for something different had grown inside her. When she'd gotten the news about her great-aunt's passing, she'd been sad, but intrigued about the thought of actually moving and doing something new with her life. Once she'd seen the pictures of the house—misleading as they were—that had been it. The place had called to her. She'd felt a pull to Shadow Valley that she couldn't ignore.

Carter shook his head. "I never would have figured it."

"Why not?"

He almost smiled. "With the way you roared into town, I figured you were too high-maintenance."

"And I'm not?"

He lifted an eyebrow, and she blushed. She'd been very high-maintenance for him.

"You have your redeeming qualities."

He caught her by surprise when he stopped to pick some of the few remaining wildflowers on the forest floor. Her heart did a little tap dance when he gave her one. She tucked it into her hair. He touched it lightly, and hot shivers ran down her neck when he traced the shell of her ear.

"So do you," she said, her voice going husky.

"Watch your step," he warned her.

She skirted around a puddle and felt his hand settle on her hip. The touch was light, but she still responded to it.

Their whole relationship had been turned upside down last night—or had everything finally clicked into place? They'd been abrading each other for so long, but now they felt in sync. She let out a long, slow exhale. They'd certainly been in sync last night.

They'd had sex, and the release of pent-up desire and feelings had felt good. *Right*. He'd surrounded her with his heat and his strength. He'd warmed her, made her forget, made her *want*...

Her mind was back in his bed when the path curved around a big maple tree and opened up into a clearing. She focused when he stopped walking, and, once she saw the view, her steamy thoughts scattered. "Oh, wow."

It was absolutely beautiful. Tall grass bent and swayed in the breeze, and a small pond reflected the trees above it. There were even a couple of migrating ducks taking a dip.

"This is what I wanted to show you," he said.

The place was a hidden paradise. Callie turned this way and that, trying to see it all at once. She could only imagine what it would look like in the springtime when violets and goldenrod bloomed for attention. It would be the perfect spot for a picnic.

They crossed over a small ridge, and her sense of wonder evaporated. There were rocks in this portion of the meadow, too tall and too ordered for nature. A bad feeling hit her in the gut, and she dug in her heels. "Is that what I think it is?"

He rubbed his thumb against the back of her hand. "It's an old cemetery. Most of the people in town have forgotten it's here."

Anger caught her unaware. Why had he brought her here? Hadn't she been through enough? "Carter, I don't want to do this."

"Come with me," he said. "It will be fine."

She didn't budge. "It's Adelaide, isn't it?"

Grass had grown wild around the area, but the tips of the tombstones were visible as the tall blades swayed. It was a peaceful resting spot, but she wanted nothing to do with it.

"She's buried here."

Callie stepped away, breaking contact. Did they always have to be on opposite sides? Couldn't he let anything go? "Take me back. Now."

His gaze was steady as he watched her. For once, though, she didn't falter under the pressure of that blue stare. She didn't justify herself. She didn't care what he thought of her. She'd walk back on her own if she had to.

"Okay," he said, surprising her. "I just thought it would help. Give me a minute, and then we'll go."

She wrapped her arms around herself as he walked away. She didn't want him to go any closer, but she couldn't bring herself to follow him. A sense of foreboding weighed heavily in her chest as she watched him navigate through the maze of tombstones. He knew exactly where he was going. Her fingernails bit into her arms, but her expectations were rocked when he found Adelaide's headstone and placed the flower he'd picked upon it.

He was paying his respects.

Suddenly, Callie felt very small. She'd learned a lot about Adelaide Calhoun this morning. The woman had made a difference in her life that few people could claim. She'd helped others and had paid the cost in the end.

Shame washed through Callie, and she started moving. Adelaide's spirit hadn't been very friendly, but she'd lived a life due respect.

Carter glanced over his shoulder when he heard her. She gave him a shaky smile when she finally stood beside him. With a gruff exhale, he pulled her in front of him and slid his arms around her waist.

"This is why I know that she wasn't at your house last night," he said into her ear. "Adelaide doesn't live with you. She lives with me."

Callie's heart pounded as she looked at the grave. "How long have you known this was here?"

"My grandpa and I would hike up here to fish in the pond, and sometimes I'd come on my own to explore. I don't know why. Maybe it was because I learned about her in school. Every so often, I'd bring her flowers or clean up her grave."

"That's why you know so much about her."

"Hey, her story had everything: spy games, subterfuge, and danger. It was like finding James Bond buried right in my own backyard."

They stood there for a long time with the grass rustling and the ducks in the pond quacking. After a while, Callie pulled out of his arms. She still felt uneasy, but she knelt down near the headstone. *Adelaide Calhoun*, it read. *1792 to 1854*. It was so little to say for such an amazing life.

Hesitantly, she reached for the weeds that had overgrown the area. The moment she started to pull them, the tension seeped out of her system. Carter came to her side and squatted down to help her. Together, they cleared everything away until Adelaide's name was visible. When they were done, Callie stood and brushed her hands on her jeans.

"Do you feel better now?" Carter asked.

She turned to him and wrapped her arms around his waist. "Thank you for bringing me here."

"Did it help?"

"You know it did."

She went up on her tiptoes and brushed her lips across his. He caught her face and slowed the kiss down, lengthening it. When he pulled back, he watched her closely. "So now you know that your place isn't haunted."

Callie frowned. "Adelaide's body may lie buried here, but her spirit isn't at rest. It's in that house."

A muscle in his jaw tightened.

"At least I know the *who* and the *what* now," she said. And he was right: knowing that helped immensely. Adelaide wasn't random noises or unexplained occurrences anymore. Callie flattened her hands against Carter's wide chest. "I just need to figure out the why."

He let out a soft curse. "I knew once you heard the stories, you'd latch on to them like a bulldog with a fresh bone."

"It's my nature. I can't help it." She'd much rather lean in than run away. She cocked her head to the side. "Can't we just agree to disagree?"

He stood stiff for the longest time, but then let out a grumble. "Why not? We seem to do that with everything else."

"Not everything." They'd found one area in which they could both agree. "It hasn't been that bad, has it?"

He touched the flower she'd tucked behind her ear. "Just promise me you'll consider what I said."

"I promise." She'd consider it, but she was going to investigate her idea more. She was tired of being scared. There had to be an answer to why Adelaide was still here. She just had to find it.

CHAPTER THIRTEEN

The best place to do research was the library. Callie had learned that during her short time as a reporter, and it was the one thing she'd actually liked about the job. Finding the stories behind the story. Figuring out people's motivations and quirks. What better place would there be to learn more about Adelaide Calhoun than the Shadow Valley Public Library?

She heard the whispers and ducked her head lower into the cubbyhole she'd found behind the stacks of books. When Carter had said he'd needed to drop by the station, she'd asked him to drop her off. She'd thought it would be harmless. Quiet and secluded.

Wrong.

People were talking. Word had gotten around town fast. Even the librarian was yakking it up. Callie stared at the page in front of her even as she heard whispers of "she saw Adelaide" and "spent the night with the police chief" going on behind her.

Problem was, they weren't wrong. The rumor mill had gotten this one right on the nose. She had seen a ghost, and she'd slept with the town hunk. Apparently, people had been waiting for this to happen for a long time. Both events. Everyone but her had known about her house, and, while she and Carter had been clashing, others had seen something else happening. Or so they claimed now…

She'd been less clued in, at least about the house. But Carter? The heat in her ears radiated down her throat. Okay, she might have seen that in the cards, too. Having the town observe their relationship was awkward, but she could deal with that. Her readers would certainly love it.

But this ghost thing…

"Focus."

She'd come here to do research, but she wasn't getting very far. The internet hadn't provided much information. Contrary to popular belief, not everything was documented there, especially small-town or old news. Town records could be a better source for what she needed. It was just a lot more work.

She let out a frustrated puff of air and tried to concentrate on the book in front of her. It was the fourth one she'd skimmed for information about the Underground Railroad, but it was more informative than the others had been. This one had an entire chapter devoted to the Railroad in Massachusetts.

She flipped through the pages and saw information about the secret symbols the Railroad had used, like quilt patterns and the language of railroad transportation as code. The network had been strong, but secretive. Everyone involved had been at risk. Adelaide must have been under so much pressure.

Callie turned the page and flinched. Speak of the devil: a photo of Adelaide stared up at her. Callie clapped her hand over it. She might have made peace with the woman at the cemetery, but that didn't mean she could forget the apparition that had floated down the hallway, yelling at her. She continued reading the text, but her eyes were suddenly drawn to the opposite page when she saw something she recognized. Her name.

Calina Calhoun.

Callie blinked. When she looked again, it was still there. Calina.

The hair on the back of her neck rose. Forgetting all about the picture, she skimmed the words. As their meaning sank in, her fear turned into the smallest seed of excitement.

Adelaide had had a sister named Calina.

What were the odds?

Slim. It wasn't a common name. Callie chewed on her lower lip and scoured the information the author had collected, but the vital piece she needed wasn't there.

She pulled out her phone. "Hi, Mom, I have a question about our family's genealogy. Where did you come up with the name Calina?"

Calina Calhoun… Calina Thompson… The pull she'd felt for the house… It was too much to be a coincidence. She began taking notes. Fate had brought her to this town and that specific house for a reason. It was time she figured out why.

* * *

The house loomed large as Callie stood on the front walk, staring at it. It looked so different in the light of day. The sun was shining and the temperature had warmed, but adrenaline simmered along her nerve endings. She remembered the storm… the abject darkness… the blob of energy… Her weight transferred to the balls of her feet. Half of her wanted to run away again, but the other half felt the pull of curiosity.

The need to go inside was so strong, she didn't know if she'd be able to stop herself.

"Hey, Callie."

She spun around to see David rushing across the street.

"What are you doing here?" he said, trying to catch his breath. A frown marred his handsome young face, and his shaggy hair couldn't hide the worry in his eyes.

"I live here."

"I know, I mean… Are you okay? Why are you alone?"

"I'm fine." She licked her dry lips. "I just… uh… need some things."

"Like what?"

Answers.

The delinquent in David knew a weak excuse when he heard one. He shifted uncomfortably and tugged on his sagging jeans. "Can't Chief Hardass go in there and get whatever you need for you? I really don't think you should go back inside yourself."

She looked at David sharply. "Chief what?"

He shrugged. "Sorry. It's what I call him. Or I did. Before you two... you know... hooked up."

Her face heated. It was what she'd called him, too, once upon a time. She looked again at the house. He was Carter to her now. Carter, who'd pulled her out that side window. Carter, who'd saved her from a falling shutter. Carter, who'd made love to her until she couldn't see straight. He'd go inside in an instant if she asked him. "Probably."

"So call him." David whipped his phone out of his pocket. "Here."

"I think I'm related to her, David."

His head snapped up. "You're what?"

"I think I really may be a Calhoun."

"Oh, shit."

"Yeah." Why else would something be pulling her toward that house? Last night, the push out of it had been inexorable. Today, the polarity was reversed. Her thigh muscles were cramping as she tried to keep herself away. "I think I'm here to help her cross over."

"Callie... I don't know about that."

She didn't either. Honestly, she didn't know what she was doing. If the sun wasn't blazing so brightly it made her squint, she wouldn't be on the property at all. Yet the lure was that strong. It was the same pull that had brought her all the way across the state.

"Go in with me," she said impulsively.

He froze. "I can't."

"Then stand in the front doorway then while I try to talk to her."

He swallowed hard and looked away. "I'm not going to help you do this."

"All right. I'll do it myself."

He followed her up the front walk and caught her arm. "Don't. Please. Landry will only blame me."

"I'll be fast."

"If I go in with you, he'll have my head. If I let you go without me, he'll have my ass."

"Then we won't tell him, will we?"

"Callie!" David let her go when she pulled away. "Ah, hell."

Summoning her nerve, Callie walked up the front path. The house looked a thousand times better than it had when she'd first arrived in town. With the lawn mowed and a fresh coat of paint, the place looked proud and stately—but she got why the trick-or-treaters had given the old Calhoun house a wide berth. The toothy pumpkins on the steps looked friendly and inviting, but in hindsight, the cobwebs and scarecrow were a bad idea.

Especially the scarecrow.

Callie felt it watching her as she walked up the sidewalk. If that thing turned its head, so help her, she was out of here.

She scooted across the porch fast. When the scarecrow kept staring straight ahead, she pulled out her keys. Carter might not have grabbed everything she'd needed, but he'd managed to collect her purse. She hadn't stopped for anything last night as she'd barreled out of the house. Her chest tightened as she stared at the ornately carved panels of the wooden door. She remembered clawing at it, trying to get out.

Her breaths went short, but determination set in. She understood things better now, and she had a goal. She needed to find a way to communicate with her long-ago relative. It was the only way she'd find out what was keeping the woman trapped in this time and space.

Before she lost her nerve, Callie unlocked the front door. Slipping the can of pepper spray Carter had given to her out of her purse, she stepped inside. Better to be safe than sorry.

The chill was gone. Sunshine spilled into the house, warming the hardwood floors. She left the door open behind her. She wanted a quick way out if she needed one.

Her ragged breaths echoed off the walls of the entryway. There was heaviness in the air; she could feel it. But it wasn't evil or threatening. It was almost... sad. If there was one thing she'd learned, it was this house's moods. Right now, with the sunlight reflecting off its walls, it seemed empty and harmless. Welcoming.

"Adelaide?" She cleared her throat. "It's Calina. I'm back. Please don't be upset."

A series of loud squeaks from upstairs made every muscle in Callie's body clench. There it was again, a faint, repetitive squeak—only it wasn't the shutters.

It had never been the shutters.

She settled her finger atop the pepper spray trigger. She needed to be careful what she wished for. "I'm not your sister, Adelaide, but I'm your niece." Several times removed, but they didn't need to get technical. "Did you know that?"

She heard the squeak again and tried hard to place it. There was something about it… Feeling more confident than she had a right to, she started to follow her ears. "I've been reading a lot about you. You're quite the heroine in the history books."

The noise was faint, but it grew louder as she climbed the stairs to the second floor. "You were on a great mission," she called, "but it's over. You need to understand that so you can move on."

The second floor was still in a bad state of disrepair, but it was warmer and brighter than downstairs. More welcoming. Nobody had chased her up here.

The constant squeak pulled Callie past her office and down the hall until she was at the door to the attic. Whatever the sound was, it was coming from the upper floor. With a shaky hand, she reached for the handle. The sound stopped abruptly when she touched it.

The sudden silence had her heart jumping into her throat.

"You can do this," she said, forcing the words past her dry lips. "It's a new day. This is on your terms."

She remembered how she'd felt at Adelaide's grave. She hadn't been scared then. She'd been moved. Why couldn't Adelaide's spirit rest?

She needed help; Callie knew it in her gut.

Determinedly, she wrapped her fingers around the door handle. It felt cool against her sweaty palm. Before she could wimp out, she turned it. The door swung open with a groan. Steeling herself for what she might find, she stepped inside.

* * *

Carter's temple was throbbing as he mounted the porch of Callie's house. Two calls from David Hughes in less than twenty-four hours. *Two*. What the hell was she doing coming back here? He'd left her at the library, never thinking that she'd come over here alone.

When he found the front door standing wide open, his chest tightened. He'd locked that door last night.

"Callie?" he called as he stepped into the entryway.

Why would she come here?

He quickly moved to the living room, but it was empty. A check of the kitchen found it quiet too.

"Callie."

His footsteps sounded loud as he hurried to her bedroom. His shoulder gave a nasty twinge when he looked inside and saw the Elvira dress still draped over the bed.

"Are you here?"

She didn't like the basement. She avoided it like the plague, and she'd been waiting to work on the upstairs rooms until winter settled in. So where the hell was she?

"Callie."

His chin snapped up when he heard movement above him. He was about to call her name again when he realized that the person hadn't answered him. Was someone prowling around in the light of day?

The footsteps headed to the front of the house. He followed them, moving as silently as he could through the living room. He stepped over a board he knew was noisy, but he couldn't avoid them all. The footsteps above kept moving. They were lighter than Callie had described. If it was her, why wasn't she answering him?

The footsteps started down the rounded staircase to the left. Carter moved to the far side where he could see, but still have cover. He was ready to act when he recognized the tall, slim form.

"Callie."

She screeched and spun around so fast that she had to grab the banister to keep from falling. "Don't do that," she said, one hand going to her heart. "I've had enough scares around this place."

"Why didn't you answer me when I called?"

"I did. You must not have heard me."

"My ears aren't that bad."

"I was up in the attic."

"The attic?" That was the last place he would have looked. She hadn't mentioned having any problems up there. "What are you even doing in this house? Why didn't you call me if you wanted to come over here?"

"Call you? It's my house," she said with a laugh. "Listen, I learned some more things today about Adelaide, and I—"

"So help me, if you say one more word about that so-called ghost..." He stomped across the entryway. "We haven't figured out what's going on in this place. I would have escorted you if you needed to come here."

"I didn't realize I had to report my every move to you."

"I haven't cleared this place as a crime scene yet. You shouldn't be here."

Which was a half-truth. He'd planned to come back for another walk-through this morning, but things had gone in a whole other direction last night. One that he couldn't have walked away from if Adelaide Calhoun herself had waltzed into his bedroom.

Callie's eyes narrowed. "I don't see any yellow tape."

His teeth set. The woman knew how to get under his skin. "I thought you were afraid of this place."

"I am. Or... I was." She wiggled her knee. "I thought I'd try communicating with her."

Communicating? Oh, good Lord. He ran a hand through his hair. "We don't need to stir things up any more than they already are. Everyone in town has been talking about what happened here. It doesn't help that it was Halloween." It was going to take weeks for the hubbub to die down.

"Happened here?" She folded her arms over her chest. "Or what happened at your place? People weren't quiet about that, even at the library."

The muscle in his temple cramped. People always talked about the town goings-on, but what had happened between them was private. It was nobody's business but theirs.

"You really should be wearing your sunglasses, Carter. Your cocky police chief shtick is much more effective that way."

"You're one to talk, honey. That ditzy blonde routine of yours is wearing thin."

Her cheeks went red.

"Fine. Whatever." She flipped back her hair, reminding him of the flirting routine she'd tried in her Mustang. "I crossed the line of a crime scene, and I ditched my police protection. What are you going to do? Ticket me?"

"Don't tempt me."

She didn't know when to stop.

"Maybe it's time you slapped the cuffs on me," she said, pushing her wrists together out in front of her. "After all, I am the town's high-maintenance menace."

She was trouble, all right. Carter covered the distance between them and caught her about the waist. She gasped when he plucked her off the second step and pulled her against him. Turning, he bumped the front door shut and settled her firmly against it. "Handcuffs aren't such a bad idea. Remind me to try them later."

* * *

Callie pressed her hands against Carter's bunched shoulders. There was fire in his eyes, but something else, too. Something hotter. Deeper. It stopped short the retort she had waiting on the tip of her tongue.

"I was worried about you," he said gruffly.

His lips came down on hers, hard with intent. His tongue plunged deep, and she held on tight. This wasn't a kiss meant for comfort. This was frustration, fear, and desire all rolled into one. He loomed over her, edgy with impatience. Edgy with need.

"I didn't want to bother you," she said. "If it helps, I brought the pepper spray."

She'd pulled her phone out probably five times on the walk over to call him, only to stop herself. She was tired of being such a scaredy cat.

"You don't have to play tough for me. That's my job."

His hold tightened around her waist, almost as if he was going to carry her out to his car again—and Callie finally got it. He was a man who liked to be in control, who needed to know where he stood in any given situation, but nothing here was as it should be. He couldn't fight against what he couldn't see. The strange occurrences in her house were affecting him as much as they were her.

His need to protect her struck a chord inside her, and she softened. She wrapped her arms around his neck and massaged the tight muscles she knew she'd find there. A groan left him, and his hands slipped under her sweatshirt to find skin.

"I really didn't want to leave that bed this morning," he said.

Neither had she.

His hands were hot and greedy as they moved up to cover her breasts. She arched when his thumbs slid under the demi-cups of her bra and rubbed her nipples. "I've got a bed here," she said, her voice tight.

He pulled her sweatshirt over her head. "The pink set," he murmured, thumbing the center of her bra cup. "My favorite."

Then he was kissing her again and getting rid of the lingerie. She pushed at his jacket. It fell off his shoulders and draped over his forearms. She made a frustrated sound, and he pulled back long enough to drop it onto the floor and tug off his own shirt.

Callie hummed in delight when all that muscled flesh rocked back into her arms. "I thought we were good at arguing." She kissed his chest. "We're even better at this."

"Couldn't agree more." He caught her zipper. Her jeans loosened, and she moaned when he pushed his hand inside them.

So much better.

"Touch me," he said.

She wedged her hand between their tightly pressed bodies. He caught her mouth in another ravenous kiss, and her thighs quivered. The bulge behind his zipper more than filled the palm of her hand. Experimentally, she squeezed.

"*Ah.* Yeah," he groaned.

He slapped his palm against the door and leaned closer, trapping her touch right where it was. His chest pressed against her breasts, and his mouth was everywhere. Against her lips, her neck, her ears...

She began to shake when his hand found its way into her panties. His touch was gentle, but determined. And curious. She opened her eyes and tried to regain her equilibrium. She couldn't see past his wide shoulders. He was everywhere. He was all she could see. He was all she could feel.

And his usually stalwart control was nowhere to be found.

Their gazes locked as she undid his zipper. The rasp of sliding metal sounded impossibly intimate in the open space of the entryway.

Oh, God. The way he looked at her.

He reached into his front pocket and pulled out a square foil packet. Callie carefully worked his briefs over his erection. It stood straight and tall, pointing right at her. She unrolled the condom over him, but gasped when he gave a sharp yank on her clothes. He had her jeans and panties down to her knees before she could react. She reached for his shoulders when he lifted her. He used his foot to push her clothes the rest of the way off. He settled her back down on the pile, but caught the back of her thigh.

"Carter," she said a little desperately when he pulled her leg around his waist.

He thrust into her, and her body melted.

He slowly pulled back, watching her reaction. Her eyes drifted shut in pleasure when he changed directions and began to push back in. He leaned down and ran his tongue across the pulse in her neck. She dragged her fingers down his bare back and felt the precise moment he gave in.

A curse left his lips, but then he was hitching her up higher until she had both legs wrapped around his waist. "Hold on, honey."

Callie arched when he began to pump in a jagged, urgent rhythm. The feel of his big cock moving inside her was electric. She moved in sync with him, and the door rattled on its hinges with every thrust.

It was raw and overwhelming. Thrilling. Last night had been intimate and comforting, but this... this was the friction that always seemed to percolate between them. To finally give in to it, to go with the flow...

She dug her heels into his buttocks when she felt herself hurtling into an orgasm. "Carter!"

He jerked, and then he was coming with her. In the silence of the entryway, in the emptiness of the old, forgotten home, energy stirred. Overhead, the chandelier blinked. The light grew stronger until it was a steady beam.

Carter looked at her, his blue eyes heavy-lidded and sensual. He brushed his fingers over her hair and caught her up to him. "Let's find that bed."

Callie wrapped herself around him like a vine and peppered kisses across his shoulder as he carried her to her bedroom. The taut muscles twitched under her lips. He put her on the bed, and she watched as he stripped. She hadn't realized it, but she'd only managed to push his jeans down to his thighs. He ridded himself of clothes, shoes, and the gun at his ankle. When he crawled onto the bed, it was to lie right on top of her. She squirmed in pleasure as she took his weight.

"Okay?" he asked quickly.

"Better than okay," she said with a sigh.

She ran her toe down the back of his calf. She felt like she'd sprinted a mile. Her heart was still thudding against her ribcage, and her skin was coated in sweat. Their bodies clung together as if they didn't want to be separated. For a long time, they lay still and quiet. She slowly ran her fingers up and down his spine. After a while, he let out a long breath that tickled her skin.

"In case you didn't notice, I went a little nuts when you disappeared." He lifted his head to look at her. "Don't do it again."

She let her hands wander lower. Mmm. *Hardass* was right.

"I kind of like it when you go nuts."

He looked pained. "Just try," he said. "For me?"

For him, she'd do just about anything right now. She let her fingers glide across his firm backside. Just. About. Anything.

He frowned grumpily, but covered her breast with his hand. He gently fondled her, and she moaned when he flicked her nipple.

"I think it's time we set a few rules," he said.

Her legs moved restlessly against his. "Rules?"

He propped himself up on an elbow. "Rule one. Until we figure out who's messing with you, you have to promise me you won't go wandering off on your own. I want someone with you."

"You told me you're understaffed."

"It could be Alice or Mamie. I don't care. I just don't want you to be alone."

"I wasn't alone. David was with me."

Carter scowled. "Don't remind me."

She brushed his hair back from his forehead. "Please don't be upset with him. He warned me not to go in by myself."

"So why didn't he go in with you?"

"I…" She didn't know. As tough as David tried to act, she couldn't picture him being afraid of a challenge. Or at least letting it show… But he absolutely, positively would not set foot inside her door. "He called you instead."

"Yeah, and that's the only thing saving him."

"Okay, okay," Callie said. She didn't know why the two had to butt heads, but somebody had to play the grownup. "I'll get an entourage."

Carter looked relieved. Leveraging himself over her, he kissed her. "Good. Now, rule two—"

"Rule *two*?"

"Rule two. If you need help with painting or repairs, you ask me. Not David."

"You can't be jealous."

He gave her nipple a quick pinch, and her back bowed. "You ask me."

"Mm." She settled back against the mattress. "You *are* good with a hammer."

To her delight, color spread across his cheekbones.

He shook his head and got serious. "I'm done playing around with this house. We have to meet halfway on things. I know you have your own ideas on what's happening here, but you've got to be more careful. Go ahead and do your research, but give a little credit to what I'm saying. Somebody—a human being—is behind these things. Pepper spray or not, you shouldn't have come here without me."

She scored lines across his shoulders and felt his muscles quiver.

His eyebrows drew together. "Why aren't you arguing?"

"Do I have a say in these rules?"

He grunted. "I should have known."

She smiled and pushed at his chest. He rolled onto his back and pulled her atop him. She liked this intimacy between them. She liked being able to talk to him. And touch him. She spread her hands wide on his chest. Touching was definitely a plus.

"Rule three," she said, tracing the line of his collarbone. "From now on, you have to promise not to get defensive when I talk about Adelaide."

His fingers bit into her hips.

"Halfway," she reminded him.

"I'll try."

She let her touch slide down his arm. There was no give to his biceps at all. "Rule four. If something is bothering you, you have to tell me. That Morton case is going to make your hair gray before its time."

He started to say something, but she stopped him by pressing a finger to his lips.

"Your stress has been showing, Carter." She bracketed her

hands on either side of his head to make sure she had his attention. "That shoulder of yours is tied in knots all the time. You need to talk to someone. Why not talk to me?" She smiled uneasily. "Some people actually seek out my advice."

He went still. "You know I care what you think, don't you?"

No, she didn't. Not really.

He slid his hand around the nape of her neck. "Well, I do. One whole hell of a lot."

He pulled her down to him, and Callie's heart tripped over itself. The kiss they shared was hot and steamy, and it melted her from the inside out. She let her weight settle on him, and any thoughts of ghosts, spirits, and escaped convicts left the room.

He trailed kisses across her cheek to her ear. "Out of curiosity, what kind of stress relief would you advise?"

"A warm seaweed wrap can do wonders."

He nipped her earlobe. "Wrong answer." His hands swept down her back and settled on her hips. "Quick, Kate," he whispered.

"Quick what?" she said, lifting her head.

Her eyes widened when he thrust up into her.

"Just quick," he growled.

CHAPTER FOURTEEN

They spent the afternoon in bed. When they weren't talking, they were making love. And when they weren't making love, Callie was working on Carter's shoulder. As tough as he was, he was putty in her hands. She nearly had the last kink worked out when his stomach rumbled.

It made hers pang, too.

"Hungry?" she asked.

"I could eat."

They had worked off a few calories. "I have beef stew I could heat up."

He watched her, his chin propped on his hands, as she moved off the bed. His gaze stroked heatedly over her body as she headed to the closet. "Now you've got me curious," he said.

"I can cook. Simple things."

She grabbed a robe. Smiling, she pulled it on. The way he watched her, she felt as sexy as if she were stripping for him. Her nipples beaded under the slick fabric, and there was no hiding her reaction. It was her summer robe, thin and short. Her heavier one was at his place.

"Shower first," he growled. Flipping back the covers, he threw his legs over the side of the bed. He came to get her, and her robe didn't stay on for long.

They shared the shower, but, in the end, probably used as much water as if they hadn't. The bathroom in the old house was small for two people. Carter buffed off and hooked a towel around his waist. He ran a hand through his wet hair, making it spike in places, before bending over to pick something up off the floor. It was her loofa.

Callie grimaced and threw it in the trash. "I must have knocked it off the shelf in the dark last night."

She'd forgotten this was where she'd been caught when the lights had gone out.

He frowned and offered a hand as she stepped out of the tub. "I'm going to find whoever did this to you."

"I don't think she can be caught."

He lifted an eyebrow, but said nothing. Instead, he wrapped her in a big terrycloth towel. Callie let her head fall back when he leaned down to kiss her.

"I'll go collect our clothes," he said, "wherever they ended up."

She watched the play of his muscles as he walked out the door—and let out a quick puff of air. It was hard to believe how much had happened in the past day. She'd seen a real-life ghost on Halloween, and now she was playing house with the cop who'd welcomed her to town with two tickets and a fine. Who would have thought it?

She reached for her blow dryer. Maybe that was the key: not thinking so much.

Carter was dressed and already in the kitchen by the time she made it back to the bedroom. Her clothes were waiting for her on the bed, and she changed into them before the warmth of the shower wore off. She glanced at the nightstand and saw that his gun was gone—secured again, no doubt, to his ankle.

She wished that he'd believe her, even just a little bit. What was happening here was supernatural, not something he could fend off with bullets or even fists. But that was her tough guy.

Hers…

Okay, maybe David was right. Carter was her cop. If it

made him feel better to act as her protector, so be it. It felt good to be on the same side—even if they didn't totally agree.

She found him in the kitchen making sandwiches. He nodded at the stove. "There wasn't enough left for a meal for two."

Callie's forehead scrunched, and she walked over to look at the pot. She could have sworn that there'd been more left over than that. She grabbed the spoon and gave the bubbling liquid a swirl. "Adelaide," she grumbled.

The missing food trick just wasn't funny anymore.

Sighing, she opened a cupboard for bowls and helped Carter get things ready. She'd just put out drinks when he turned from the counter. "I almost forgot. I found this on the staircase out front."

"Oh…" She carefully took the old, yellowed envelope. She must have dropped it when he surprised her. She was happy that it hadn't gotten bent. "I forgot about that."

Understandably. Her attention had gotten derailed when he'd stormed into her house, all hot and bothered and hormonal.

"What is it?" he asked.

She glanced up at him. "Rule three?"

He leaned back against the counter and folded his arms over his chest. "Adelaide?"

"It's a letter to her, the real-life woman who lived in this house." She put the envelope down on the table where it couldn't get spattered. "I found out today that we're related."

He went so quiet that she got uneasy. The stew on the stove hissed, but neither of them moved.

"You're serious?" he finally said.

She nodded. "That's why I got so excited and rushed over here without telling you. I'm a descendant of her sister—who was also named Calina."

The goosebumps Callie had gotten at the library returned, and she rubbed her arms. "I don't think it's a coincidence that I'm here. I think fate brought me to Shadow Valley for a purpose, to help Adelaide's spirit find a way to rest."

He watched her, saying nothing.

A hard knot formed in her chest. He'd promised. "This house has some kind of hold on me, Carter. I felt it the first time I stepped inside. Yesterday, it pushed me out, but today, it pulled me back."

He dipped his head and ran a hand through his hair. "I'm not angry with you, honey. I'm just worried about you. I thought we'd cleared up that confusion."

She knew. The picture in the hallway of the fruit basket... It still looked nothing like her.

She fiddled with the silverware. He just didn't understand, and it hurt. "Did you know that Adelaide had a secret lover?"

The stew finally got his attention. He turned off the burner and reached for the bowls. "How would you know something like that?"

"I found some old love letters." She pointed at the envelope on the table. "That's what that is. His name was Peter. He was a banker, but he knew about Adelaide's double life. He didn't like the way she was sneaking around during the night doing dangerous work. He was afraid she'd be caught— or even worse, that he'd give away her secret, and she'd get caught because of him."

Carter set the bowls of steaming soup onto the table and sat down next to her. "I didn't know the library had something like that."

"They don't."

A slow, soft creak came from overhead.

He looked up. He waited for a second, but the sound didn't come again. "Then where did you find them?"

"Here. In my attic. That's why I was up there. I found an old trunk, filled with her things." Steam rose from Callie's stew, rising in wispy swaths. It hadn't taken her long to find the old travel case. Once she'd summoned the nerve to open the door and climb the stairs, she'd been drawn right to it.

Carter straightened when another drawn-out squeak came radiating through the rafters.

She stirred her soup calmly. Ah, the old shutter trick. Good times.

He sat still, holding his soup spoon like a weapon. "Are you sure they're really Adelaide's belongings? Or could someone have put them there, wanting you to find them?"

"To do what? Gaslight me?" She took a drink of water. Was that his excuse for the ghost she'd seen, too? Not even a Hollywood guru could have made that special effect. "I'd never even heard of Adelaide until last night. Besides, look at how yellowed that envelope is. It's old. They all are."

A hint of another squeak traveled down through the walls. Just a hint, but it was enough to push her cop out of his seat and up the stairs. Fast.

Callie was right on his heels. "That's the sound I told you about, the one that's not the shutters. I hear it all the time."

"Stay with me, but stay behind me."

She grabbed the banister but yanked her hand back quickly. It was ice cold.

She reached for Carter instead, laying her palm against his back as he stopped on the landing before the attic. They'd gone up the stairs fast, and she tried to swallow her loud breaths. He knelt down to pull his weapon out of his ankle holster and then reached for the door handle. Callie backed off, but he pulled her close and put her hand back on his shoulder. Standing off at an angle, he opened the door slowly. It swung open without a peep. Vigilant and silent, they started up the staircase.

The storage space awaited, still and empty.

"Has anybody been up here?" he asked. Callie saw nothing threatening, but he wasn't lowering his guard. "Other than you and me? Or Raikins?"

"*I've* never been up here until today," she said, peering around his shoulder. When she'd painted the exterior, she'd done nothing more than peek in the porthole window at the front. That had been enough for her.

The open space didn't seem so scary now.

The bare, dust-coated light bulb hanging from the ceiling was still lit. She'd forgotten to turn it off when she'd heard

Carter calling from downstairs. With the vaulted ceiling closing in, the room felt claustrophobic and smelled musty. Odds and ends lay about, belongings that previous residents had left behind. Bedrails were propped up against a wall, and a small table held a lamp that had seen better days. A rocking chair sat in front of the porthole window, taking advantage of the autumn view outside, but off to the side of the room was a trunk. An *old* trunk.

It had been impossible to miss.

Callie started to go around Carter to show him what she'd found, but he stopped her with a bar arm. Moving carefully around a threadbare curtain that hung from the rafters, he checked the other side. Frowning, he holstered his weapon. "Who did you tell you were coming here today? Somebody at the library?"

"Nobody."

"Hughes?"

"He talked to me outside and then called you." Callie dropped to her knees in front of the trunk. She didn't know how long she'd spent up here, going through its things, but the stack of letters she'd already read showed it must have been a while. The trunk was a time capsule, full of long-forgotten treasures. Inside, there were a pair of brass candlesticks, an antique hair clip, and an old-school primer. A tea set was carefully packed in newspaper and cushioned underneath by a handmade quilt.

"The Underground Railroad used quilts as signals." She pointed at the star sewn onto the top patch. "That means the North Star trail."

"That should be in a museum." Carter dropped down on his haunches next to her. "How did it survive up here with all the renters coming and going?"

He was careful not to touch, but Callie couldn't hold herself back. She gathered up the letters, tucking the one she'd taken back into its spot. The group had been bound together by a red ribbon.

"These are Adelaide's things," she whispered. "They're not

some trick."

The heirlooms were too old to be fake. There was too much weight of importance around them.

Somehow it didn't seem right to talk too loud. She started sorting through the yellowed envelopes, looking at the dates. She found the last one and opened it carefully.

Carter rose and looked around the room. He didn't seem satisfied with the explanation. He wandered about, testing the sturdiness of the bedrails and the glide of the drawer in the tiny table. Every so often, he'd stop and bounce atop a floorboard.

"Oh, no." Tears suddenly pricked at Callie's eyes. "He broke up with her."

"Who?"

"Peter." Sorrow seemed to come over the space at the sound of the name, and she rubbed her arm against the chill. "The secrecy and danger got to be too much for him. In the last letter I read, he'd moved to Ohio, but I thought he'd come back. But he's not."

The writing on the page before her blurred. "Here, he's wishing her the best, but telling her it's time they moved on—without one another."

Carter watched her from the window. "Easy, honey. It happened over a hundred years ago."

Easy wasn't an option. The feelings she had seemed magnified somehow… as if they were coming from outside her rather than in. "I don't think Adelaide died from pneumonia." Callie had to swallow back tears. "She died of a broken heart."

The rocking chair suddenly let out a mournful wail.

Callie scrambled backward, landing on her butt—only to realize that Carter had pushed it.

He jerked his hand back. "Damn, that's cold."

"That's it!" she said. "That's the sound I've been hearing."

He rubbed his fingertips against his thumb. Pulling the sleeve of his shirt down, he moved the chair deliberately forward and then back. Another squeak emitted from the rocker's old joints.

It was enough to make Callie's hair stand on end. She got to her feet and wiped her eyes. "Carter, please," she whispered.

He was already crouching down to check the floorboards. "The floor seems level."

"Carter, move away from that."

He waved his hand in front of the window, stopping at a certain point. "There's a draft. That's probably the problem. I can fix it."

There was no way a tiny wisp of air could move that thing. The old rocker was handmade and solid. She didn't care how crooked the floorboards were or how hard the wind blew. "We need to go. We shouldn't disturb her like this."

He rubbed a hand across his jaw. He nudged the chair again, but when he saw the way she flinched, he moved away from it.

And away from the presence she felt there.

She caught his arm as soon as he was in range. Hugging the letters tightly to her chest, she pulled him toward the door. In all the time she'd spent reading those letters before he'd arrived, she hadn't been uncomfortable, but now the dread was seeping right down to her bones. "Let's go back downstairs and finish our meal."

"It's all right," he said. "There's nothing to be afraid of."

She caught his hand to make sure he didn't dawdle. He paused to pull the chain on the overhead light, but she led him down the stairs and closed the attic door firmly behind them. They made their way back to the kitchen, but, as if on cue, a *clunk* from the basement sounded once they got there. Callie jumped back, bumping into Carter, but air started blowing through the kitchen vents.

He wrapped his arms around her. "Relax. Deep breaths."

Callie stopped and tried to center herself.

"Is this what it's been like for you here?" he asked.

She let herself lean back against his big body. "It's worse when it's dark outside."

But not always…

He sighed, and his hold tightened. "Maybe I've been coming at this wrong."

"What do you mean?"

"Strange sounds, footsteps, and cold spots."

"Don't forget the blinking lights and the falling shutters."

"Which can be explained…"

"But—" She turned around in his arms. She'd thought he was beginning to understand. She'd thought he was beginning to see.

"*After the fact*," he said, giving her a squeeze. "I always arrive too late. I never experience it like you do."

"You saw the shutter."

That muscle in his temple twitched. "Yeah, I saw the shutter."

He gently rubbed his thumb over the spot on her head where it had hit her. "I've got an idea. What if instead of you staying with me, I stay with you? Here, so I'm in the moment and able to respond."

"And see Adelaide?"

"And catch the bastard who's been playing with you."

Playing with her?

"You think this is a game? Why would anyone try to scare me like that? Other than because it was Halloween, and they thought it would be a good prank?" Now that she considered it, it would have been Shadow Valley's ultimate prank. *Aagh*. She balled her hands up against his chest. He had a point.

"I don't know anyone who would do that to you, but it's time we found out." He rubbed her back. "So, what do you think? Can I move in?"

She hadn't even considered where *she* was going to spend the night, but one thing was for certain: she was going wherever he was going. He made her feel safe—not to mention distracted and interested in things other than ghosts. The town was already talking about them, no matter where they stayed, but if he moved in here, were they asking for trouble?

The light coming through the kitchen window was low on the horizon. She hadn't realized how late it had gotten. They'd spent so much time immersed in each other that the autumn day had passed. Dusk would be arriving soon. She either needed to pack now or prepare for a night back here, in the very house she'd run away from.

The fear inside her was still raw, but hadn't she learned more today? Things that had made her curious enough to come back? Adelaide seemed to have accepted her presence. She'd even led Callie to a part of herself the world hadn't known about.

Callie looked at the letters she still held in a vise grip. "Let's stay here."

"We'll leave if it gets to be too much for you," he promised.

She lifted an eyebrow. "You ran pretty fast when you heard one little squeak, buddy boy."

He cocked his head. "Are you sure about this?"

"I came here to communicate with Adelaide, to learn more about her."

"What are you going to do with those?"

She looked at the yellowed envelopes with the careful printing. She hadn't thought about it. She'd acted on instinct when she'd taken them, but suddenly she knew. She'd been meant to find these letters. "I'm going to write Adelaide's story."

The whole tale had yet to be told. It was up to her to finish what her great-aunt had started.

CHAPTER FIFTEEN

Moving in did the trick. Once Carter set up residence, the house went quiet. There were still the normal sounds of an old house settling and birds screeching in the woods, but nothing that couldn't be explained away. The furnace still thumped occasionally, but he hadn't noticed any cold spots. The lack of activity made Callie happy—and ticked her off at the same time. It was like when you took your car to the shop, she'd told him, and it refused to act up for the mechanic. He had other opinions on the subject, like maybe having him in her bed was a deterrent for bad actors of the human type.

It had been days now, and he hadn't seen or heard anything that would change his mind. It only made him more confident that he was right—that somebody had been messing with her head. Or intent on doing worse.

He turned up the heat in his cruiser and cocked the steering wheel to fight against the wind trying to blow him off the road. He'd had to drive across the state for a court appearance for Fleiss, the escapee he'd helped catch. Charges had been filed for the credit card the convict had stolen and the Winnebago he'd broken into and made his home for a few days. More charges were being considered, but Fleiss had yet to give up any information on Morton.

Carter was pretty sure he didn't have any.

The more he heard, the more certain Carter was that Morton had broken off on his own. A smart move, considering his compatriots. The guy was good at covering his tracks, and he didn't get sloppy. He didn't stay in one place too long and changed up his routine.

His intelligence was the reason why he was still out there.

Carter rubbed the back of his neck. Callie was right. The search had gotten under his skin. His department needed to keep on top of things, but they weren't the only ones responsible for finding Morton. Every cop in the state was hunting him down.

He glanced to the passenger seat of the car when his phone rang. He answered as soon as he saw Callie's name. "Hey," he said softly.

"Hey, yourself. Where are you?"

"About an hour out. Sorry, this took longer than I expected."

"That's okay. How did it go?"

Carter frowned as a semi passed him, drifting way too close to the center line. "They threw in an extra charge for the swing Fleiss took at me. I appreciated that."

"Bastard," she muttered.

He grinned at the outrage in her voice. He liked having her on his side.

"The FBI has also moved Morton up on its ten most wanted list."

"FBI twit."

His grin pulled wider. He probably shouldn't have shared that, but he trusted her to keep his opinion between the two of them. "How did your pies turn out?" he asked.

She went quiet. "Mamie's turned out okay."

Meaning hers hadn't.

At least the baking lesson had kept her busy. Things had been going well at the house, but that didn't mean he'd forgotten rule one. He'd asked Mamie to stay with her today while he'd made the trip. "I'll have a slice of yours."

"I left it out for Adelaide."

As a lure. He sighed. She'd taken to pestering the spirit to try to get it to react. What a ghost was supposed to do with a pie, he had no clue.

"I'll be at the café when you get here," she said.

He frowned. It was late for Mamie's to still be open, and he'd thought they were going to do the baking at her house. "Everything okay?"

"Mm-hm."

Something wasn't right. He could hear tension in her voice. "You sure?"

"I'm just working on my column."

Now he knew something was off. She went into a cave when she wrote. He knew well enough from watching her do research on Adelaide.

Adelaide.

He pushed harder on the gas. "I'll be there soon."

"I've missed you today," she said.

He shifted in his seat. Now he really wanted to get back home. "We'll make up time tomorrow," he promised. "No work."

"No work," she agreed.

The urge to turn on his lights and rev the engine was strong, but Carter made himself keep to the speed limit. They hadn't gotten any precipitation yet, but the wind was whipping and the temperature had dropped. Snow was on its way.

He hunkered behind the wheel and tried not to keep looking at the clock. When he was within range, he turned up his police scanner to see if there was anything that warranted his attention, but it was quiet. The route finally began to twist and turn until it descended into Shadow Valley. He passed the spot where he'd pulled Callie over that first day and understood her need for speed, but he had to slow down even more. The wind could be tricky here, especially when it got like this. Sometimes the gusts swirled above the valley, while other times they scraped through like an ice cream scoop.

He was driving down Main Street when he spotted a silver

car parked in front of Mamie's. Callie's.

The Mustang was halfway into an illegal parking zone.

For once, he was happy enough to see her that he just might not fine her.

Feeling uneasy, Carter did a U-turn at the empty intersection and parked next to her. Wind pummeled him as he opened the door, and he pulled his bomber jacket up higher around his neck. It was one of those nights where the wind was dipping low, strafing the town square. The howl was at a low roar, and the café sign creaked and swayed. The tips of his ears were numb when he finally made it inside the diner.

All but one of the booths were empty, and the lights in the kitchen were off.

"Oh, Carter," Mamie said. "You finally made it. Were the roads bad?"

"It kept things interesting." He narrowed his eyes as he took in the two of them. They were huddled together in the booth. Mamie had a cup of tea in front of her, while Callie had her laptop open. "Why is the place still open?" he asked. "I thought you had the day off."

Mamie looked up at him, and he could see the strain around her eyes. "We're not really open. We were just waiting for you."

"Why?"

She glanced across the table at Callie.

It was then that he noticed the bag on the seat beside her. "What happened?" he asked.

Mamie bit her lip and stirred her tea.

"Callie?" he asked.

She didn't answer. There it was again, the tension.

"Don't make me ticket you for the way you're parked outside."

She straightened in her seat and looked out the plate-glass windows. "What's wrong with the way I parked? I'm not in front of the fire hydrant."

He'd interrogated enough people to know when to back off. He also knew when it was best to approach from a different angle. "It's halfway into a no-parking zone."

"But there's nobody else on the street."

"Which makes me question why you didn't choose any of the legal spots." He moved the overnight bag from the seat to the floor and slid into the booth beside her. "That Mustang isn't suited for winter, especially in these parts. You should start driving my truck."

"But I like my car."

"You can like it just as much if it's sitting in the garage."

She shivered. "You brought the cold in with you."

He hooked a finger under her chin and made her look at him. "Tell me what's wrong."

She pressed her lips together.

"Callie?"

"She missed you," she finally said.

He glanced across the table at Mamie, who blushed and quickly shook her head. "Not me, dear. Although you're certainly one of my favorite people."

"You know darn well who I'm talking about," Callie said, her voice catching. "*Adelaide* missed you."

"Now, wait—"

She poked him in the shoulder. "Rule three."

"All right." He raked a hand through his hair and was surprised to find it damp. Something was coming down outside. He took off his coat and tossed it over a chair at the next table. "I'm listening."

She looked at Mamie again, who reached over and squeezed her hand.

"I thought our visit to Adelaide's grave had changed things," Callie said in a small voice. "I thought that we had come to an understanding, especially after I read her letters. Things had been good all week. The moment you left, though, she started acting up."

Which meant that somebody had been watching them closely enough to know when he was out of town. The back of Carter's neck prickled, and he started mentally ticking through the list of people who had that kind of access. "What do you mean, 'acting up'?"

"She knows you. I think she likes having you in her house." Callie closed her laptop and ran her hands through her hair. It didn't look like the first time she'd done that. "She's been restless ever since I moved into her space. Looking back, I can remember things that happened—the squeaky shutters, the thump in the basement, *Halloween*. It's worst when I'm alone. She's quiet as a mouse whenever you're around, though, and she got upset when you left."

"How could you tell? Did you hear footsteps again? The rocker in the attic?"

"She slammed the kitchen cabinet doors," Mamie said in a rush.

Carter frowned. Mamie had seen it too?

He wrapped his arm around Callie's shoulders. She was stiff as a board. "When did it happen? Any idea why?"

She leaned into him and let out a shaky breath. "We'd just pulled our pies out of the oven. We were talking and cleaning up. We started to put things away, but suddenly the room went cold."

Mamie tapped the table. "After the furnace made that noise in the basement."

Callie nodded tiredly. "Right. It thumped, and then it got cold. Before we could check the thermostat or do anything else, Adelaide let us know that the baking lesson was over."

Mamie's eyes went big. "Those doors slammed one right after the other, Carter, just like Adelaide had run down the room. And it was so cold in there! Cold as it is outside right now, mark my words."

One of them had probably bumped a door by accident, and things had grown in their minds from there. But he could see that neither of them would be open to that logical explanation. They were feeding off each other's fear even now. "I'm glad you decided to come here."

"Not before the television turned on."

He swung his head toward Callie.

"We left the kitchen in a hurry, but then the television

turned on in the living room. It freaked me out because the newscaster was right in the middle of a report on Morton. It felt like Adelaide was telling me that she knew you weren't there."

"Ah, honey." He pressed a kiss to her forehead. "You've had problems with that thing before, though, haven't you?"

"Once. When David was there." She pointed at him fast. "Don't even say it."

He didn't have to.

He rubbed her arm again. As sorry as he was that she'd been scared, he liked that her fighting spirit was coming back. "Did you see anyone else in the house? Did you notice any unfamiliar cars outside? Were the doors unlocked?"

"It was Adelaide, Carter. It's always Adelaide."

He didn't know what to say to help her. He'd searched that house countless times, and he'd yet to find any evidence he could follow to ease her mind. The second set of fingerprints hadn't yielded any better results than the first. What could he do? He'd told her once he couldn't fight a ghost, but he really, really needed something he could get his hands on.

Across the table, Mamie cleared her throat. "Well, since you're here now, I think I'll just head off upstairs to bed. It's been quite the day for this little old lady."

Callie straightened. "I'm sorry to get you caught up in this."

Mamie smiled and brushed off the apology. "They say that life is slow in small towns. Now I can prove them wrong."

The windows rattled when another gust of wind came through, and Mamie bobbled her tea. Callie reached over to steady the cup, and Carter scooted out of the booth. He offered Mamie his hand. "Thank you for being with her today. You go get some rest. We'll make sure to close up when we leave."

"You're good kids." Mamie moved more carefully than normal as Carter helped her up from her seat. She smiled down at Callie. "I'm so happy you found one another, especially since I won the pool."

Callie blushed and began straightening up. "Help her

upstairs, Carter. I've got this."

Carter led Mamie to the back staircase and helped her up to her apartment above the diner. He took her key from her shaky hand and helped her open the door.

She bit her lip. "You won't tell anyone if I hide under the covers?"

"Your secret is safe with me. But don't worry. I'll get to the bottom of this."

She patted him on the shoulder. "We already know what's causing this, Carter. Just listen to Callie. That's what she needs."

He dipped his head as the door closed. The wisdom of elders.

By the time he got back downstairs, Callie had cleaned up the table, packed up her computer, and put on her coat.

"Come here," he said.

She moved into his arms quickly, tucking her face into his chest.

"Tell me the rest," he said against her ear.

"It's Adelaide, Carter. I don't know what she wants, but I think she's getting frustrated. She's becoming more and more powerful, and it's starting to scare me."

That much was obvious. Shudders were running through her body. When he'd left town, she'd been more confident. She'd thought that they'd figured out the key to Adelaide's unrest. She'd had a plan, and things weren't bothering her. "She didn't try to hurt you, did she?"

"No. I was just happy she didn't lock me in my room again." She paused for a moment and pulled back to look at him. "Wait a minute. Did you just say 'she'? I thought you didn't believe in ghosts."

He sighed. Mamie's words were ringing in his ears. Callie didn't need him to fight with her; she needed him to help her. In whatever way he could. "It's not important what I believe. Right now, I care more about what you think. We've done things my way—maybe it's time we choose yours."

"What do you mean?"

"Aren't there people who look into this kind of thing? You know, with gadgets and night cameras?"

Her eyes went wide, and a silly smile settled on her lips. That alone was worth the concession. "Are you serious? You want to call in the *Ghostbusters*?"

He winced. He was never going to live this down, not in Shadow Valley, that was for sure. "It wouldn't hurt to consult professionals who might be able to see something we're missing."

Like scams.

It went against every grain of logic inside him, but he was willing to do just about anything to take the fear out of her eyes. It had been there for too long. He was still going to call an electrician about the TV and drag Ernie's cousin back for another look at the furnace, but he'd play along for her sake. "We can make some phone calls and see if anyone is interested in studying the place. It's got some historical merit with the connection to Adelaide Calhoun. We should be able to get someone with some decent credentials, I'd think."

The worry lines vanished from her face. "I'd like that."

"Okay, I'll get on it tomorrow." It was at least something he could do for her. He brushed his lips over hers. God, he'd missed her today. "My place?"

"I was hoping you'd say that."

He swung her bag over his shoulder and tucked her up against his side as they headed for the door. "I'm going to need you to do one thing for me before that happens, *miz.*"

A corner of her mouth twitched. "Move my car?"

"It's killing me."

CHAPTER SIXTEEN

Today was the day.

Callie paced around the living room. The research team was coming for a visit. Carter had found a group that specialized in paranormal research—in Salem, naturally. When it came to historical paranormal phenomenon, that was the gold standard, after all. Dr. Bennett and his team were scheduled to arrive any minute.

She straightened the pillows on the sofa. When Carter had first suggested the idea, she'd been all for it. She still was, except… Things had been going really well. Just like she'd predicted, Adelaide had been happy ever since he had returned. Why upset the apple cart now? It would be easier just to keep him around full time. That sounded like a great plan.

Callie stopped pacing and stared down the hallway. She knew why they had to do this. Adelaide might have calmed down, but she was still in limbo. They needed to help her if they could. Callie just hoped that having a bunch of strangers traipsing through the place wouldn't upset the spirit too much before they could figure out what they needed to do.

A knock on the door made her jump. She turned, but Carter was already crossing the entryway. He answered the door, and she relaxed when she saw Alice and Mamie.

"Come on in, ladies," he said. "They're not here yet."

Callie waved, but her friends were abnormally subdued as they crossed the threshold into the house. It was quite a contrast to the way they'd jumped around the diner when she'd relented to their constant pestering and told them they could come see the real "cleansing." If that was what was going to happen today... She didn't really know.

"Take a seat," Carter said. "I'm sure they'll be here soon."

The two stood uncertainly in the entryway. After a while, they shrugged out of their coats and tiptoed into the living room. They sat down so close together on the couch that their shoulders brushed.

Callie knew how they felt. There was a different feel to the house tonight. She hated to even quantify it, but it felt almost... defensive. Like Adelaide knew something was coming.

"There's a van pulling into the driveway," Carter called.

She hurried to look over his shoulder out the window. "There are more of them than I expected."

"Hopefully, that means it won't take as long." He let the curtain drop. "I want this to be over."

"You and me both." She reached for his hand. She knew he thought this was a waste of time, but she appreciated him enduring it for her.

He wrapped his fingers around hers. "I can send them packing if you want."

She hesitated for a moment. "No," she said, tugging on his hand to stop him. "I want to do this."

"Are you sure?"

"Will you stay close by?"

"So close it will be embarrassing."

She smiled because she knew he wanted her to. "Let them in."

There were footsteps on the porch, but Carter opened the door before anyone could knock. "Paranormal Research Guild?" he asked.

"That's us," a gray-haired man said. "I'm Dr. Bennett. We

spoke on the phone."

"Chief Landry."

Carter shook the man's hand, and Callie bit her lip to hide a real smile. There was her tough guy. She knew the posturing was to keep the visitors in line, but she appreciated it. She wanted the truth, too, not a con job. She gave the researcher a once-over. He looked respectable enough. He wore glasses and a full beard, but it was tidy and trimmed. He looked like he should be teaching chemistry somewhere, not hunting ghosts.

She stepped forward. "Dr. Bennett, it's nice to meet you. I'm Callie Thompson."

"It's a thrill to meet you. Several of us are big fans of your Quick Kate column."

She lifted an eyebrow. She hadn't considered that. Had her celebrity factored in to their swift response? Would it affect their findings? She pulled out of the handshake and rubbed her hands together. "Thank you. Please, let me show you around the place."

Open, she reminded herself. She needed to be open to this, because she really didn't have any other options left. Besides, Carter had already cornered the skeptic market. She saw the way he was staying back, observing everything. Nobody was going to pull one over on him.

Mamie and Alice were much more receptive. Their cheeks flushed with excitement when they saw the researchers and all their equipment. One man set an electronic device on the table by the sofa as he unloaded his things. Alice eyed it like a two-year-old wanting to touch. "What do you think it's for?" she croaked in a whisper that everyone within two blocks could hear.

"Maybe it's an ectoplasm detector," Mamie whispered back.

"It's a digital thermometer," the man said with a grin. He had tattoos on his neck and leather cuffs around his wrists.

"Ooooh!" Alice and Mamie were in love.

"The temperature sometimes falls when there's a presence in the room," Bennett explained. "It's just one of many phenomena we try to capture when we're investigating a house.

If you have any questions about our equipment or procedures, feel free to ask."

Callie perched on the edge of a chair, but Carter wasn't letting down his guard. He propped himself up against the wall and folded his arms across his chest. Honestly, she liked him having her back.

Alice and Mamie began cooing over something new that the tattooed guy was showing them. "It's an electromagnetic field detector," Mamie said in delight.

"EMF, Mamie," Alice said. "We gotta get the language down."

Callie was surprised when another knock came at the door. Everyone who'd been invited was already here. Now was not a good time for surprises. She saw Carter's eyebrows draw together, and she followed when he went to answer. "David!"

Carter came to a standstill when he found David Hughes on the porch. "I don't even want to ask."

David seemed taken aback too, but he straightened his shoulders. "I heard you guys were going to try to contact Adelaide tonight."

"Yeah. So?"

"I think I should be there."

Carter let out a quick bark of laughter. "I think not."

David looked almost relieved. He started to turn away, but Callie hurried to stop him. "No, wait. Come join us."

She put a hand on Carter's shoulder. She knew he was already on edge, and her young neighbor always seemed to push his buttons, but she needed all the support she could get. Carter's muscles bunched, but he stepped aside. She caught David's hand when he looked unsure. For a moment, he resisted, but then he entered, albeit uneasily. "Go on in," she told him. "Let me talk with my cop."

"Really?" Carter said as David trudged to the living room, his head on a swivel. "Like we don't have enough going on tonight?"

"I know you two don't get along," she said, "but his BS detector is nearly as good as yours."

Carter stopped. "Good point."

"I have them every now and then." She went up on tiptoes to kiss his cheek, but he turned his head and caught her kiss with his lips. His arms wrapped around her, and his hand tangled in her hair. Callie let herself sink into the protective embrace. "Should we get this dog and pony show started?"

"Can't be soon enough for me."

They rejoined their visitors in the living room. Callie took a seat again, but Carter chose a new spot against the wall, one where she could see him. David had found a chair in the far corner, and he was quiet as he sat down to watch. Too quiet. She looked at her neighbor more closely. He looked almost green.

"This is Paloma," Bennett said. He gestured at a redheaded woman. "She's our psychic medium. We can take all kinds of physical measurements, but her intuition and ability to communicate help us make sense of the data."

Paloma nodded at the group, but she was already wandering around the room and waving her hands through the air. Every once in a while, she'd come to a stop if she *felt* something.

Callie would have sworn the woman was blitzed, but Alice and Mamie were star-struck.

"Look at her," Alice said in her not-so-quiet whisper. "She's fantastic."

"Did you see the crystals in her earrings? I wonder if they help." Mamie turned to Alice as she patted her ears. "We should have brought crystals."

Bennett picked up a clipboard and adjusted his glasses on his nose. "Maybe we should start at the beginning. Ms. Thompson, Chief Landry told me some of the phenomena you've experienced, but I'd like to hear it from you firsthand. What specific things have you noticed that make you think there might be a presence in the house?"

Might be?

"Please, call me Callie." Unexpectedly nervous, she hooked her hair over her ear. "There have been quite a few things, actually."

"Like sounds? They tend to be the most common."

She nodded. "There are squeaks, whines, and thumps. I've heard the rocking chair in the attic. The basement can get quite noisy, too, and the television comes on by itself."

She saw Carter roll his shoulder. She'd gotten him there. Ernie's cousin hadn't been able to find anything wrong with the wiring.

Bennett's eyebrows lifted. "It sounds as if you have a very active entity."

"Yes, I can feel the energy." The medium settled a hand over her chest and inhaled deeply. "It's young, very mobile."

Carter coughed.

Bennett gestured with his pen. "Please continue."

Callie rubbed her hands up and down the arms of the chair. Where did she even begin? "My bedroom door locks by itself. Doors slam, food disappears, and there are cold spots."

"Wait," Carter said. "Food disappears?"

She glanced over her shoulder. "I told you that."

"No. No, you didn't."

"I left the pie out for her."

His eyebrows lifted. "To eat? I thought you wanted to see if it would fall onto the floor or something. If I'd known that was going on, I would have dusted for fingerprints in there."

"Oh, dear," Mamie said. She flushed when the attention turned to her. "You know me and kitchens. I polished that place to a sparkle after we finished baking."

"It's all right," Callie said. Nothing had ever turned up with the fingerprints, and why would it? Ghosts didn't leave fingerprints. She shifted in her seat and tried to get her thoughts back on track. "The most distressing incident, though, happened on Halloween night. I saw her."

"Saw her? How do you mean?" Bennett asked. "Was it a dark shadow? Or movement in the corner of your eye?"

"Oh, no. I saw her straight on, rushing down the hallway at me."

The researchers all stopped what they were doing.

"A full-bodied apparition?" Bennett's eyebrows jumped above the rims of his eyeglass frames. "You say this was a female spirit?"

"Yes, it was Adelaide Calhoun." Callie picked up a file from the coffee table. "I put this together for you. She used to live in this house back in the 1800s. She worked with the Underground Railroad freeing slaves. There's a picture of her in there."

"Yes, yes. The Underground Railroad. I picked up on that, but I didn't quite know what it was." Paloma turned in a slow circle with her fingers fluttering in the air. "She's adventurous. There's a daring quality to her."

Alice and Mamie nodded in quick agreement.

"Where, exactly, did you see this apparition?" Bennett asked. His voice had risen a notch. "Was it this hallway here? How long did she manifest? Did she interact with you, or did she not seem to notice you?"

Tattoo Man grabbed one of his electronic detectors.

"Everybody, ease up," Carter said in a low voice.

They all stopped on a dime, including the medium.

Callie dug her fingers into the armrest. The energy in the house had risen. She could feel it. That was dangerous, especially with Adelaide. The spirit was easily riled. "It's all right, Carter. They need to know. It's why they're here."

She pointed to the hallway. "Adelaide was over there. She started out at the end of the hallway and came toward me. She lifted her hand, and… and told me to run."

"She *talked* to you?" Bennett scribbled furiously on his clipboard. "It's very rare to have a combined visual and auditory experience. It takes a lot of energy for an entity to do that."

"She was full of energy that night," Callie said with a nervous laugh. Suddenly, Carter was there, squeezing her shoulder. The contact eased the band of tension surrounding her ribcage. "She yelled, 'Run, Calina. Run.' So I ran."

"Of course you did." Bennett's brow furrowed as he looked down the hallway. Dusk had settled in, and the shadows were growing.

"There's residue of her rage in the air," Paloma said, giving a dramatic shudder.

A sudden thud from the basement made everyone jump.

Paloma moved to the doorway between the kitchen and the living room. She knelt and began to move her hands experimentally over the floor. "She's over here. The floor is practically jumping. My toes are numb."

"I've got something over here, too," Tattoo Man said from the far side of the room near the bookcase. "The temperature just dropped almost ten degrees."

Paloma took a deep breath and closed her eyes. "Come to us, Adelaide. We mean you no harm. Let us know what's upset you so."

She turned in a slow circle, and the room of people fell silent as they watched her. Including Carter. He didn't look happy, and Callie's hope fell. This was not what she'd asked for. Did this woman really expect anyone to fall for her act?

Then again, maybe Callie had asked for too much. Maybe the real deal didn't exist.

The possibility made the pit of her stomach grow cold. What would she do then? This had to work. She had no backup plan.

"Come to us, Adelaide," the medium repeated. She lifted a hand to her forehead and began to shudder. "Come to us. We welcome you."

"Lady, you are so full of crap."

David was suddenly on his feet. Anger and disgust radiated from him. He was focused on the woman with all the drama, but he took a step back when heads spun toward him.

Paloma let out an offended gasp, while Alice croaked, "Rotten boy."

Inside Callie, though, something began to resonate.

"David?" She slowly stood. It wasn't like him to make himself the focus of attention. Yes, he acted out, but usually he was ducking his head and trying to avoid confrontation. At least with Carter around—and Carter was planted right behind her with his muscles bunched and bad attitude intact. "What is it?"

On cue, the teenager's chin dipped. He fidgeted as he looked for an exit. "Nothing. Sorry, I gotta go."

She stepped forward, blocking his way. She knew this kid. She trusted him. "Tell me."

He rubbed the back of his neck as he stared at the floor. "Adelaide Calhoun isn't floating under the floor of the kitchen."

Paloma let out a huff. "How would you know? You don't have the gift."

David's head came up.

"No, but I do have the *curse*." His hand shook as he pointed toward the bookcase. "Adelaide Calhoun is standing right over here, and she's laughing her fool head off at you."

* * *

Callie's attention went to the bookshelf. The man with the thermometer took a cautious step back, and Alice and Mamie clutched at each other. Carter, though, kept his eyes on David.

"She's laughing," David said numbly. His gaze darted over the onlookers, and his face went pale. He looked like a six-year-old who'd just been pushed out to center stage.

Carter felt the hairs on the back of his neck stand on end. The kid was a troublemaker, but this wasn't his style. This... wasn't a performance. Carter looked toward the bookcase. He didn't see anything. He didn't—

Wait, there it was. He recognized the charged electricity in the air. He'd always just thought the house was dry and static-prone, but it was only now he realized it wasn't that way all the time.

"I'm outta here," David said as he turned on his heel.

"Wait!" Callie rushed over and caught him by the shoulder. "Tell me about her."

David wavered as if the need to get gone was strong. "What do you want to know?"

"I... I..." Callie froze.

Carter felt like he was teetering on the edge of something.

None of this made any sense to him, but he went all in. For Callie. "You said Adelaide was standing. Can you see her?"

David's hands tightened into fists. "Yeah, I can see her."

"You said she was laughing. Can you hear her?"

The poor kid looked like he wanted to be sick. Callie caught his hand. Carter wasn't surprised when David's clenched fist opened and his fingers wrapped around hers.

"Sometimes." He rubbed his head. "There's a lot of static, though. It's hard to understand."

Carter let out a slow breath. He was a skeptic, but he trusted his gut. Right now, his instincts were ringing so badly to get Callie out of the room, away from danger, that he could hardly hold himself back. She couldn't run this time, though. This time, she had to stay. He kept his voice calm. "Have you seen Adelaide before?"

"Lots of times. In the window upstairs."

"Is that why you would never come inside?"

David shrugged. Carter could understand why he wouldn't admit out loud that he'd been scared.

"Why tonight?" he asked.

"To protect Callie."

"From Adelaide?"

"From these *quacks*."

Paloma let out a huff and flipped her flame-red hair over her shoulder.

"It's all right," Bennett said, trying to calm everyone. "Tell me what you see, son."

Paloma didn't like losing the limelight. She stamped her foot on the floor to remind everyone that she was still in the room. "I still sense something below."

The nut job. Carter rolled his eyes, but not before he caught the expression on David's face. It was fear. Not fear of anything he was seeing, but fear of not being believed.

"What does our equipment say?" Bennett finally broke in.

"My money's on the gypsy," Alice croaked. "That kid's never told the truth a day in his life."

Mamie turned on her friend and crossed her arms under

her hefty bosom. "Would you put a sock in it? I'm so tired of listening to you berate that boy."

Alice's mouth dropped open so wide, a 747 could have flown through it. Mamie ignored her and turned back to David. "I believe you, hon."

David wiped his brow, and his shoulders relaxed an inch.

The researcher with the tattoos cautiously approached the bookcase. He looked down at the monitor he had in his hand. "The EMF's jumping all over the place, and I'm still registering a cold spot. It's freezing over here."

The researchers snapped out of their stupor and went to work. Cameras started flashing and digital recorders started rolling.

"Bring that equipment over here," Paloma said. She waved her hands in a circle around her. "Right about here."

The research team started to move away. Everyone spun in their tracks, though, when a book hit the floor.

Carter wouldn't have believed it if he hadn't seen it. The book hadn't slipped off an edge; it had tilted out of its place amongst all the others and tumbled down. There just hadn't been anybody around to nudge it.

He pushed Callie behind him. "What's she want?" he asked David. "Why is she still here?"

Paloma gave up with a flounce. She threw her hair over her shoulder and stomped into the kitchen.

"Phony," David said.

"Show some respect," Carter snapped.

David blinked in surprise. "Not me. Adelaide called her that."

Callie tried to work her way around Carter, but he looped his arm around her waist to hold her back. That didn't stop her from peeking around him. "Can you talk to her, David?"

"I… I don't know. I've never tried."

"Can you? Ask her why she keeps trying to scare me out of the house."

David gathered up his nerve. He looked across the room. "Why do you—"

He tensed.

"She can hear you." His brow furrowed. "It's hard to make out what she's saying."

"Try," Carter practically growled.

"It's something like 'family.' Protect?"

"She knows I'm family," Callie whispered.

"She's pointing at the chief. Something about a flower?"

Carter's chin snapped back as if the kid had jabbed him.

"Does that make any sense?"

"Yeah," Carter said in a raw voice. He glanced at Callie, whose brown eyes were huge. Too much sense.

"What else, David?" Bennett said. "Tell us everything you're hearing."

The teenager ran a hand through his hair. A sheen of sweat was on his forehead. This was taking a lot out of him.

"There's something she needs to do. She's worried." He shook his head before anyone could ask. "She won't say what, but she's tired of waiting."

Suddenly, his eyes popped open.

"What?" Carter demanded. He caught David's shoulder when he wobbled.

"She said, 'Be careful. Danger.'"

"Oh Lord, help us." Mamie grabbed Alice with one hand and started fanning herself with the other.

"What kind of danger?" Carter asked. They were entering his territory now.

"People need to know. Can't be found." David pressed his hands to his head as if it hurt. "Hide. People are searching."

Carter was in full police chief mode now.

"Hiding. Hiding. She keeps repeating the word *hiding*," David said.

Down in the basement, the furnace thumped. Paloma examined her manicure. "I told you so."

"Could that be another spirit?" Bennett asked.

David looked woozy as he stared at the bookcase. "I don't have that much control over it."

Bennett signaled his team. "You two, get down there. We'll

keep working up here."

"She's getting frustrated. I'm losing her." David's voice was thin, and he pressed his fingers to his temples. "Hide. Run."

"The Underground Railroad!" Alice squawked.

"Of course," Mamie said. "She hid slaves on their way to freedom."

Callie pounced on the file of information she'd collected. "She thinks she's still back in the 1850s."

"It makes sense," Bennett said. "Maybe she hasn't been able to pass over to the other side because she thinks she still has work to do."

"No," David said softly. "She's shaking her head."

He slumped, but Carter caught him before he went down. He hefted him into a nearby chair. He pushed the kid's head between his legs so he wouldn't faint, but David pinned him with a look.

"She left, but she said one last thing." The color was gone from the teenager's face, and his eyes were unblinking. "She pointed at you and said, 'Protect her.'"

Carter clenched his teeth. "You'd better not be messing with me."

David stared at the floor. "Yeah, this was fun for me. A real blast."

Mamie jumped to her feet. "I'll get you some water, hon."

Footsteps sounded on the basement stairs, and the research team returned.

"Did you find anything down there?" Bennett asked.

The guy with the tattoos shook his head. "We took some pictures and did an EVP session, but didn't get any responses. There wasn't any reaction on the EMF meter."

"All right." Bennett rolled up his sleeves. "Then we'll concentrate on the data we took in this room. Let's all take a moment to think. How can we help Adelaide complete her mission? We need to figure this out if we're going to help her."

"What if the mission isn't for Adelaide?" Carter couldn't believe he was participating in this, but there was one thing that made sense. He turned to Callie. "What if the mission is for you?"

Her eyes rounded. "The letters."

"And the quilt."

"Can you explain?" Bennett asked.

"Some of Adelaide's belongings are in the attic," Callie said. "I'm writing her life story, but maybe she wants more?"

"Spirits have been known to attach to physical objects. Can you show us? I'd like to take some readings around her belongings."

The entire group moved to the back staircase, but out of the corner of his eye, Carter saw David push himself unsteadily out of the chair. He didn't want to let Callie out of his sight, but there were plenty of people with her, including Alice and Mamie. He decided to follow David.

"Hey," Carter called. He caught up to David in the entryway.

David spun around. He looked like he'd been through hell. An embarrassed look came over his face before he turned defensive. "Freak show's over, man."

He grabbed the door handle, but Carter pushed the door shut. They came face to face. The kid was getting tall. Hell, Carter could remember an eleven-year-old who'd hardly come up to his chest. Now, they were nearly eye to eye. Maybe it was time to start treating the kid like a man.

"Want to tell me what just happened in there?"

"God, can't you ease up just once?" David ran a hand through his slick hair. "I've got a killer headache going on here."

Carter cocked his head. "How long has this been going on? How long have you been able to see these things?"

David pressed his lips together.

"How long?"

"Ten."

"Ten what? Ten weeks? Ten years?"

"Since I was ten, okay? Is that what you wanted to hear?"

Not really. Carter had seen what had happened in that room. The kid looked like he'd been run over by a truck. If it took this much out of him now, if it scared him that much, how would he have reacted at the age of ten? "Did you ever tell anyone about it?"

David's face turned sour. "What do you think?"

His parents. A colorful curse passed through Carter's lips before he could stop it. They'd threatened to send David away on more than one occasion. Only now did he understand the true impact of what that meant. They weren't planning on sending their son to any military academy.

Carter shook his head. He was starting to get some answers to questions that had been bothering him for a very long time. "Is this why you act the way you do? Is this why I get calls about you practically every weekend?"

David's tough-guy look finally faltered. "I just want to be normal, man."

"Having a juvie file two inches thick isn't normal, pal. Normal teenagers don't even have a rap sheet."

Shame showed on David's face. It was subtle and quickly hidden, but it had been there. Carter had seen it.

The kid shoved his hands into his pockets. "I don't know how to handle it, okay?"

"Have there been others besides Adelaide?"

The kid shrugged, which meant "yes" in Carter's book.

"How often does it happen?"

"Too much, okay?"

"Maybe you should see somebody about it."

David might as well have come up swinging. His fists clenched and his shoulders pulled back. "I'm not crazy. I'm not going to see a shrink."

"I didn't mean a shrink."

"I think he meant me." The voice came from the archway behind them.

Carter looked over his shoulder. Most of the group, including Callie, was standing there. He didn't know when they'd shown up or how much they'd heard.

Bennett stepped forward. "I might be able to help you, son."

"You?" David said. "Help me? That quack psychic was able to fool you."

Carter rolled his shoulder. Nice. Real smooth.

Bennett let the jab roll off him. "She's proven effective before. You do have a lot more experience with Adelaide."

David's chin was still held high. Carter could feel him edging toward the door, ready to run.

"I've heard about your type," David said flatly. "You'd try to test me like a lab rat. Nobody's attaching electrodes to me. Nobody."

Bennett rubbed his chin. "Electrodes. Now, that might be interesting."

David's eyebrows shot up until he figured out that he was being teased. He gritted his teeth. "Seriously, man. What do you think you can do?"

The researcher pushed his glasses up on his nose. "From what I've seen, you have a highly developed sense there. If we study it, you'll understand it better. That would be comforting to me. If I had the ability you have, I would be scared to death."

David shrugged, but Carter could see that the guy had hit the nail on the head.

"With more understanding, we might be able to figure out a way for you to control it. We're conducting some very interesting work with people like you right now."

David went very still. "There are others like me?"

"Not many, but yes. There are others like you. You might not all have the same abilities or sensitivities, but you are not alone."

Carter reached up to rub the back of his neck and glanced over to Callie. Her eyes were full of tears. She'd been right: David had needed someone to listen to him. He was just lucky the right people had been here to hear him. Carter knew that if he'd learned this on his own, he wouldn't have believed it in a million years.

Now, though, he was reconsidering.

"I told you the boy was special," Mamie said in a dramatic

whisper to her friend.

"Ack," Alice said with a wave of her hand.

David had ears just like everyone else in the room. In fact, he'd already proven that his sense of hearing was better. "Mrs. Gunthrie, you know how your garden tools keep moving around in that shed of yours?"

"Is that you?" Alice snapped.

"No," he said with a smirk.

"Oh!" Alice croaked like a frog when she got the message. "*Oh!* You! Mamie, I told you something funny was going on in there!"

The group broke up into smaller chunks as Bennett and David went outside to talk. The researchers planned to stay the night, and they began discussing where they should set up all their equipment. Carter heard Mamie and Alice talking to them about EMF meters and the tool shed.

"How are you doing?" he asked Callie.

"Better," she said with a tired smile. The lines of stress around her eyes had faded, and her body didn't seem as rigid with stress.

"Yeah?"

"Yeah."

If all this mumbo jumbo was helping, that made it worth it. Carter brushed his lips against her temple. She slipped her arms around his waist and leaned into him.

"Thank you," she said.

"For what?"

Her brown eyes went soft. "For making this happen, but most of all, for what you did for David."

"You liked how I busted his chops?"

"I liked the way you gave him a second chance. I told you he wasn't a bad kid."

Carter sighed. "I didn't do it for him."

"I know. You did it for me... and Adelaide." Callie rested her head against his chest. "I hate to think of her being stuck like this. We have to help her, Carter."

"Relax, honey. We are."

"The poor soul has been waiting for years. We have to put things right. It's what she's been waiting for."

* * *

They hadn't understood!

Adelaide dropped her head back and nearly howled in frustration. She'd come so close. She'd finally made contact, yet the connection had been cloudy. The boy had tried. He'd tried so hard. She paced around the attic, too full of frustration to sit in her chair. Her strength was waning, but desperation kept her holding on.

Things had not yet been made right. Her message hadn't been clear enough, but she didn't know how to communicate with the police chief to let him know. And now there were others, strangers running around her house with their shiny gadgets and strange behavior. She didn't know them. She didn't want to talk to them. They couldn't help her.

She sank to her knees before the trunk filled with her belongings. Her treasures. Her heart. Her shoulders slumped. Weakness was swiftly overtaking her. She needed to rest and regain her strength. If she could. This time, she might have gone too far... used too much...

Footsteps sounded on the staircase, and she let go. She'd find a way back.

She had to find her way back to him.

CHAPTER SEVENTEEN

Adelaide was gone.

It had only been a few days since the research team had conducted their study. They still hadn't presented the results or provided any evidence, but Callie could feel it. The house had gone dormant. There were still creaky floorboards and drafts from uncaulked windows, but there hadn't been any squeaks from the rocking chair in the attic. The cold spots were gone, as was the sensation of being watched. Even the furnace had been acting better.

Still, she was surprised when she looked in the mirror. She hadn't realized how much the stress had affected her, but the dark circles under her eyes were gone and she felt lighter. Her creativity and good humor had returned. She was pumping out good columns faster than ever, and the research she was doing for her planned book on Adelaide was fascinating.

This. This was the life she'd dreamed of when she'd moved across the state—only better.

She pulled Carter's old T-shirt over her head and let it slide down her body. She reached for her hairbrush, but a spark of static electricity snapped when she pulled it through her hair. "Ah!"

She quickly put the brush down. Okay, so little things could still make her jump. Still, she was happier than she'd been since she'd first moved to Shadow Valley. Adelaide had settled down, and things with Carter were going better than ever.

He was even trying to be nice to David.

Callie looked in the mirror one last time and fluffed her hair. Her stomach fluttered as she left the bathroom and walked down the hallway. The newness of their relationship hadn't worn off yet. In fact, without Adelaide or cop business pressing on them, it had come to the forefront. They were finally able to concentrate on one another, and she got all jittery inside when bedtime rolled around.

She found Carter sitting on the side of the bed, waiting for her. His feet were bare, and he'd already taken off his shirt. Her mouth went dry. She liked the look of his body, but she liked the feel of him even more. When he looked at her, her knees went a little weak.

"You make that old thing look so damn sexy," he said.

Her breasts felt heavy under his look. Slowly, she walked toward him. He caught her by the hips and pulled her between his spread legs. She settled her hands on his shoulders and began searching for knots. They were fewer these days, but the one on his shoulder blade was stubborn.

"How did your meeting with the museum guy go?" he asked.

"He was excited to see what Adelaide had left behind."

"So your mission is complete?"

"I guess." She'd kept the letters, but the curator had picked up the rest of Adelaide's things this afternoon. The treasures in that old chest had made the man's eyes sparkle. He'd gushed about the importance of the find and had thanked her for the donation so many times that it had gotten to the point where it was embarrassing. "I hope she can rest in peace now."

Carter tilted his head back to look her in the eye. "Why are you so sad? I thought you'd be relieved."

She started to deny it, but stopped when she realized it was true. It really made no sense. Some of Adelaide's stunts had terrified her. She knew now that the ghost had just been trying to get her attention, but, back then, she'd been truly scared. Her nerves were still on the ragged side, but she couldn't deny her feeling of letdown. "I don't know. I guess the house feels lonely without her. I'm worried if she was able to cross over."

What if they'd just chased her out of the house? What if she was wandering homeless now or at the cemetery so far up in the hills? Had they done the right things to help her? The message had been so unclear.

"David is sure she's gone?"

Callie smiled and threaded her fingers through Carter's hair. It was funny how such a simple question could mean so much. "He walked through the house after the museum curator left. He couldn't find a trace of her."

"Good."

"He's doing a lot better. I think that finding Dr. Bennett was a godsend for him."

"I'll have to hold judgment on that one." Her breath hitched when Carter slid his hands under the long T-shirt and caressed the backs of her thighs. "I haven't had to pick the kid up in days, though. I guess that's something."

"Hardass," she said with a light shove to his shoulder.

He fought back with a quick pinch to her bare bottom. The sting made her go right up on her toes, and her fingernails left little half-moon indents in his skin.

He rubbed comforting circles on her backside. "Did you get your column turned in on time?"

His touch wasn't comforting at all. Heat pooled between her legs, and she spread her fingers wider on his chest. His muscles jumped when she brushed his nipples. "My editor was thrilled when I sent in two."

"Does that mean you'll have extra time in the morning?"

She dropped her head back when his touch became infinitely more intimate. "Will you?" she asked breathlessly.

"I'll make it."

He slowly parted her and pushed a finger inside. She clutched at his shoulders when he pressed his face between her breasts and nuzzled her. He'd learned just how she liked to be touched, but it was more than that. He'd established his place so firmly in her life; she'd begun to crave his body, his mind, and even his elusive sense of humor.

She closed her eyes and concentrated on breathing, but when he began pumping his finger in and out, she saw a flash of color behind her eyelids. She pushed against his shoulders, and he toppled back onto the mattress. She crawled right on top of him. Straddling him, she worked the T-shirt up her body and over her head. He caught her hips tightly as she let it fall onto the floor atop his shoes.

"It's been a while since you gave me a ticket," she said as she began to rock against the bulge behind the zipper of his jeans.

"You haven't done anything illegal."

"Can we change that?"

"I thought you'd never ask." He rolled her onto her back and swept his hand up her body to her breast. He plumped it up and then his mouth was on her. He dragged his tongue over her nipple, and Callie squirmed on the bed sheets.

"You have the right to remain silent," he said, "but don't let that hold you back."

She laughed softly as she reached for his zipper. His hips swung toward her, and she'd just gotten it halfway down when the phone rang.

"Shit," he said.

She dropped her head back against the pillow. "Not now."

He leaned his forehead against her chest as he tried to rein himself in. His breath swept against her nipple, and she bit her lip when it tightened almost painfully.

The phone refused to be ignored.

He grabbed it from the nightstand and nearly broke the screen when he jabbed at it. "Yeah?" he barked.

She watched the change come over him. Whatever the call was about, it was for Chief Landry. She could feel the difference in the tension in his muscles as she ran her hand down his back.

"Are you sure?" he said. "Settle down, now. I can't

understand you."

He glanced her way, and she could see something was wrong. She could hear it in his voice.

"Alice, slow down and breathe," he said. "Put Sherman on the phone."

Callie flinched. Something had happened at Alice's place? She pushed herself up onto her elbows. What was wrong? Had somebody been hurt?

Carter saw the questions in her eyes, and he lifted a hand to hold her off. "Can you give me a description?"

Her heart began to pound when he swore again.

"Are you sure you just winged him? Where did he go?"

Her eyes went wide. *Winged him?* Had somebody been shot?

"No! Don't go after him. Stay inside, lock up the house, and wait for me to get there." Carter sat up and swung his legs off the bed. "I'll be right over. For God's sake, don't shoot me when I knock on your door."

Callie scrambled up until she was kneeling on the bed. "What's wrong? What happened?"

He was already searching for his clothes. He zipped his jeans back up as he looked over the floor. "Somebody tried to steal Sherman's truck. He heard someone dinking around, so he grabbed his shotgun and headed out after the guy."

"Oh my God. Who was it?"

"Nobody knows. He ran off into the woods."

A lead balloon dropped in her gut. She took her T-shirt when Carter handed it to her and tugged it on as he put on his shoes. He walked over to the closet to get the long-sleeved work T-shirt he kept there. She knew his bulletproof vest was in his truck.

She didn't like this. In her head, she knew he assumed risk every day when he put on that uniform and walked out the door. She just hadn't expected him to have to face this level of danger. This was Shadow Valley, not Boston.

"I don't have a good feeling about this." Suddenly freezing, she pulled the comforter over her legs. She didn't want him to leave.

"It's my job. To protect and serve." He strapped on his gun that she'd gotten used to seeing on her nightstand. "The guy got caught up to no good, and now he could be hurt. I need to take care of things."

"I know. It's just that I…" No, she wasn't going to do this. If they were going to make anything of this relationship, she had to accept all of him. That included his job. "Please, be careful."

He stopped long enough to plant a hard kiss on her lips. "Lock the house up tight. I'll be back as soon as I can."

"Call me," she said. "Now go help people."

* * *

It wasn't a good night to be out in the elements. Another cold front had swept into town, and the steering wheel of his truck was cold to the touch. The cold didn't bother Carter. It was the mess he was stepping into that had him concerned. He wasn't quite sure what he was facing. Sherman had shot a guy. There just weren't any good outcomes to a scenario like that.

He pulled out his phone. Bill had the night shift tonight, and he was playing catch-up right now. They needed to coordinate, and he didn't want to step on any actions that had already gotten underway.

"Hey, chief," Bill said. "What's up? I thought you had the night off."

What's up? Carter shook his head. Hell, Alice hadn't even called the station.

"I just got a call from the Gunthries. Somebody tried to steal Sherman's truck. He shot the guy."

"*Shot him?*"

It had been so long since Shadow Valley had had a shooting that it probably wasn't even in the records.

Carter braked at a stop sign, but kept going around the corner when he didn't see anyone on the streets. "The guy ran off into the woods. I'm going to check it out."

"I'll come back you up, but I'm way out on Route 8, dealing with an OUI."

"Call everyone else in first. This doesn't have a good feel to it." They had a wounded suspect out there. Wounded and hiding in the woods… It wasn't the best of situations.

The Gunthries lived on the opposite side of the town square from Callie, but still back up against the tree line. When he turned another corner, Carter saw their place was lit up like a Christmas tree. All the outdoor lights were on, and there was a flashlight sweeping the backyard.

"Put out an alert to the community," he told Bill, although he was sure the message was already spreading. "People should make sure their doors are locked and stay inside. Maybe we'll get lucky and somebody will spot him."

Sometimes social media had a purpose. It wasn't that late; people were still on their devices. They didn't know if this guy was armed, but he should be considered dangerous. The last thing they needed was another civilian to get surprised by him.

Carter pulled up to the house and shook his head as he stepped out of his truck. "Sherman," he called toward the flashlight. "I thought I told you to wait inside."

Alice's six-foot-tall beanpole of a husband shuffled over to talk to Carter. The wind tugged at his coat and pants, but his shotgun was as steady as his flashlight. "It's my property. I'll do as I please."

As he'd already proven… Carter wandered over to the old beater truck the would-be thief had tried to steal and crouched beside a small pool of blood. "What happened here?"

"Like I told you on the phone, Alice and I were watching our show on the DVR. That's when I heard the door of my pickup open. I've been meaning to oil it for some time now." Sherman pulled his jacket up tighter around his neck. "Well, I knew right off what was happening. Nancy from next door had clothes stolen off the line. That hooligan came back for my truck."

Carter went still. He hadn't made that connection, but his administrative assistant did live next door to the Gunthries. He let his flashlight sweep over the old Ford. It wasn't locked, and he wasn't surprised to see the keys in the ignition. "So you decided to grab your shotgun?"

Sherman's spine straightened. "You know I did. He wasn't ready for that, let me tell you."

"Did you hit him bad?"

"Got him in the arm. Maybe the side."

There were drops of blood leading up the driveway. Carter followed the trail as far as he could with his light. It led off into the woods behind the Gunthries' house. In the dark, the red splotches were hard to see. If it had snowed, they'd be in better shape.

"Did you get a good look at the guy?"

"Ugly son of a gun."

"Did you recognize him?"

"He wasn't anybody from around these parts."

Carter pulled a notebook out of his jacket pocket. "Can you give me a description?"

"He was a big guy. I'd say he was about my height, maybe two... two twenty. His hair was shaved real close to his head."

Carter took the description down, but it didn't ring any bells. He hadn't seen anybody like that around town. Newcomers and visitors tended to stick out. "What was he wearing?"

"Now why would you ask me that? I'm no fashion maven."

Carter lifted a hand when his phone started ringing again. "Hold on. Let me get this."

It was Jackson, his officer with the bum arm. He must have come in to coordinate the search. Good idea. "Landry here."

"Chief," Jackson said. For someone who'd just come onto the case, his voice was ragged. "I know you're busy, but I've got some new information you should know."

Carter tensed. Ah, hell. Were they already too late? "What happened? Did somebody find the guy? Is anyone hurt?"

"No. I don't know. It's not that. Maybe now's not a good time to tell you, but I was fooling around with those fingerprints you sent to the lab from Callie Thompson's fuse box."

Carter's attention focused like a switch had just been thrown.

Jackson took a deep breath. "I know they said the results were inconclusive, but I tried playing around with the prints. You know, like matching the partials up with the ones Raikins took to get a more comprehensive one. And... Well... You're not going to believe this."

The tension at the back of Carter's neck threatened to strangle him. "Jackson, if you don't tell me, I'm going to come right through this phone and tackle you."

"I tried a side-by-side match with that larger print, using one set of fingerprints instead of the whole database." The static screamed when the officer paused. "Now, I'm just learning. It's only a seventy-four-percent hit."

"Whose prints did you run?"

"Morton's. Hell, Carter. They're Morton's."

The nausea hit Carter hard and fast. For a second, his vision blurred, and he reached out for the truck to steady himself. "Are you telling me that Clive Morton was in Callie's basement?"

"I don't know for sure. I'm saying I'm not an expert on this, I was just messing around, and the match is far from conclusive—but close enough that I'd want to know if it was my girlfriend's house."

Carter's instincts went into overdrive. He had to get to Callie. Morton had been in that house with her. She didn't know, and he'd broken rule one.

He'd left her alone.

He was making a beeline for his truck when logic prevailed. He'd just left the house. Nobody had been there except the two of them, and he'd locked the door behind him. Those prints had been taken a while ago.

But locked doors hadn't stopped the noises in that place.

He rubbed his throbbing shoulder as he looked at the trail of blood. He couldn't deal with this now.

He went still. Morton. Damn it, where had his head been?

"Hold on, Jackson." Carter dove inside his truck and grabbed one of the FBI's wanted flyers from the glove compartment. "Sherman, was this the guy you saw?"

Sherman lumbered over. He held the piece of paper at arm's length as he shined his flashlight at it. "By golly, that's him."

"Why didn't you say so? We've been looking for this guy. He's an escaped felon."

"I've been on the road, chief. I heard about those escapees, but I didn't see any flyers and I don't watch the news much. Too much politics."

Carter's brain quickly clicked into gear. Morton had been behind all the petty thefts. Why hadn't he seen it before? The clothes from Nancy's line, the church money, and now Sherman's truck. The answer had been sitting under his nose the entire time.

"Jackson, Sherman just ID'd Morton. Where is my backup?"

The woods pulled at Carter like a magnet. Everything inside of him wanted to go tearing off after the guy, but he knew better. It was too dark in those woods. There was little chance he'd be able to find Morton on his own out there, unless Sherman had gotten him worse than he thought. The guy must have been navigating these trails for weeks. He'd know where to go to hide or where to seek refuge.

Hell. *Callie.*

"Everyone's just been put on duty," Carter said. "Call the surrounding communities and get us some help. We need to sweep these woods, and we need to do it fast." He ran a hand through his hair. Thoughts were flying at him from every direction. "We'll need dogs, floodlights, the works. Direct everyone to Sherman and Alice's house. You'll coordinate things from the station."

"I'm on it, chief."

He couldn't forget about Callie. If he wasn't sure she was safe, there'd be no way he could concentrate. As soon as he hung up, Carter called Bill.

"Bill, turn around. I want you to go over to Callie's. Stay with her until you get word from me. Jackson got a hit on those prints. They're Morton's. Sherman just confirmed he's the guy he shot."

"Are you kidding me?" The sound of squealing tires came over the phone, followed by a siren. "Don't worry, chief. He won't get near her."

Carter took a deep breath. He had a lot of things to do, and he needed to do them right. He couldn't let this guy slip away again.

"You all right there, Landry?"

Carter looked at Sherman. The guy stood there, his shotgun pointing at the ground. He was ready to defend what was his. Carter understood the feeling. His brain focused. It was time to be the police chief. "I'm good."

Time passed quickly from that point. He busied himself cordoning off the area as he waited for his people to arrive. The woods were dark as he wrapped tape around a tree near the point where the blood splotches disappeared.

Morton just better hope he wasn't the one who found him. The bastard had been in Callie's house. Had he been the one who'd been scaring her all along? Making sounds, using her things, and trying to get into her bedroom? Carter tamped down the fury that threatened to consume him.

He was just pulling out a map of the county when two of his officers showed up. He nodded at them and spread the map over the hood of a police car. If Morton had gone off trail, it would be hard to find him without dogs, especially if he managed to stop the flow of blood from his wounds. If he was heading somewhere specific, though, the map might help. Carter pulled out a pen and circled the place where the convict was last seen.

His phone rang again, splintering his thoughts. "Landry here."

"Chief, it's Bill."

The map was quickly forgotten when he heard the shakiness in Bill's voice. "What is it?"

"You'd better get over here quick."

"Is he there?" Carter's world tilted on its axis. "Does he have her?"

"No, it's…"

"Spit it out, Bill."

"The Hughes kid says it's Adelaide. She's going nuts."

CHAPTER EIGHTEEN

Callie couldn't sleep, not after Alice's call. What was happening over at the Gunthries' place? She couldn't believe there had been a shooting here, in Shadow Valley, of all places. Had they found the man? Was he hurt badly? Not knowing was driving her crazy.

Grabbing her phone, she quickly texted Mamie and David to make sure they were safe. She was secretly relieved when David texted he was home playing video games. She knew it hadn't been him... although he had been known to poke around the Gunthries' tool shed. She shook off the thought. That would have been bad. So very bad.

Mamie took longer to talk down. Callie briefly considered running down to the café to stay with her, but thought better of it. Still, she couldn't just lie here worrying, especially with Carter out there in the middle of it. Whatever *it* was.

She pushed off the covers and went to the closet for her robe. There had to be something she could do to pass the time as she waited for the phone to ring.

The floorboards creaked as she walked to the bedroom door. The peanut butter cookies in the kitchen were calling her name. If this wasn't the time for stress eating, she didn't know what was. She grabbed the doorknob, but nearly stubbed her toe again when the door didn't open.

She looked down quickly. The doorknob was stuck.

Her breath caught in her lungs, but she swiftly tamped down the surge of fear. It had to just be locked. Carter was cautious that way.

She reached for the lock, but snatched her hand back when she received a jolt of static electricity. "*Ow!*"

She rubbed her hand. That had been the second time tonight. Eyeing the door anxiously, she tried again. This time, she was able to touch the thumbturn, but she couldn't move it. It wasn't just stuck—it was jammed tight. So was the door handle itself. She used her sleeve to get a better grip, but her hand slipped off before it so much as budged.

Tingles started in her belly. "This is not happening. Not again."

She sprang back when the television started blaring from the living room. The volume turned up to full, and she clapped her hands over her ears.

"Oh, no. Please no."

Upstairs, the rocker started squeaking. She didn't know how she could hear it over the din, but she could. The knot that formed in her stomach was cold and hard. She backed away from the door, shivers running down her spine.

Outside her bedroom, the tumult rose. Doors began slamming. In the living room, something hit the walls. She hunched her shoulders with every crash. Were those her books? Through the crack under the door, she could see the lights flashing on and off, on and off.

Inside her bedroom, though, all was still.

The hair on Callie's arms rose. Adelaide had wanted attention before; this was different. Something was wrong. Very, very wrong. The whirlwind of noise and activity seemed to gain strength. She was in the eye of the storm but couldn't wait for it to turn on her.

"Stop it," she begged. "Please, Adelaide."

The maelstrom rose around her. Energy pumped through the house. Appliances turned on and off. Callie hopped onto the bed when moans started coming up through the floorboards from the basement.

"Why?" She was shaking so hard that her teeth clattered. Why had the spirit come back? Hadn't she completed the mission Adelaide left behind? Wasn't she doing as the spirit had asked?

"Stop it," Callie cried. "Stop it or tell me what's wrong."

It made no sense. Adelaide had been so quiet that they'd thought she'd left. Or was at least content. Why now? What had made her so upset? So angry?

"It's Carter, isn't it? Are you upset he's gone? He's coming back, I swear. He'll be here soon."

The promise didn't help. The noise grew to a deafening roar. Callie lurched toward the door and yanked on the handle. She braced her foot against the wall for leverage. She'd rather be out there in the middle of everything than caught here.

Nothing worked. She couldn't get out. She was trapped alone with Adelaide's irate spirit.

The windows. She'd gotten out that way before. She spun around and flew across the room. Her hands shook as she undid the latch and pulled the windowpane up. It slammed back down with such force, she shielded herself for fear it would shatter.

"Adelaide. Quit it! Let me out of here. I'll go. I promise I'll leave and never come back."

Braving her fears, Callie dove to the window and began to pull with all her strength. A face in the window startled her. She jumped back so quickly, she stumbled over her own feet and fell to the floor.

The face wasn't her reflection, and it wasn't Carter. It was David.

* * *

The tires of Carter's truck screeched to a stop outside of Callie's house, and he was out and running practically before he threw the transmission into park. Bill was standing on the front sidewalk, gaping at the house with wide, terrified eyes. Carter felt the hairs on the back of his neck rise when he looked at the place.

It was possessed.

Shutters flapped. Lights flickered. Every electronic device in the place sounded as if it had been turned on.

He ran across the lawn to where Bill stood. "Where's Callie?"

"I don't know. I couldn't get in. She wouldn't let me."

Carter didn't have to ask who "she" was.

"Circle the house," he ordered Bill. "There's got to be a way. We've got to get inside and help her."

If Carter wasn't seeing it with his own eyes, he wouldn't have believed it. This was bad... and something he wasn't sure how to fight. He laid his hand on the gun at his hip and started around the house. They had to get inside. Callie could be trapped and hurt for all he knew.

He saw a figure at the side of the house on the ladder propped up against her bedroom window. He nearly pulled his gun before he saw it was David Hughes.

"David," Carter yelled. His breath fogged in the cold winter air. "Is she in there?"

The teenager's head snapped around and, for once, he looked happy to see him. "She's trapped. Adelaide won't let her out of the room."

Carter had seen and heard too much not to believe what the kid was saying. He hurried over. "Is Adelaide in there with her?"

"No. I don't know where she is." David stopped and closed his eyes tightly as if he were in pain.

"David!"

"She's angry." His eyes were glazed when he opened them. "Adelaide's lost it."

"Let me up there." Carter held the ladder as David scurried down. He took the rungs two at a time on the way up. When he looked through the window, he found himself face to face with Callie.

"Carter!" She began pounding on the window. "Get me out of here."

She yanked on the handle, but the window wouldn't move. He tried to help her, but couldn't get a good grip. He pushed, pulled, and banged with the palm of his hand before he finally gave up.

"Back away," he yelled as he pulled out his gun. He turned the butt end to the glass and brought it crashing down hard.

It bounced off the window like a Super Ball.

"This isn't working," he said, breathing hard. He saw her palms press against the window, and he lifted his hand to lie against hers. "Breathe, honey. Try to stay calm. I'll be there as soon as I can."

He hated it, but he looked away from her tear-filled eyes and quickly descended the ladder. His stomach twisted at the thought of leaving her, but there was nothing useful he could do from up there. "Keep talking to her," he barked at David. "I'm going inside."

"How?"

He didn't know, but he was going to find a way.

He met Bill back on the front lawn. The officer looked even more white-faced than he had before. "There's no way in," Bill reported. "Everything is sealed tight as a drum. Nobody's getting in, and nobody's getting out."

Like hell.

Carter's determination gelled with the ball of rage in his gut.

This was going to stop. He was going to protect Callie no matter what the spirit bitch threw at him. He'd kick the front door down. TNT it, if he had to.

His steps faltered on the steps to the front door. "Protect her," he said slowly.

Adelaide had told him to protect Callie.

But he'd left her side...

All at once, the pieces of the puzzle locked into place in his head.

"You're doing my job for me," he whispered.

That was it. He didn't have a doubt about it. Callie was in trouble, so Adelaide had done what she could.

He sprang into action and covered the porch in two steps.

Bill caught up to him as he grabbed the door handle. "It won't open. I tried."

"Adelaide, let me in," Carter said.

The door swung open and the house dropped to a deadly silence.

Carter didn't miss a beat, but Bill sucked in a breath and backed into the porch railing. Carter grabbed him by the shirtfront and pulled him inside. He wasn't waiting for any more backup.

The entryway was empty, but Carter pulled his gun and held it at the ready. He swept the rooms with an eagle eye as he headed straight to Callie's room. The stereo and the television had gone quiet. Books were on the floor, but he stepped between them, undaunted. He halfway expected to find Adelaide in the hallway, ready to kick his ass, but it was clear.

He holstered his weapon.

"Callie." He grabbed the bedroom door handle and wrenched it. Pain shot through his wrist when it held solid.

"Carter!" He could feel her presence on the other side.

He twisted the handle again. It was no use.

"Back up," he yelled. "I'll kick it in."

He took a step back and let loose with his foot. It landed hard against the wood, jarring his entire body, but the door held. Bill snapped out of his stupor. He lowered his shoulder and, together, they attacked.

The door held strong as a fortress.

Moans started up from the basement, and Carter tried again. Had he read Adelaide wrong? The moans built in strength. Was she not forgiving him?

"We've got to get Callie out of here before Adelaide starts acting up again," Bill said.

"Adelaide is the one holding the door closed." Carter's frustration mounted. Why had she let him in only to block him out?

Protect her.

That was the message she'd directed straight at him. What else had she said?

237

Hiding. People are searching. That was it. She'd thought she was still working for the Underground Railroad.

Moans echoed up from the basement, and he ran a hand through his hair. He couldn't think if she kept doing that.

His hand stopped at the back of his neck.

Wait. Could it be?

Oh, fuck.

Instinct had him arming himself again. "We need to search the basement."

Bill shook his head. "We need to help Callie."

"Callie's fine." Carter was certain of that now. Adelaide had her safe.

Good, old Adelaide—vigilante for truth and justice.

"Chief—"

"He's here," Carter said. "Morton is here." ——————

* * *

Callie felt her panic threaten to overwhelm her when Carter called through the door, "Hold on. We'll be back."

Her body went limp, and she rested her forehead against the wood. She looked down at the handle through a sheen of tears.

She'd had enough. No more. She couldn't take this anymore.

She'd done everything she could do, but it just wasn't enough. She was tired of being scared, tired of looking over her shoulder, tired of jumping at every little thing.

No more.

"Did you hear that, Adelaide?" she whispered. "It's over."

Anger gathered strength inside her. She slapped the door with the palm of her hand and pushed herself away. Standing in the middle of the room, she opened her arms wide. "I give up. You win."

She turned around in a slow circle. For once, she wanted to see the spirit again. She knew it was listening.

"You know what, Adelaide?" Her voice got louder. "I deserved better than this."

The house stood quiet, but she could feel the energy still

pulsing. It swirled around her. Lifting her finger, she pointed at her unseen guest. "You never gave me a chance, yet I did everything I could for you. Have you looked at this house, *your* house? I worked my fingers to the bone to make it a home. You saw me do it."

Callie didn't care if Adelaide didn't like what she was hearing. The spirit couldn't scare her anymore. She was past that stage, and she was brimming with indignation. "I moved into this house, and, when I discovered you were here with me, I tried to accept it. I was open to the idea. I tried everything I could to get along with you. When books started flying and rocking chairs started creaking, I did my best to deal with it."

She grabbed a pillow from the bed and hurled it across the room. "I'm doing what you wanted. I took your things to a museum, and I'm writing your story so everyone will know. I would have done that no matter what you did to me. Do you know why, Adelaide? Are you listening to me? I did it because I was proud of you."

Another pillow received a solid kick. "I thought so much of you, but you still terrorized me." With a deep breath, she folded her arms across her chest. "I don't think much of you now."

Suddenly, Callie felt Adelaide's presence in the room. The air sizzled with energy, and the temperature dropped. She held her ground. "Do your best. I'm not afraid of you anymore. I'm taking your power away from you, Adelaide. I'm the one in charge now."

The energy ebbed and flowed. Callie could feel the struggle and knew she was winning.

"I'm leaving," she said flatly. "You can have the house. You can pull your little stunts that you think are so funny, but I won't be here to see them. I won't hear them. And do you know what, Adelaide? Neither will Carter."

They'd gotten to the heart of the matter. Callie could tell because the pillow she'd just kicked flew back across the room. She didn't even blink. When it came to the police chief, he was one thing she wasn't giving up.

"I'm sorry that Peter left you," she said, "but you can't have Carter. I love him."

The room went quiet.

"He's mine," Callie said softly, "so get out of my way and open that door."

She stood straight and tall. Her heart pounded in her chest, but she wasn't going to show any signs of weakness.

Time slowed...

And the lock softly clicked.

* * *

Carter pushed open the door to the basement and stepped back. The lights were already on. Adelaide was being helpful. Holding his weapon at the ready, he scanned whatever area he could see. He saw no movement, so he slowly eased onto the staircase. Bill moved into position behind him.

Carter pushed onward. He knew he was right about this. Step by step, they moved down into the basement. The moans had stopped. Even the furnace was quiet. The old, dank room echoed their footsteps as they moved about the room.

"It's empty," Bill said. "Like always."

"No, it's not," Carter said through clenched teeth. There might be nothing to see, but that didn't mean that nobody was here. Giving up the advantage of surprise, he began to bang his fist along the wall.

"What are you doing?" Bill asked. "The house has a ghost. You tried to get Adelaide to cross over, but apparently, you just pissed her off. We should grab Callie and go. We need to be over at Alice's right now."

Carter knew that Bill thought he'd gone over the edge, but his emotions weren't controlling him. His thinking was laser-focused. He *knew* what he was doing. Adelaide had told him plain as day; he just hadn't understood her at the time.

"Adelaide used to work with the Underground Railroad. There's a good chance that she hid slaves in this house."

The light dawned in Bill's eyes. "You think there might be a secret room down here?"

"Help me find it."

Starting on opposite sides of the room, they each began pounding on the walls. There had to be something down here. There was no other way to explain how Morton's fingerprints had gotten on the fuse box.

Sweat broke out on Carter's forehead. Adrenaline had his system jumping. One break. All they needed was one stinking break.

He knocked on the wall, and his ears keyed in on a hollow sound. "Over here. Behind these shelves."

Bill hurried over. Together, they tried to move the heavy wooden bookcase. It wouldn't budge. It had been nailed to the wall. "There's got to be a switch or a lever," Bill said.

Carter's hand brushed over a piece of metal. "I've got it. Stand back."

He tugged on the lever and there was a loud click. The bookcase swung open like a door when he pulled on it, and he heard a familiar *thump*. Bill quickly pulled out his flashlight. In its beam, a small room was revealed.

Carter's pulse pounded in his ears. The room was empty, but somebody had obviously been living there for quite some time. There was a cot in the corner with new sheets and a blanket much like the one Nancy had described. A pile of clothes on the floor looked like they would suit her husband. A Coleman Lantern sat on a crate in the corner along with a radio, and a towel hung over the back of a chair.

The towel matched Callie's set.

Something inside his chest went cold and hard. It went subzero when he saw an empty Tupperware container sitting beside the radio. He'd put the leftover pizza from last night's dinner in that container himself.

"Where is he?" he growled.

He pushed aside a hanging blanket and found a tunnel. Pulling out his flashlight, he slowly followed its trail. He hadn't gone ten feet when he saw a heap lying on the ground. With his gun ready, he focused the beam of light.

The heap was Clive Morton.

CHAPTER NINETEEN

"Don't shoot," Morton said as he held up his hand to block the light. "I'm unarmed."

Carter wasn't about to let down his guard. He held his weapon steady as he swept the beam of light over the convict's prone body. Morton didn't appear to have anything in his hands, but that didn't mean he wasn't dangerous.

Blood had pooled on the earthen floor of the old tunnel. Carter threw a quick look down the shaft. It led out to the woods, but it wasn't the sturdiest of places. Someone, probably the man in front of him, had tried to brace the walls with pieces of lumber, but the old tunnel looked as if it could cave in at any moment.

Carter's stomach turned. Morton had been able to come and go as he pleased, with Callie none the wiser. She'd been upstairs only a few feet away from this scum for weeks. How many times had she been up there alone? Vulnerable? Scared? His shoulder throbbed so hard, it made his teeth clench.

"Watch him," he said to Bill as he crouched to search Morton.

"Damn, I know that voice." Morton tipped his head back until it leaned against the wall. "Just my luck. Honey's boyfriend is the police chief."

Red flashed in front of Carter's eyes. Just how close had the guy been? Close enough to listen to them, obviously. Had he been watching them? Had he been watching Callie?

He searched the man and checked the wound. Sherman had caught him high on the side, up near the ribcage. Blood made the material of his shirt stick to the wound, but pulling it off would only increase the blood flow. Either way, it wasn't a lethal shot.

"Here," Bill called.

Carter caught the towel and pressed it against the seeping wound. Morton hissed with pain. *Good*, Carter thought.

"Use that to apply pressure," he said.

Morton coughed and hacked up more phlegm. Carter couldn't find an ounce of sympathy inside him. This slimeball had terrorized Callie for weeks… probably intended to do worse.

"Officer Raikins, call for an ambulance." Carter narrowed his eyes on the escaped convict. "You're going to be hurting for a while. The nearest hospital is in another town."

Bill keyed his radio, but when he put out the request, he didn't get a response. "I'm not getting a signal down here."

"Then go upstairs."

Bill didn't move. "Considering the circumstances, maybe I should stay here."

"Go. Call. An ambulance."

Bill backed out of the tunnel reluctantly, but Carter didn't take his eyes off Morton for a second. There hadn't been any ghosts in the basement. It hadn't been the furnace clunking. It had been the hidden door—and this clumsy ox.

Why hadn't he seen it sooner?

Carter stepped back. He couldn't think of the guy here in the house. Not with Callie. Not if he wanted to stay sane. "I take it you're responsible for the little crime spree that's hit our town in recent weeks? You took a lot of chances. Stealing clothes and hitting a church? You're not the smartest guy in the world."

Morton cackled. "I was smarter than you."

A muscle pulsed in Carter's temple. That jab hit a little too close to home.

"Hey, a guy's got needs," Morton said with a laugh. "I had shelter, but I needed clothing. And a man's not a man if he doesn't have a few dollars in his pocket." A smile slowly slid onto his ugly face. "Speaking of needs, honey's a decent little cook."

Rage hit Carter smack dab in the middle of his chest. "Shut up."

"She's a hot-lookin' number, too, albeit a little skittish."

"I said *shut up*."

Morton spat on the floor and wiped his mouth with the back of his hand. "So tell me, chief. Do you call her 'honey' because of that pretty blond hair? Or does she taste that sweet between those sexy, long legs?"

"Enough!" Carter roared. His finger twitched on the trigger. "Don't talk about her. Don't even think about her."

Morton just sneered and laughed. "I was ready to fill in for you anytime. In fact, I tried, but her bedroom door was always locked. Too bad, really. There doesn't seem to be much she doesn't like."

"You son of a—"

"*Carter.*"

The sound of Callie's voice cut through the red fog, but it only intensified Carter's fury. The thought of that animal touching her, watching her, stalking her... It made him sick.

"Carter, back off. Please!"

His muscles strained. Morton had tried to get into her room. What had he intended to do on Halloween night when he'd turned off the power?

* * *

Callie caught Carter by the arm. Every muscle in her body was taut as she waited for him to get himself under control. She'd heard what the man on the floor had said. It made her queasy, but Carter... The look on his face frightened her.

"It's not worth it," she said softly.

"Stay back," he ordered her. His blue eyes were so icy. She

took a half-step back when he placed himself between her and the intruder. "Go upstairs with Raikins."

There was no way she could go when there was the chance that he might do something stupid. She wasn't going to let him ruin their future. "Come with me. Bill's right here on the stairs. He can watch him until the ambulance arrives."

"Hey, honey," the man on the floor called. He coughed, and the sound gurgled in his throat. "Thanks for letting me use your shower. You've been a great roomie."

For the first time, Callie looked at the itinerant man who'd made her house his home. *He'd* been in her shower? Her skin crawled, and she gratefully hid behind Carter's wide shoulders. All along, she'd just thought she had a leaky showerhead. The full scope of the situation began to hit her. The man had shared her shower. He must have used her soap and shampoo. Had he used her razor?

She nearly gagged.

"Go upstairs," Carter said. "I've got this."

"Bill," she called. She shuddered with revulsion as she looked at the man again. She couldn't take her eyes off him, even though his scraggly, bloody appearance repulsed her. She'd been living with a total stranger, and she hadn't even known it. "Bill, get over here."

Footsteps thudded on the staircase. They slowed when Bill took note of the tense situation. "The ambulance is on the way, along with the state troopers," he said with forced calm. "Chief, why don't you go upstairs and direct them? I'll take care of Morton."

"I'm not leaving until he's strapped down to a gurney."

"Morton?" Callie's throat tightened. Her gaze quickly flashed to the man bleeding on the floor. That was *Morton*? The world tilted on its axis, and her knees gave way. She clutched at Carter as she started to go down.

"Whoa," he said as he spun around to catch her.

She couldn't help it. She'd seen the news reports. She'd watched Carter work the case. She knew how dangerous Morton was, and he'd been living right underneath her nose.

She'd done laundry right outside this very room.

Carter caught her around the waist and ushered her out.

Bill stepped forward. He had his gun trained on the wounded man.

"That's the guy you've been looking for?" Callie asked.

"That's him." Carter led her across the basement, intentionally blocking her view of the secret room. A room with free access to the woods behind the house... an entry that anyone could have used to enter her home... and had.

"My radio was in there," she said inanely. She tripped on the bottom step of the staircase and would have fallen if he hadn't taken her weight. "And my towel. His blood was on my towel."

"I'll have the place cleaned out tomorrow," Carter promised. He led her up the stairs one step at a time. "We'll board up the access tonight."

"He used my shower," she said. The thought was disgusting. Another thought occurred to her, and her outrage grew. "And he ate my food. Ghosts don't eat food."

Carter stopped at the head of the stairs and grabbed her by the shoulders. "Don't do this to yourself. Don't think about it." A crack finally appeared in his armor. "I can't take it."

Callie turned into him. She ducked her head into the crook of his neck and wrapped her arms around his waist. He let out a shuddering breath and pulled her closer. He held her until she began shaking so badly that she couldn't stop. With a curse, he swept her up into his arms. He carried her into the living room, sat down hard on the couch, and buried his face in her hair. "I'm sorry," he said.

She couldn't stop trembling. She burrowed against him and squeezed her eyes shut tight. It didn't help. She couldn't block out the images of Morton wandering around her house. Carter reached for the blanket draped over the back of the sofa.

His old camping blanket. He pulled it around her shoulders, and she huddled into it.

"He was here before I was," she said as thoughts began assembling in her head. "He was the one who opened my boxes and went through my things. He *slept in my bed* before I got here."

Carter was still holding her like a vise when the ambulance pulled up to the house. "Basement," he said coldly when the paramedics hurried into the living room.

"That's it," he said. "We're not waiting to watch them wheel him out of here."

He ushered her to her room so swiftly, Callie didn't remember standing on her own two feet. Moving to the closet, he yanked clothes off hangers and tossed a sweater and jeans at her.

"Carter?" she said uncertainly.

"I need to get you out of here." He ran a shaky hand through his hair as she hurried to get dressed. "This never should have happened. The clues were right there in front of my face. I should have figured it out sooner."

"Figured what out? That an escaped convict was hiding in a room that even I didn't know was attached to my house?" She threw him a look that was almost angry as she opened the dresser and found some socks. "I live here, and I didn't have a clue."

"But it was my job to find him." He closed his eyes. "It makes me sick to think about what could have happened."

Callie paused. "But nothing did happen. He stole some food and borrowed some shelter, but he didn't do anything to me. Don't think about the what-ifs."

"I should have been here to protect you."

"You *were* here. How many times did you stay with me? You were here even when you didn't like me."

"I always liked you."

"You caught him, Carter." She framed his face with her hands and looked him in the eye. "You figured out he was down there, and you got him."

He shook his head. "It wasn't me; it was Adelaide. She was trying to tell us about him all along. She knew what was happening. She was trying to protect you."

Callie's breath caught. Was that what had happened

247

tonight? Had Adelaide been protecting her when she'd trapped her in the bedroom? Her mind raced. Was that why the spirit had locked her door every night since she'd moved in?

A memory exploded inside her head. She'd forgotten about the footsteps on Halloween night. There had been sounds in her kitchen, but she'd been so preoccupied with the glowing ghost at the end of the hallway that she hadn't paid attention. Morton had been coming for her, but Adelaide had run her out of the house before he could get to her.

"Oh, Adelaide. I'm so sorry." Callie pulled back from Carter and looked around the room. She couldn't feel the spirit's energy anymore. "I didn't know."

A clatter from the basement made her flinch, and the look on Carter's face hardened. He grabbed the blanket and caught her hand. "Let's go."

"Wait," she said as he rushed her out of the room. She managed to sweep up her shoes on her way out the door, and he grabbed her coat.

Outside, she made him stop. She sat on the top step of the porch to put on her socks. Her toes were quickly becoming numb from the cold. Carter's footsteps were heavy as he paced in a small circle on the lawn and waited for her.

She tried to hurry, but she couldn't keep a grip on her shoelaces. Her hands were shaking too badly. A crowd was gathering outside her house. The flashing lights from the squad cars matched her rapid pulse, and her blood pressure went up as her neighbors pushed in on them.

"Callie?" someone called.

She braced herself. She wasn't ready for the onslaught of questions that would surely be coming her way. She looked up, prepared to tell the person to go away, but relaxed when she saw David. He didn't need to ask any questions; he'd been there. She reached for his hand. "David, thank you."

He dropped onto the steps beside her. "I didn't do anything this time. You did. I thought you'd want to know… You finished Adelaide's mission tonight."

Callie began working on the other shoe. "I know. She was

trying to protect me from Morton. She wanted him out of the house."

David folded his hands and rubbed the back of his knuckles with his thumb. He seemed unsettled. "That was part of it, but it wasn't the reason she's been stuck here for so many years."

Callie paused. She hadn't thought of that. She slowly looked at David. "What are you talking about?"

"You fought for him. That's what she told me, anyway." David cracked his knuckles. "I saw what you did, the way you stood up to her. You fought for what you wanted."

He looked at her with confusion in his eyes. "She said that she didn't."

"Oh my God. *Peter.*"

Carter finally lifted his head. "What about Peter?"

Callie was flummoxed. Adelaide had been waiting for love to come back to her home. That had been her mission. Callie finished with her shoelace and stood. She wrapped her arms around her waist as the cold seeped through her coat. "I understand what she meant, David. Thank you for relaying the message."

Carter looked back and forth between the two of them, but didn't ask again. He sized up David for a long moment before sticking out his hand. "You came through again tonight. I appreciate it."

Callie's eyes widened. David looked at the outstretched hand with as much surprise as she did. After a long moment, he returned the handshake. Talk about something to mark on the calendar.

David turned to go home, and Carter held out his hand for her.

"Thank you," she said softly. "That meant a lot to me."

He shifted impatiently. "Can we get out of here now?"

She followed his gaze as he looked over her shoulder. There was movement in the house. They were bringing Morton up from the basement. "Now would be a good time."

Together, they crossed the lawn. Carter helped her into his

truck before getting behind the wheel. The engine roared to life when he turned the key, and people moved to get out of their way as he backed out of the driveway. In seconds, they were moving down Highland, away from the scene.

She glanced at him. His attention was focused straight out the front windshield. His jaw looked like granite, and his mood was still edgy. She could feel the frenetic energy bouncing around the truck's interior like a ping-pong ball.

"Carter, stop it. This wasn't your fault. I was the one who kept insisting that Adelaide was the source of the noises in the house. I wouldn't listen to you when you tried to tell me otherwise."

For a long while, she didn't think he was going to respond.

"I should have checked it out better," he finally said in a flat voice.

She sucked in her stomach. She might be one of the nation's most popular advice columnists, but she didn't know how to handle this. He was closing in on himself again. She had to find a way to get through. "You had too many things on your mind. Your cases were pulling at you."

"Case," he said. "It was one case, and I couldn't even see that."

"I was distracting you."

His eyes flashed, this time with a different inner light. "You're right about that."

She felt a glimmer of hope. Reaching out, she took his hand.

Emotion suddenly clogged her throat. Things really had turned out for the best, even though he couldn't see it. He'd done his job: he'd stopped the bad guy—and she'd saved him in return. She hated to think about where they'd be right now if she hadn't been able to stop him in the basement. With the way Morton had been taunting him, the outcome could have been much worse.

She lifted his hand and kissed it. She'd been so scared when she'd found him standing over the bleeding man. The look in his eyes had been chilling. She understood it, though. He was as protective of her as she was of him.

He cleared his throat. "What was David talking about back there? What did he mean when he said 'you fought for him'? Did Adelaide attack you?"

Callie let out a sound that was half a laugh and half a sob. "Not exactly. Looking back, I think I attacked her."

He glanced at her sharply, but then his gaze snapped back to the road. "How do you attack a ghost, or do I even want to know?"

Tears sprang to her eyes. God, she loved him so much, it hurt. "You fight with words. I told Adelaide I loved you."

His head whipped around, and the truck swerved. He hit the brakes and pulled over to the shoulder.

"Want to run that by me again?" His voice was so raspy, it made goosebumps rise on her skin.

"I had no idea Morton was in the house," she said. "I thought Adelaide was upset because you'd left. She likes you, you know. She always has."

He didn't say anything, just sat there watching her with those blue eyes.

"I wasn't going to let her have you. I told her that you were mine. I loved you, and she'd better get out of my way." Callie shrugged. "She unlocked the door."

Carter reacted fast. One second, she was strapped into the passenger seat, and the next, she was in his lap. It was a familiar move, one she was beginning to like a lot. He pulled her in for a blistering kiss, and the depth of emotion behind it shook her. It went on forever until he ran a line of kisses over to her ear.

"I love you too," he whispered.

Her heart skipped a beat.

"I've been in love with you ever since you roared into town in that Mustang of yours. I fell hard, and I fell fast."

He pressed his face into the crook of her neck, and she threaded her fingers through his dark hair to hold him close. Both their hearts were pounding fast.

"Move in with me," he said roughly.

"What?"

"Full time. Sell the house. Turn it into a B&B. Or a museum. Hell, burn it to the ground. I don't care. Just stay with me."

His eyes were solemn as he looked at her. It was the same look that she'd considered unemotional when she'd first met him. Now, it nearly brought her to tears.

"Let's just do it," he said. "We love each other, and we're already living together."

"But that was because—"

"Because I wanted you near. Marry me."

That knocked the wind out of her.

He waited uneasily until the tension stretched thin. "Damn it, Callie. What more do you want? We're compatible, we balance each other out, the sex is great, and—"

"Yes."

His eyes narrowed. "Yes, the sex is great, or yes, you'll marry me?"

She grabbed him by his police jacket. "Both."

She swung a leg over his hips and straddled him. The kiss she planted on his mouth was so long and hot, the windows of the truck were steamed over when she came up for air. "Take me home, Carter."

His lips curled into one of those rare smiles. He reached for the gear shift and threw the transmission into drive. The wheels spun as he hit the gas. Callie let out a shriek of laughter as she climbed off him. She knew he was in a good mood when he didn't order her back across the seat and into her seatbelt. Instead, she snuggled up close to him and ran her hand up and down his thigh. "So tell me, does a police chief's wife get any perks?"

He caught her hand when it came too close to his crotch. "You've already seen my perks, honey."

She chuckled softly. "I was thinking more along the lines of immunity."

"Immunity?"

"From any more tickets."

"Immunity, my ass," he growled. The grin he threw at her was wicked. "Ticketing you is half the fun."

EPILOGUE

Far away upstairs in an attic, a hazy figure clapped her hands together and smiled. She'd been waiting for true love to come to her home for so long that she'd begun to think it would never happen. This house needed love. It couldn't survive without it. That was why she'd stayed.

Slowly, she walked to her window. Love had escaped her in life, and she'd regretted the loss every day. She hadn't been able to leave until she'd gotten it back.

Now it was here, and the winds of change were blowing her way.

She looked out the porthole window and saw that it had begun to snow. The whiteness made everything look so clean. So pristine. She'd seen too much darkness.

Movement caught her attention, and she looked down to see an ambulance pulled up at the curb. Its red lights flashed against her white snow, marring it.

She didn't like the red.

She backed away. It would be gone soon, and it would take the dark spirit with it.

Then she could go.

She sat down in her rocker one last time and pushed against the floor with the tip of her toe. The chair gave out a haunting, but comforting squeak. She closed her eyes and felt the love swell throughout the home. It reached out to every nook and cranny. Finally, her mission was complete.

A door banged shut downstairs, and she smiled. "Peter," she whispered.

The hazy figure faded, and Adelaide Calhoun crossed over forever.

ABOUT THE AUTHOR

When taking the Myers-Briggs personality test in high school, Kimberly Dean was rated as an INFJ (Introverted-Intuitive-Feeling-Judging). This result sent her into a panic, because there were no career paths recommended for the personality type. Fortunately, it turned out to be well suited to a writing career. Since receiving that dismal outlook, Kimberly has become an award-winning author of romance and erotica. She enjoys the freedom and creativity allowed in writing romance, especially with all the interesting cross-genres that have been exploding on the scene. When not writing, she enjoys movies, sports, traveling, music, and sunshine.

Follow Kimberly at:

Website https://kimberlydean.com
Twitter @KDean_writer

To get the latest information about upcoming work, join Kimberly's newsletter at http://kimberlydean.com/newsletter/

4970883R00160

Made in the USA
Lexington, KY
29 March 2019